the Carrion Eaters

the Carrion Eaters

EVAN H. RHODES

𝔰𝔡

STEIN AND DAY/*Publishers*/New York

Any similarity to persons living or dead is purely coincidental.

First published in 1974
Copyright 1974 by Evan H. Rhodes
Library of Congress Catalog Card No. 73-90694
Designed by David Miller
Printed in the United States of America
Stein and Day/*Publishers*/Scarborough House, Briarcliff Manor, New York 10510
ISBN 0-8128-1652-8

for
Isabel Leighton Bunker
who made it possible

My thanks to Sabina Iardella and Michaela Hamilton for their help with this book.

E.H.R.

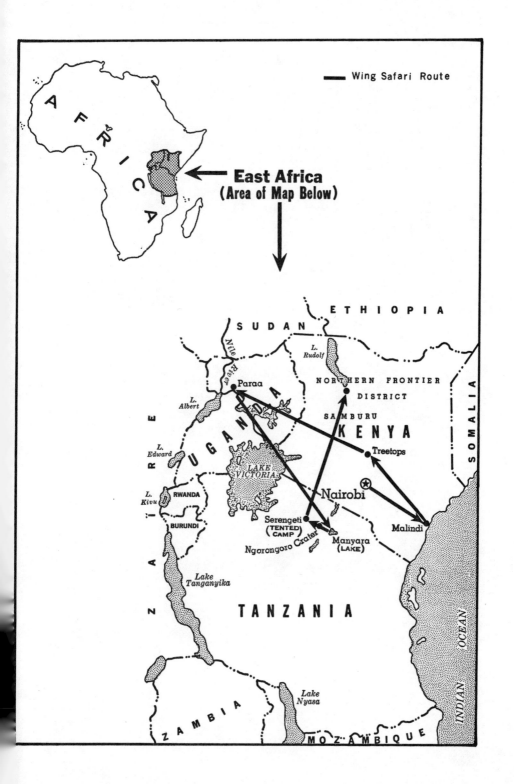

Wing Safari Route

AFRICA

East Africa
(Area of Map Below)

SUDAN   ETHIOPIA

Nile River   L. Rudolf

Paraa   NORTHERN FRONTIER
                         DISTRICT

L. Albert   SAMBURU
                              KENYA

UGANDA   Treetops

L. Edward

LAKE VICTORIA   Nairobi

L. Kivu   RWANDA

ZAIRE   BURUNDI   Serengeti
                                                 (TENTED CAMP)   Malindi

Ngorongoro Crater   Manyara (LAKE)

SOMALIA

Lake Tanganyika

TANZANIA

Lake Nyasa

INDIAN OCEAN

ZAMBIA   MOZAMBIQUE

the Carrion Eaters

1

Late in February, the wire services reported a plane lost over the northern wastelands of East Africa. Seven passengers were aboard the twin-engined craft piloted by Keri Stephenson, a courier for a photographic wing safari popular among wealthy Americans.

Finding them was imperative. Tourism was the second largest industry of the region, and adverse publicity could severely affect the economy.

Two days later a search plane, drawn by a signal fire, spotted the wreckage on a barren escarpment deep in the Northern Frontier District, where Shifta bandits had been attacking remote villages.

From the outset the authorities were suspicious. The aircraft was considered one of the safest, the pilot responsible. How had they possibly strayed so many miles off course?

The main office's weekly reports on the safari revealed that there had been an incident on their boat trip to the headwaters of the Nile. Everybody had assumed that it was simply an accident. But now—

Their suspicions intensified when the rescue party reached the site of the crash. A fully clothed skeleton with a crushed skull was found laid out in the aisle of the wreck. Two bodies, half-eaten by the look of them, were recovered at the base of a cliff. One person seemed to have died of internal injuries. Another was never found. Of the three rescued passengers, one died on the flight back to Nairobi. Six people dead in less than two days.

The case took an uglier turn when the two survivors accused each other of murder.

Piecing together information from notebooks, photographs, a journal, the pilot's log, and the conflicting testimony of the two who lived, the authorities reconstructed the following sequence of events.

2

Speeding along the macadam road gouged into the sienna earth, the Land Rover left Nairobi behind in the shimmering heat. Six members of Wing Safari #7, on their baptismal game run, sat beneath the two open roof hatches which would be their observation posts when animals were sighted.

Keri Stephenson, their guide, was driving. Behind him, under the front roof hatch, sat Sarah Shallott, her husband Simeon, and a dark-complected man, Farragut W. Hardy.

Beneath the rear roof hatch sat Edna Goddard Carlyle, a church steeple of a woman in her late sixties, her finely honed face giving her an air of authority and isolation. Next to her a gangly teenager squirmed around trying to get comfortable. Roland was long-limbed, angular, and full of undirected energy, but his eyes had a vacant, almost stunned look.

"Do sit still," Edna said.

Roland stiffened and clasped his hands.

Edna turned her intent gaze to Keri's profile. Blond, disheveled good looks; sensitive, she thought. But she had expected somebody a little more mature. Keri couldn't be more than thirty-five. Edna mistrusted people who operated on charm. And charming he was, from his lilting British accent to his perfectly-aged bush jacket.

Keri caught Edna staring at him and smiled into the rear - view mirror.

"Last year Sim and I finished off South America," Sarah was saying, "and the year before that . . ."

Edna estimated that the Shallotts were about fifty. Sarah knew she was pretty and never missed a chance to make herself prettier. Artful makeup and constant animation were two of her weapons. Simeon had the knack of the chameleon, Edna decided. His features were regular, his weight exactly right for his average height. He would have been handsome, except for the continual pucker of his mouth. Like a milk snake's, Edna thought.

Sarah finished, "So this year we decided to do Africa. I have a feeling that this is going to be the most wonderful vacation of all. Aren't you excited, Farragut?"

Stocky, in his late forties, Farragut had a high forehead blotched with freckles, crisp, brown hair and large, dark eyes. Definitely painted with the tar brush, Edna thought.

The Rover hit a pothole. Farragut clutched his bulging camera cases. "This isn't exactly a vacation for me," he said.

Roland stood up and stuck his head out the roof hatch. Ahead, the road arrowed across the plains of Athi toward a crescent of green and mauve hills. Wild flowers bloomed everywhere, cumulus clouds raced overhead, and the air smelled like a harvest of lemons. Roland felt the wind tear at his hair, the hot sun beating down on his head, and then found himself, for some unknown reason, getting an erection.

A white-banded gazelle appeared out of nowhere, chased

the Land Rover for a hundred yards, and then streaked into the bush. "Did you see that?" Roland yelled.

"Roland, get down from there before you decapitate yourself," Edna said.

Roland gritted his teeth and obeyed. The vacant look came back into his eyes.

Sarah turned and tugged at Roland's sleeve. "I think it's perfectly grand for somebody so young—seventeen, did you say?—to be on *safari*." She imbued the word with all the mystery of the Dark Continent. "'N' at right, Sim?"

Simeon nodded automatically.

"'N your mighty lucky that your—how did you say you're related?"

"I don't believe I did say," Edna replied. "Roland is my grandson, though he's been raised to call me Edna. We believe in treating each other as equals, don't we, dear?"

"Yes, ma'am."

"In the strict legal sense I'm also his guardian," Edna continued. "His parents died when he was an infant."

"Oh, what a tragedy," Sarah said. "How?"

Roland's eyes darted to Edna. But if she heard Sarah's question she didn't react. No use, he thought, I'll never find out.

Guardian, Edna reflected. As she recalled the troubles back in New York, her left arm began to ache. She shifted the weight of her large carry-all. Lord, would there never be an end, she thought. Expelled from school after school. Violence in everything he did. And this last episode that had nearly crucified her.

She knew Roland was at that point where his life could go in any direction. And so, as she had done before, Edna put aside every other obligation and devoted herself to him, gladly, she told herself. Roland was all she had left.

The doctors had urged a complete change of scenery. She

had investigated all the possibilities before deciding on this wing safari. Edna felt that somehow, she must make this trip a definitive experience for him. He couldn't help responding to the adventure. I will save him, Edna thought, if only from himself.

"This air!" Sarah took a deep breath. "The last time I felt so lightheaded was on my honeymoon. Speaking of which, Keri, I forgot to ask—"

"Happily," Keri said. "Fifteen years. Three children."

"'N'at nice?" Sarah said with a touch too much enthusiasm. "Got two of my own from my first hubby, now divorced. Just goes to show that one mistake needn't ruin your life. Walk proud and eventually God will send a Simeon across your path."

I may just throw up, Roland thought, and as Edna's eyes met his, for once he knew they were of a mind.

Farragut reached over the back of his seat. "That's a beautiful movie camera you've got there, Roland."

Roland leaned forward eagerly. "Thanks. Edna got it for me. Say, do you know anything about this zoom mechanism?"

"Roland," Edna interrupted, "I thought you promised to read the instructions thoroughly?"

"I did, but—"

Farragut busied himself cleaning lenses.

"But," Edna repeated kindly. "Is that what you'll settle for, a life of buts? Roland, you have only one responsibility on this trip—that camera. Wouldn't it be a pity if we didn't have a record of this experience?"

Edna proceeded to explain the features of the Baur Super-8 while Roland sank farther and farther into his seat. No point telling her he was just trying to be friendly. The moment was gone.

Sarah tapped Keri on the shoulder. "Weren't there supposed to be two more people with us?" she asked, a little disappointed with her companions.

"They'll be joining us tomorrow," Keri said.

Simeon snapped alert and pointed to an eerie-looking tree in the savannah. "Yonder at two o'clock! Bird I've never seen before is perched in that tree I've never seen before."

Edna let the binoculars fall from her eyes and reached into the maw of her carry-all; out came her book, *East African Birds*. "Hooded vulture," she said, putting a check alongside a picture. "The tree is a baobab, sometimes called the devil's tree. Right, Keri?" Without waiting for an answer she put another check in her book, *East African Trees*.

"Right on both counts," Keri called over his shoulder. "Done your homework, eh? Or are you a company spy assigned to keep me on my toes?"

Edna's laugh was almost girlish. "Just an ordinary tourist. But we will do what we can to keep you on your toes."

"Simeon," Keri said, "you must have the eyes of a fish eagle to see that far."

"It's an undisputed fact that Simeon's got the sharpest eyes in Missouri," Sarah said. "Course, we live in Bel Air now because of Simeon's work. Edna, where do you hang your hat?"

"During which season?" Edna asked.

"Oh," Sarah said.

"What is Simeon's line of work?" Edna asked.

"Why Sim's the chief fund-raiser for the western division of our Mother Church," Sarah said.

"He should talk to me about it at some point," Edna said. "Perhaps my foundation can help."

Simeon nodded.

"Will everybody please pay attention?" Keri said. "Up

ahead is the Nairobi Preserve. Bit of instruction before we go in. Most animals are indifferent to cars. They don't associate their smell with danger. But under no circumstance is anybody to get out of the Rover during a game run. The instant you're divorced from the vehicle you're just another animal to the predators. Everybody got that?''

Edna looked to see if Roland was paying attention.

"Okay," Keri said. "Let's go."

3

The Nairobi Preserve encompassed forty square miles of plain and bush where prey and predator lived in natural balance. Following park regulations, a game warden took over the driving chores from Keri.

They bumped over the savannah, criss-crossing trails, stopping to allow Edna to check off a flame tree aglow with scarlet blossoms. Next, a lilac-breasted roller. The click of Farragut's Nikon startled the bird, and its emerald wings blurred against the deepening sky.

It was nearly five P.M.—"Perfect game viewing time." Keri explained. "The herds will have roused from their siesta and there should be a great deal of activity until dusk."

A mood of anticipation fused the group as they scanned the terrain. Sarah snapped the brim of her Aussie hat to a rakish angle. Simeon warbled a call to the maribou storks roosting on a bleached stump. The Land Rover came to a river and followed the line of fever trees whose strange flat canopies obscured the banks.

"Look—under that bush," Simeon said.

"What are those adorable things?" Sarah asked as the Rover slowly rolled toward a litter of pups that yipped excitedly at her waving fingers.

"If they could reach your hand," Keri told her, "those adorable things would bite it off."

"You're funning me," Sarah said, jerking her hand back. "Don't mean to sound boastful but we do breed shih tzus for a hobby, and I pride myself on having a way with pups. 'N'at right, Sim?"

"I'm sure you do," Keri agreed. "Those pups, however, grow into hyenas."

As if in confirmation, a cub let out a wailing laugh that flushed birds and small game from cover.

Roland focused the movie camera and zoomed in for a close shot. They were a mottled brown with oversized ears cocked on snub-nosed heads. Their low hindquarters gave them the skulk of a criminal. Roland stared through the rangefinder into the most hopeless eyes he'd ever seen.

Then he got wind of them and pinched his nose. "Wow! They smell like they're made out of dead armpits."

"Luckily," Keri said. "It's the only warning other animals have before hyenas attack."

"Aren't they just scavengers?" Edna asked.

Keri shook his head. "A popular and very erroneous idea. True, they'll eat anything. Tires, carrion, human corpses. But they're also the most ruthless hunters in Africa. Look!"

The dam came loping toward her den, the struggling body of a small Thompson gazelle clamped in her jaws.

Keri said, "The female rules here, usually the oldest. I'd rather face a pride of lions than a hyena clan. One swipe of *simba*'s paw and you're done. But with *fisi*, well, the filthy beasts prefer to eat their prey alive.''

Edna watched the gazelle being rent limb from limb long after the others had to turn away. ''Is it true that they're hermaphrodites?'' she asked.

''Now how in the world would you know something like that, Edna?'' Sarah asked.

''They have something of the same mystique as werewolves and vampires,'' Keri said. ''Actually, the female's labia are so overdeveloped they hang down like the male's scrotum. Hence the difficulty determining sex.''

''Not much different than the brazen young that one sees today,'' Simeon said. ''Running around in long hair and pants, even to Sunday service. Where will this godless unisex business end?''

'' 'N'at's right,'' Sarah agreed. ''I'm certainly glad to see that you've got a sensible haircut, Roland.''

Roland wished he still had his long hair.

''Some natives believe that hyenas are the embodiment of evil,'' Keri went on. ''There's a saying I grew up with, 'When a man goes mad the time of the hyena is upon him.' ''

The rising and falling wail of the hyenas followed them as they drove deeper into the game preserve.

They hadn't gone very far when Simeon exclaimed, ''Will you look at that? There, at eight o'clock.''

''*Twiga*,'' the driver said, grinning. Poking above the dappled shade of a sausage tree were the long necks of two giraffes.

''*Pole, pole*,'' Keri cautioned the driver in Swahili and he shifted into low.

The Rover rocked over the tussocks to creep within

twenty yards. Heads popped out of the hatches. Edna thumbed furiously through her book of East African animals.

"What kind of giraffe is that?" she asked. "Masai? Rothschild? Reticulated? How tall? Is it true they're mute?"

"Masai," Keri answered in a hushed voice. "Eighteen feet. World's tallest land mammal. And yes, for the most part, they're mute."

Knobby legs splayed at knock-kneed angles, the two animals were rubbing their necks together with a look of bliss.

"Heaven!" Sarah exclaimed. "Have you ever seen anything so innocent?"

"Two by two Noah led them into the ark," Simeon said.

Keri chuckled. "Not those two, I'll wager. Take a closer look. See, they're both male. Deserved or not, giraffe have a reputation for being sui-genderistic."

"Sui who?" Sarah asked.

"Queer," Roland told her.

"Now, Roland, how in the world would you know a word like *that?*" Sarah asked.

"My analyst—" Roland began, but Edna cut him off with a "Roland!"

Sarah glanced at Simeon and raised her eyebrows.

A third giraffe appeared on the scene, moving in dainty slow motion. The two males stopped rubbing their necks together. One arched his nose down to the female's loins, whereupon she promptly peed in his mouth.

"No wonder they're mute," Farragut said.

With an awkward leap one male mounted the female while the second male cavorted about, trying to mount either of them.

"It's the male's way of knowing when she's ovulating," Keri told them. "Otherwise he wouldn't waste his time mounting."

Lights! Action! The world's tallest land fuck. Thank

God you're automatic, Roland thought, as he heard the camera cartridge whirring within.

"*Roland!* You needn't bother filming that," Edna said. Her long, veined fingers reached out and covered the lens.

Roland put the camera down.

Keri explained that such specialized sexuality was usually the sign of a diminishing species.

"Knock-knock," Simeon said. "Who's there? Giraffe. Giraffe who? Giraffe-a see a dream walking? Well I did," he sang.

Sarah threw back her head and laughed. The trio of giraffes disengaged and gallumphed away, their legs covering forty yards at a stretch. Farragut, who hadn't finished focusing, gave Sarah a baleful look.

Keri pointed to a hillock and whispered, *"Kongoni."*

As though conjured from the rise a herd of fawn-colored hartebeest grazed toward the sunset. Their hindquarters stood a trifle shorter than their forelegs, and each had a slight hump where the neck joined the shoulders.

"Why you cute little gossips," Sarah said. "Just look at them nodding to each other."

"Colonies of flies spend their entire lives living up in their nostrils," Keri said.

The leader, a large male of about three hundred pounds, stood alert, nose to the gentle wind.

Keri looked to the sky where the sinking sun limned the clouds. "Dark soon. They know it's killing time." Then he nudged the driver and said, *"Bas, bas."* The game warden jammed on the brakes. "In the grass," Keri said softly. "Just to the left."

Against a background of mauve vetch two cheetahs sat back to back, heads high, like guardians of an ancient temple.

Farragut fumbled with his camera, changing lenses.

Keri kept his voice low. "Cheetahs are somewhere between a dog and a cat. They have footpads like dogs, semiretractile claws, but kill with their fangs."

"How come the hartebeests aren't scattering?" Roland whispered.

"They know the cheetahs have just eaten," Keri answered. "Don't ask me how, but when a predator gets ready to kill he gives off a distinctive odor."

"A smell of death?" Edna asked.

Keri nodded. "If the animal doesn't get that message on the wind, he knows that for the moment he's safe."

"Keri?" Sarah called out. "My binoculars are stuck. Can you—?" Her glasses clanked against the metal door.

Startled, the cheetahs bounded away, their lashing tails disappearing into the scrub.

Farragut had just finished reloading. He slapped his hat against his leg. "Of all the silly—"

Pink spots appeared on Sarah's cheeks. "Really, I'm sorry, but how was I supposed to know?"

Keri spoke up hastily. "My fault, I should have warned you. The slightest noise can spook the game. Now I think we've seen enough for one day."

The sun sent a fan of rays through the clouds, bathing the landscape in a weird glow. The breeze shifted and vegetation enfolded with the first signal of dusk. The driver barreled toward the exit. About a quarter of a mile ahead they again saw the herd of hartebeests. They'd stopped grazing. All were alert.

Keri scanned the plain with his field glasses. "They're frightened, that's certain. Hold on, something's moving."

"About a hundred yards dead ahead," Simeon said.

The Rover halted. Roland could only see waving grass. He hiked himself out of the hatch and stood tiptoe on the seat. Then he caught sight of the lioness stalking through the gray-green scrub, belly low, head thrust forward. She halved the distance stealthily. Roland inched up until his butt rested on the car roof. He pressed the camera trigger, zoomed in on the sinewy tendons, the topaz eyes.

"Roland! Get down off there immediately."

As one, the entire car shushed Edna. Keri turned to see what had alarmed Edna, but three pairs of legs blocked his view.

The cat was less than a hundred feet away. The leader of the hartebeests swiveled in the lioness's direction. At an unseen signal from him the herd began to drift away while he stood his ground.

Other cars had also seen the hunt, and there were a dozen or so strung out after the creeping cat. The vehicles were a dead giveaway of her position and the hartebeests moved faster in their rocking-horse motion. They did not panic, but kept a respectable distance between themselves and the killer. The sentinel brought up the flank, his horns like a tuning fork divining the slightest change in her position.

"I'm not at all convinced that lioness is really hungry," Edna said. "Or she'd be after them with a little more verve."

"No," Keri said, "she's famished. See her stomach pouch? A sure sign she's recently thrown a litter. She doesn't dare leave her brood alone much longer, because hyena like nothing better than lion cub. But with these cars following, I doubt she'll make a kill. She and the cubs will go hungry tonight."

"But that's inhuman," Sarah said. "Why doesn't your nice game warden make the cars stop?"

Farragut said, "We're one of the cars, aren't we?"

Sarah shrugged off his remark.

Roland had squirmed out of the hatch until he was sitting square on the roof, so excited he thought he would pop. He did a fast scan with his camera. At the northern horizon a jet from Nairobi's airport climbed, leaving its silver signature in the sky. A million years below were the scrub plain swallowed by gathering darkness, the golden lioness stalking through secret thickets.

The cat brushed by the Rover. Roland's finger tightened on the camera trigger, fixing her. God, she was beautiful. The lioness ... the scurrying antelope ... Whose side am I on? he wondered.

Without warning the camera stopped. All the film had been exposed. Roland's heart sank. His shaking fingers tore at his pants pocket for another film cartridge. He put the camera down on the roof.

The lioness bolted from ambush in a headlong dash.

"Driva!" Keri barked, and the Rover shot forward.

The abrupt move sent the camera skittering off the roof. Roland yelled, lunged and missed. He recalled Edna's admonition. "You have only *one* responsibility on this trip—" and without another thought he leaped off the roof after the camera.

Edna screamed. Keri shouted for the driver to stop, but in the confusion the warden kept his eye on the streaking lioness.

Roland landed in a spiny bush with a crackling thud. Thorns dug into his body, a line of fire ripped his cheek. A moment later he heard an anxious voice from the pinwheeling sky. "Are you all right?"

"The camera!" Roland managed to gasp.

Keri shoved it under his nose. "Here's the bloody thing! Now into the Rover with you before we get run over by these damned cars." He hustled Roland into the front seat.

"What a foolish thing!" Sarah clucked, " 'n after Keri explicitly—" Simeon assured Roland that a merciful God protects even madmen. Farragut told Roland he was lucky he hadn't broken a leg and missed the rest of the trip. The game warden rounded it out with some choice curses in Swahili.

Roland braced himself for a scathing reprimand from Edna. He could not have been more surprised, or relieved, when she said nothing.

4

"But didn't you realize the danger?" Keri asked. "You could have cracked your skull."

"I guess I didn't think," Roland answered, shrugging. "Anyway, if you lived with Edna—well, going after the camera was the *least* dangerous thing I could do."

Keri had taken him to a doctor on the outskirts of Nairobi, who assured them that Roland was made of India rubber. Now Keri quickened their pace through the shadowy lanes that led back to the hotel. He should have taken a car; it was too late to be out on foot. But a quiet moment alone with the boy had definitely seem indicated.

Their route took them through a native quarter of ramshackley mud huts. Vendors hawked their wares in the jumble of honeycombed *dukas* where pungent smells met and mingled—meat and fish frying over braziers, musty clothing mended by cross-legged tailors, the sweat of people barely scrabbling out their existence.

"How come everybody looks like they weigh eighty pounds?" Roland asked.

"Because most of them do." Keri said. " 'And the poor shall never be out of the land.' That's the Bible, I think. We'll have to check it with Simeon."

"Another one of those down-head bits from the Good Book?" Roland muttered. "You know, Keri, they've invented this machine in the Peace Corps? It scoops up earth, fires it, and in one stroke builds a wall that's as durable as brick. Costs a *fraction* of the price of an ICBM. Or, for that matter, what this safari is costing."

"Delighted to see you've a social conscience," Keri said. "However, you have been out of your silk diapers long enough to know there's a bit more to human motives than sweetness and light."

"Hey, wait a minute. Just because Edna's rich doesn't mean—" Roland broke off and grabbed Keri's arm.

A leper with no legs propelled his trunk along the dirt lane with wooden blocks clutched in his fists. He looked at Keri with a gap-toothed grin. *"Jambo, bwana."*

"Jambo, mzee," Keri greeted him. "How goes it for you?"

"Na taka kufa." The native answered, shrugging.

Keri replied, *"Shauri a mungo,"* then inspected the hand-made zebra-skin tobacco pouches the native proferred. Keri chose one and put some shillings into the gnarled hand. They parted.

Roland looked back at the stump of man rocking along at his tortoise pace. "What did he say?"

"Same exchange we've been having for years. I ask him how he is. He says it would be simpler if he could die. I tell him that's God's affair."

Roland lengthened his stride to keep up with Keri. "Poor guy's right. I'd rather be dead than crawl around like that."

"Perhaps," Keri said. "Though they tell me it's a totally different cup when you're faced with it. The urge to live ..."

"Talk to Edna and she'll tell you I've got the opposite little wish."

"Well, after your little acrobatic act ..."

Keri stuffed the tobacco pouch into Roland's pants pocket. "Present for you. And speaking of pouches, what *does* your grandmamma have in that tote bag she carries about?"

"The world," Roland said.

His fingers closed around the pouch in his pocket. "So you're going to win me over?" he said abruptly. "Make sure I'm a good little boy the rest of the trip? Okay, how much did she spill?"

Keri grinned. "Honest little beggar, eh? Fair enough. She suggested that you were—erratic. Gotten yourself into quite a mess back home. She stayed mum about it, though. I liked her for that." He waited a bit. "Not ready to tell me either? Suit yourself. But we will be living in each other's pockets for the next few weeks, so we might as well try to make a go of it. And most lads your age—"

"I know," Roland interrupted. "Would gladly trade one nut for a trip like this. Maybe that sounds ungrateful, but I'll let you in on a little secret. I'm scared out of my head."

Keri put his arm on the boy's shoulder. "Don't worry," he said, smiling. "I haven't lost a tourist in the bush yet. Anything specific bothering you?"

Roland's breath came out in puffs in the frosty mountain air. "I can't shake this awful feeling. Ever since Edna told me we were coming here, I've been having these dreams about snakes and crocodiles. And I've been seeing a shrink long enough to know what that whole bit's supposed to mean."

"Hold on," Keri said. "Most Africans think a croc's a croc; forget the symbols. He is our second largest killer."

"Oh, great. Who's the first?"

"Crafty bit of baggage named Homo sapiens."

Roland tapped his forehead. "Come to think of it I remember reading once that Africa had the highest murder rate in the world. Even more than New York. Hey, is that why you've got us walking so fast?"

Keri cleared his throat. "Now, Roland," he began, trying to turn the whole thing into a joke. "Surely you've had premonitions before? And *nothing's* happened?"

"That's what scares me," Roland answered. "Based on the law of averages alone, one of these days I'm *bound* to be right. I tell you, between science and superstition they've got you coming and going."

"I do believe I've a bit of a wag on my hands," Keri said, delighted that the boy was opening up. Once his guard was down he was likable enough; quite unlike the pampered offspring of the rich that Keri had expected. Keri also realized that Roland was genuinely frightened.

Suddenly Roland stopped in his tracks and gawked at two approaching native boys robed in black. They were holding hands and caressing each other, and their eyes shone like bits of obsidian in their ebony faces. They passed with a whisper of silk.

"They're from a remote tribe," Keri told Roland as he hustled him along. "It's simply their way of telling the world they've declared their love for each other."

"What about the cops?" Roland asked.

"What about them? In their society homosexuality is the preferred way. Something to do with food availability and keeping the birthrate down."

"I'll lay you odds it works." Roland replied.

·31·

Keri ruffled the boy's hair. "I've always thought of homosexuality as something like the measles," he said easily.

"You get it; get over it. Then you're immune."

"Oh, yeah? What about the German measles?"

Keri laughed and put his arm around Roland's shoulder. "I was only talking about the *pain* of homosexuality."

Then he saw the boy's troubled, guarded eyes. Hadn't Roland fagged for an older classmate, gotten that whole question out of the way? Or didn't they do that in America?

Roland ducked out from under Keri's hand.

Now they were out of the native quarter and into the European commercial district. The stores were dark and shuttered. *Ashkaris* in long, red robes patrolled the alleys. Moonflower trees seemed to pulsate beneath the street lamps.

Roland leaped up, snagged a bud, and handed it to Keri. "Little present for *you*."

Keri shook his head. " 'Pluck a flower and you trouble a star.' "

Crushed, Roland said, "What's that supposed to mean?"

"Think about it, it may make sense someday. English poet name of Thompson gets the credit. And, incidentally, *those* flowers happen to be poisonous."

Roland flung the bud away.

At the corner, Roland stopped at the open door of a bar and peered into the dimly lit interior. The Rolling Stones blared from the jukebox. A coffee-complexioned woman with a gold tooth crooked her finger at Roland.

"This place what I think it is? Hey, Keri, what do you say? Least I can do is buy you a beer for saving my life."

Keri snagged Roland's ear and hustled him off. "You raunchy lout, trying to lead an old man astray. Edna would have my head. Besides, my heart already belongs to Livvie and Sadly.''

Roland's eyes questioned him.

"Livvie's my wife. You'll meet Sadly when we get to the Serengeti. Extraordinary female."

"Really? How old?"

"Old enough for you, I guarantee it."

"That's great. Because I tell you, I never thought of myself as a sex maniac—except during exams, maybe. But ever since I got here, wow!"

Keri grinned. "I know. Most tourists come down with it. It's a curious combination of the altitude and nature in the raw. Take cold showers."

When they got within a block of the hotel, Keri began to breathe easier. But Roland's high mood seemed to evaporate.

Keri, sensing the change, said softly, "What's wrong?"

Roland jammed his hands into his pockets. "Nothing. Everything." He paused. "I guess a lot of it has to do with Edna."

"You're joking!" Keri exclaimed. "That heavenly dear—"

Roland cracked his knuckles. "That's what everybody says. Don't get me wrong, I love her. Well, respect her. I'm too scared of her to love her." He frowned. "How do I explain? See, Keri, Edna lives in an Iron Maiden."

"Come off it, boy," Keri said, "or I'll think you've really gone dotty."

Roland cracked his knuckles again, harder. "Maybe I have. Because the minute she says *don't*, then I've *got* to."

"Do you know my oldest son by any chance?" Keri asked. "*Why* must you?"

·33·

"Because if I didn't I know I'd wind up in that Iron Maiden along with her. All she wants is for me to think like her, act like her, walk her straight and narrow."

Keri tried to keep the irritation out of his voice. "If you feel that strongly, why did you agree to come?"

Roland stopped at the deserted sidewalk cafe in front of the hotel. His body tensed and a look of loneliness crept into his eyes.

"I guess I'd better level with you about what happened," he whispered.

5

"Edna's got this huge summer place out on Long Island, one of those old-line, fancy communities," Roland began. "Nearby, there's this railroad spur operating between two terminals, about five miles apart. No passengers, only cargo. A computer runs the whole thing. The railroad set it up as a test case.

"About a quarter of a mile from the terminal closest to Edna's estate the tracks cross a ravine. Not too deep, fifteen, maybe twenty feet. But enough of a drop so you could break your leg."

Or neck, Keri thought.

"One night, me and my best friend Howie had nothing to do. Edna really hates Howie. Thinks he's common. She's even forbidden me to see him, so, like I said, he's my best friend.

"Anyway, for a kick Howie and I decided to walk the trestle over the ravine, see if we couldn't beat the train into the terminal. It was really simple, all you had to do was run on the railroad ties. In fact, we beat the train in by more than five minutes."

"Whose idea did you say this was?" Keri interrupted.

Roland rubbed his chin. "Howie's, I guess, because he's the one who thinks of everything. But this was just one of those ideas you start talking about and then all of a sudden you're doing it.

"The next time we tried balancing ourselves on the rails, like walking the high wire—Howie on one rail, me on the other. For balance we held onto each other's hands across the track. Turned out to be kind of scary, but that's what made it such a kick.

"Before you knew it we were doing it a lot, maybe once a week, always at night. We got so good at it we didn't have to hold hands anymore, just kept our fingertips barely touching as we walked the rails."

The hair on the back of Keri's neck bristled.

"The final challenge was to cut down our time. Soon we were beating the train in by only three minutes, then two. Like Howie said, with no conductor on the engine, it was really like beating the machine.

"Then one night—" Roland swallowed hard. "We tried to cut it too close. Maybe a speck of dust got into the computer and threw it off. You can't trust them—I don't care what anybody says!

"We were just over the middle of the ravine when we saw it coming. I was all for jumping into the gully then and there. But Howie yelled, what was I, chicken or something? He grabbed my hand and started walking faster and faster on the rail; I could barely keep up with him. We started to feel the vibrations coming up through our shoes. Howie was yelling that we were going to make it, we *had* to. But the train was already starting across the ravine."

Roland rocked back and forth, punching his palm over and over. "I looked behind me. The engine was bearing down so fast that I panicked. I jerked my hand free and jumped. When I landed I looked up and saw Howie laughing like crazy and teetering on the rail. The engine began to slow down as it approached the terminal and Howie leaped at it, trying to get a foothold on the guard rail. I guess he figured that if he was up front when the train pulled in that would be as good as beating it. And this time without anybody's help.

"He lost his footing. His arms were flailing, grabbing at anything. He touched the third rail. I saw him hanging there, dancing with electricity. And then he fell. He didn't die. But he's kind of like a vegetable. When I go to visit him at the hospital he just sits there and smiles."

Tears welled in Roland's eyes. He stood staring up at the waning moon.

Keri took a couple of deep breaths. There was far more to Roland's story than just a boyhood prank gone bad. For Keri, it was another case of the young deliberately challenging life. Sky-diving, motorcycle racing, drug overdoses. Even the fantastic mortality rate on the highways almost always involved the young. And it was happening all over the world.

Keri handed Roland his handkerchief. The boy would definitely bear watching.

Roland blinked and said, "They booked me for malicious mischief, trespassing, destruction of property, and about ten other things. But it didn't mean too much to me at that point because I'd flipped out.

"Edna pulled strings and I was released in her custody. The judge ordered me held for psychiatric observation. Think of it as a learning experience, he said. That kind of publicity in an uptight town can be pretty grim, and Edna got the brunt of it. All those whispers about 'poor Edna' and about how history was repeating itself."

"How so?" Keri asked, his brow wrinkling.

Roland shook his head slowly. "Wish I knew. My father died when I was very young. Right after that my mother deserted us, Edna told me. But any time I try to find out more about what happened—" he shrugged. "So now you know why she almost had kittens this afternoon. But then I was going after her camera, I swear!"

"All right, then, I believe you," Keri said, trying to sound convinced.

Roland studied his sneakers. "Keri, what do you think? Can somebody learn to be sane?"

"No experience with analysts," Keri said with forced lightness. "We've none here, only the *real* head-shrinkers. Trouble with analysts is that their premise is always, 'You're wrong!' Which is a lot like original sin, don't you see? When all the proper man wants is a simple direction that will lead him to the three f's."

Roland brushed his hands across his eyes. "Okay, I'll bite."

"Fame. Fortune. And if I said 'fucking' Edna would probably fall into a tizzy, so I won't." Keri thought for a moment. "I've so often wondered if the names analysts apply to human behavior really tell us anything about ourselves? What do you think?"

Roland managed a smile. "Why ask me? Would you ask a lemming for directions?"

Keri threw back his head and laughed. Then he sobered. "Tragic for you, I know. But, Roland, you've got to treasure your friend's memory, not his ghost. Why not start fresh? I can promise you this. Keep your eyes open and this safari may change your entire life. Shall we give it a try?"

Roland grabbed Keri's hand impulsively and gripped it hard. Then, with the sudden recollection of the two natives, he dropped it as though it were a snake.

6

"We're off!" Keri said, herding his group across the run-way toward the twin-engined plane they'd be using for the next month. Lettered on the fuselage was the name, *Solar Bark*.

The new couple had joined the safari that morning. Angus Hawkins's delightful off-center smile titillated Sarah, cheered Roland, and immediately put Edna on her guard. She inspected him carefully. Angus was a powerful-looking man with graying dark hair and green eyes. Deep lines scored his features, but despite his obvious dissipations he would still have been an extremely handsome man. Were it not for his eyes, Edna decided. Bewildered, like the eyes of a child lost in the body of a man. She dismissed him and turned her gaze to the girl walking with him.

Apple Romano was in her mid-twenties, leggy, in a yellow and green shift that moved with her in a clinging flow. At the hotel and now at the airport she had riveted the attention of every male. Including Roland's, Edna was distressed to note.

Of course, Edna thought, calculating Apple's assets, in my day such flamboyance would never have been considered beautiful. Her best feature was her hair, sable in color and twining to her breasts in witches' locks. But her lips were too full by far, and her eyes looked strangely unfocused. Why was every male within range vibrating to this girl?

One big bite, that's all I want, Roland thought, feeling his teeth on edge. He watched Apple, trying to pick out the best spot.

While Keri loaded the luggage, Apple became aware of Roland and involuntarily returned his gaze through oversized sunglasses. Her eyes moved from his face slowly down to his sneakers.

Angus noticed her appraisal and the blood crept up his neck. Gripping her arm, he hustled her into the plane. As she climbed aboard, Apple automatically started to cross herself. Her fingers froze midway and her hand dropped to her side. Roland loitered in the aisle, waiting to see where Apple would sit. But Edna had already had a word with Keri, who poked his finger in Roland's back. "Get on with it, now. You're to help me fly."

Roland strapped himself into the copilot's seat. Sarah, Simeon, Farragut and Edna sat directly aft of the cockpit partition in two pairs of facing seats. Behind them, in tandem, Angus, then Apple.

Simeon complained that his head touched the ceiling so he and Sarah changed seats. "It will keep you from flying backwards, my angel," Simeon told Sarah with a kiss. It also gave him a better view of the rear of the plane.

Edna's eyes darted about, searching for a safe place for her carry-all. Finally she managed to wedge it under her seat.

Sarah twisted around to Angus. "Sim and I were just saying that we couldn't be happier having you aboard, 'n' at right, Sim?"

With a cautious glance at Apple, Simeon nodded.

"Everybody strapped in?" Keri asked, coming down the aisle. He yanked at all the seat belts. Returning to the cockpit, he revved the engines and raced the plane down the strip. The *Solar Bark* angled into the air.

After looking out the window a few minutes Sarah turned and smiled lavishly at Angus. " 'N' what was it you said you did?"

Angus told her he was a vice president of an American conglomerate. "In charge of foreign development and sales."

Edna recognized it as a fairly stable corporation, selling on the Big Board at approximately twenty times its earnings, if she remembered their last statement correctly.

Angus had spent the last year in Africa, "Scouting the markets, blocking out promotional campaigns to make the natives aware of our products. And that's all I'm going to say about business for the next couple of weeks."

Sarah glanced at Apple, who was leafing through a fashion magazine. " 'N' what about—?"

"Why, she's my, umm, coordinator," Angus said. But his grin implied more.

Sarah rattled on about the progress that men of Angus's caliber would bring to poor, underprivileged folk. "Refrigerators and air-conditioners and—" all the while stealing furtive glances at his muscular body.

Farragut listened in silence.

Angus felt his eyes closing. Another drink, that would straighten him out. He sucked on his lower lip. Christ, they'd really tied one on last night. Then, as he remembered what had happened later in bed, his gut knotted.

Never! He'd never had any trouble before. If anything, he'd worn a couple of people out. Angus thought back, trying to pinpoint exactly when he'd begun to misfire. Oh, maybe a couple of isolated times, just before he'd met Apple. But it was just after Apple's husband had died that it had gotten bad. Understandable enough, Angus reasoned. It had been one of the worst messes he'd ever been through in his life. And God knows, she was still taking it pretty hard.

Drinking had helped for a while. Then a couple of weeks ago the front office "suggested" that he take a vacation. Too bad he hadn't been able to book them on a hunting safari. Bagging Apple and some big game, that would have recharged him. But the government had clamped down on hunting permits, and they'd wound up with this bunch of sewn-up pussies.

Shelled out a small fortune, too. Well, the support check to his ex-wife and kids would be late this month. It was worth it; anything was worth it to get the old rock back. And Apple sure knew how to turn him on. He wished he could get a better handle on her. One minute as innocent as a kid in a convent. The next, playing so rough . . .

His hand fell back to touch Apple's knee. She rapped his knuckles with her cigarette case. Angus tightened his fingers around her kneecap until she winced and uncrossed her legs. His touch continued with rough tenderness, growing more exploratory as the plane droned on.

7

The next days were a whirlwind as the group flew from game park to game park. At Keekorock a beige ostrich hen whirled into a fantastic fan dance, trying to lure them away from her nest. At Tsavo, a bull elephant charged in mock attack when their car ventured too close to the herd. At Amboseli a herd of impala stotted straight up in the air, then arched across the plains in graceful, twenty-foot leaps.

"I just think these game runs are thrilling," Sarah announced one evening at cocktails. "And this safari would be complete if only we had—" and quickly arranged a bridge tournament. She couldn't have been more unhappy to discover that Angus didn't play. And that Farragut did.

Angus and Apple kept to themselves. They drank a great deal, went to bed early. There was always a lot of noise from their room.

Which made Roland's loneliness seem even worse. He'd come down with a severe case of the tail wagging the dog, and was beginning to wonder if the muscles in one arm were getting lopsided. Yet, the release was less satisfying.

If only there were some young people around, he thought. Everybody looked like they were heading for the elephants' graveyard. He would have settled for some raps with Keri, but the courier was always busy preparing the next routing. And every time he tried to get the least bit friendly with Apple she turned him down cold.

The group flew to Malindi on the coast and spent two days sportfishing in the Indian Ocean. Simeon fancied himself a buff, but it was Farragut who caught the prize of the day.

In their room after dinner, Angus rubbed his glowing body with sunburn lotion. "Do my back, honey, will you?" he asked.

Apple paid no attention to him. She was staring at a crimson oleander shrub. On one of the leaves, two praying mantises were beginning their ritual dance of sex.

"Wait for me, I'm going to clean up," Angus said, goosing her on his way to the bathroom. In the shower stall he bellowed a show tune in a husky, pleasant voice.

Apple inched closer to the plant. Standing on their back legs, the insects looked so human. The male would advance, then dart back, always keeping well out of the range of the female's powerful jaws. Suddenly he hopped onto her back, his body twitching. In the frenzy of sex his guard relaxed. The female reached over her shoulder and bit his head off. The headless male continued copulating until climax. Only then did he die. The female shrugged him off and settled down to devour the rest of her lover.

Apple resisted an urge to squash the avaricious queen. Why? she asked herself. That was the insect's way. But she, Apple ... With that came the unbidden memory of the gentle creature who had been her husband less than a year ago. Who would still be alive today had she not sinned. . . .

Angus strode back into the room, his taut stomach glowing above the towel wrapped around his waist.

"What are you doing?" he asked.

"Nothing." Apple opened the window and flicked the insect out into the garden. For a long moment she looked up, losing herself in the dark, racing clouds and the young moon that lay in the sky like an odalisque.

Why am I so hooked on her, Angus wondered, as he stared at her enormous, liquid, brown eyes. They were set in lashes as thick as weeds, and the way they never quite focused on him intensified her elusive quality. Sure, the fact that he'd managed to corral somebody twenty years younger was gratifying. But there was more. Somehow Apple reminded him of the way he used to be—sensual, beautiful, so alive. And that she seemed unaware of her attractiveness turned him on even more.

Yeah, she sure had something that kept the guys sniffing after her. Even that scrawny kid, Angus thought, chuckling to himself.

"But I've got you," Angus said, wrapping his arms around her. He nuzzled her neck, licking the salt off her skin. No doubt about it, he'd gotten fond of her. Maybe even a little dependent—he broke off the thought. He'd never been a supplicant in love, and he wasn't about to begin now.

Apple squirmed out of his embrace. Taking off her safari jacket, she began to brush her hair.

Angus made them another round of drinks. Apple took a tranquilizer with hers. Then Angus unwrapped the towel and began massaging himself. His vigorous rubbing vibrated every part of him. Apple looked away. Caught his swinging reflection in the mirror. Turned from that. Saw its ghost in the windowpane.

·45·

Angus came up behind her and pressed against the curve of her back. "I know how tough it's been for you these past months," he said softly. "But, honey, you've got to forget it. It's done—over with—an accident. Nothing you can do will change it. And all those priests you keep running to can only tell you the same thing. Why torture yourself to death? Come on, I want to give you a present. Top, bottom, front, back, you name it tonight."

"We can't solve it your way," she said dully. "I shouldn't have come with you."

He caught her ear lobe in his teeth and ran his finger down her cleavage. "A little French roll, hmm?"

She plucked his hand away. "Leave my breasts alone, they're antisocial tonight."

"That's okay, my penis is manic-depressive."

She laughed in spite of herself. But when he pinched her nipple she turned with a cry and tried to knee him in the groin.

"That's more like it," he growled. He pushed her down on the bed and burrowed his head in her lap. "Anybody home? Can Apple come out and play?"

"Go away. She's not feeling well."

"Then I'll just slip in for a short visit." With his left arm he pinned her shoulders while his right hand worked at the zipper of her pants.

Apple shut her eyes and called on every resource to fight the rousing heat spreading through her body. Her tongue flicked to the corners of her mouth. Sweet Mary, she prayed. Give me the strength to say no this once.

When she did not respond the anger flared in Angus. His teeth sank into the fleshy part of her inner thigh. She broke free and sprang at him, her fingernails raking at his crooked grin. He shoved her down again.

"Tell me you didn't like that," he said. "Go on, try and tell me."

Her eyes seemed to look through him. "You are fooling yourself, Angus," she said. "You are too old to be playing like a juvenile."

Stung, he sat back on his haunches. "There's not an ounce of fat on—"

"Old!" she cried. "Older than yesterday. Older tomorrow. Old!"

The flat of his hand caught her across the mouth.

"Last night," she plunged on, "you couldn't even—"

Her hair lashed wildly as his pendulum hand continued, each time draining more reason from her until her eyes glazed over and with an automatic motion she lifted her face to meet the blow, caught at last in its triumph.

Her flushed, sagging body told him she was ready. Angus had never been more ready. Over her feeble protests he chivvied her out of her clothes.

Her words were muffled by his driving torso. "Is with thee ... blessed art thou among ..."

They went at each other then, each intent on his own goal.

8

In the cottage directly opposite Angus's and Apple's, Edna stood at her darkened window. The events of the past half hour had turned her to stone.

At last she snapped her binocular case shut and with a shudder went to the shower. She turned the hot water on full force and stepped in, letting it lash her thin frame. Her veined, translucent skin turned pink.

As she dried herself, she breathed silent thanks that Roland had been assigned the cabin behind hers; he could not have seen anything. This time. She must talk to Keri—she must guard Roland from—Edna broke off and steadied herself. Control, she warned herself. *Knowing* the enemy had always proven the better part of the battle.

Edna slipped between the clammy sheets of her bed and began to ponder the enigma of Apple Romano.

She had everybody else on the safari safely categorized but Apple continued to elude her. Men were literally *drawn* into her orbit.

Edna closed her eyes. Roland, yes ... but more than Roland's safety was at stake. That girl was a direct threat to Edna. To everything she had worked so hard to develop in her life.

Edna wondered what she had been like at Apple's age. Her mind wandered back through the decades, centering at last on the family estate and coming to rest in that nightmare room where she had first learned the Goddard lesson.

Her father's bedroom. An enormous octagonal chamber built to accommodate his treasury of first editions. On her seventh birthday her father had set her up on the fireplace mantel. Behind her, the elaborate maritime clock tolled the hour. She looked at the alabaster hearth miles below, and was frightened.

Goddard held out his arms. "Jump," he said. "I'll catch you. Don't be afraid. There's a lesson I want you to learn."

She pressed tightly against the wall.

"Jump!" Her father smiled, his fingers beckoning.

Her heart sang with trust and she jumped. The alabaster flew up to meet her, smashed into her left arm. She lay there, stunned. The physical pain was minor compared to the pain of betrayal.

He picked her up and set her on her feet. "Stop crying," he commanded. "You're a Goddard, and it's time you learned the Goddard lesson. Remember it and you will never lack in life. Never trust *anybody*."

It wasn't until some weeks later that the governess noticed that Edna favored her left arm. Doctors diagnosed it as a recurrent paralysis rooted in some hysterical syndrome. It displeased Goddard, and Edna fell from his favor. He had no time for imperfection.

Edna learned to disguise her weakness, carrying flowers or her garden hat in her left hand, then a purse which gave way through the years to a carry-all she was never without.

Throughout her girlhood, on the occasional visits home

from boarding school, Edna avoided her father's room. The sweep of black Italian marble floor leading to the massive Elizabethan four-poster bed gave the place a funereal look that had always depressed her. But the day came when it seemed eminently appropriate, for there lay her father dying of intestinal cancer.

For three years Edna put aside her fear and helped nurse him. She was tireless, learning everything from changing dressings to administering morphine. In his lucid moments, Goddard told her again and again how her grandfather, a whaling captain, had amassed the first Goddard fortune.

"When his clipper ships unloaded their cargoes in the penal colonies of Australia, there was very little in the way of goods to bring back. The ships rode high, they would capsize without ballast. So he directed his captains to fill the holds with earth. That's right, common dirt! And he brought that dirt back here. Everybody laughed. But he used it as land fill in the marshes of New York's harbor. Built docks and wharves and storehouses on that new land he had created himself. They stopped laughing when they had to pay rent. The land value skyrocketed. Yes, a real mover of continents your grandfather was."

Goddard recounted how he had followed the Christian ethic and increased the gift of the talents tenfold. Oil and timber and copper and lead he had torn from the virgin America. Gradually Edna's fear of the man was replaced by respect for the force he was. A force that made all other men seem mundane.

For a thousand days and nights Edna sat by his bedside, listening, while her brothers and sisters, six in all, pursued polo, yacht-racing, lawn tennis, balls, kisses, and all the other inutile things her father despised.

In straightforward ways, clever, insidious ways, Edna pointed out to her father that all he had struggled so hard to build would be reduced to sixths at his death. Meanwhile she delighted him by quoting the latest prices of silver and of wheat futures; made sound sense when talking of the business possibilities of the new fad, the automobile. With an uncanny combination of expertise and intuition she learned to predict the rise and fall of the stock market and parlayed a sum he had given her as a bet into a small fortune.

But no matter what the bet, no matter what the dare, no matter how often she made him forget his pain she kept reminding him that the empire was about to fall. The estate was monumental, so money was not the issue. Edna was after a different, a whiter whale—power. And the common currency of power was people.

One winter evening she came into his bedroom and placed on the counterpane the new will she'd had drawn up. She also had the foresight to bring along two senior partners of the old law firm.

Edna's brothers and sisters were provided with handsome trust funds for life. But the bulk of the estate—the tremendous fortune, the interlocking corporate directorships and all the powers in them—all fell to her.

Goddard stared at his daughter and realized for the first time what he had spawned. He was frightened.

Edna sensed his indecision. Leaning over him, she murmured, "I'm doing it for you. For your name. For the memory of who and what you are. I will not fail you, I swear it. Trust me, father."

She put a pen into his hand.

Though it weakened him severely, Edna propped him up. She guided his hand, almost willing him to sign all the copies. As page after page was initialed, she felt her pulse beat dully through her body. Her skin tingled; she felt lightheaded and heavy in her limbs all at once.

At last he fell back, exhausted. She kissed him lightly

on the mouth, then pressed until her lips were bruised. Her nostrils contracted against the awful stench of the disease, a smell of death. She started out of the room, the copies of the rolled will clutched in her left hand.

Dimly, she heard one of the nurses cry out, "Miss Edna! Your father!" And the hollow footsteps running across the marble as everybody rushed to the bed.

Edna did not rush. She knew. Her fingers closed against the fine parchment, crushing the roll of paper. Her heart raced, her body burned with the most profound sensation she had ever known. She was aware of every part of her body, even her arm. She could not bear the feeling.

She sagged against the wall, pressing her throbbing flesh against the cold, impersonal marble. Alone in her victory, she experienced the only physical consummation of her life.

9

The capstone of the safari's first week was an overnight stay at Treetops, the hotel built in a grove of Cape chestnut trees in Kenya's plateau country. They were to fly there from Malindi, but a late fuel delivery had put them behind schedule. At last they were airborne.

Keri flipped on the cabin intercom. "I've radioed ahead to Nyeri for special transportation," he said. "But even so we may not make it."

Unless they reached Treetops before dusk, he told them, there was no hope of getting in. With darkness the herds and the predators completely surrounded the hotel in the trees.

Sarah, unable to lure Angus into any worthwhile gossip, had unhinged the dropleaf table and plumped for a rubber.

"All my life I've hankered to spend a night there," she said to Simeon. "Two spades, your bid, Edna."

Edna watched the colored pieces of pasteboard flash before her eyes. Diamond on diamond, heart on heart, king on queen, and always the face of the couple kept intruding. Angus's perverse smile, the chest hair curling from his open collar, and Apple, traveling around with him, not even pretending to be married . . . Edna felt her skin prickle with the flagrancy of it all.

And here Roland was just at that vulnerable stage. Edna began to question her judgment in not having hired a private plane for the trip. But that had seemed so insular. She'd wanted Roland exposed to a spectrum of people—within reason, of course. She had assumed that the extravagant cost would insure that everybody on this safari would be top-drawer. Well, so much for money these days.

Already she had noticed Roland gravitating toward Apple and Angus. What was it that drew him to the base and vulgar? A trait from his mother's side, no doubt, for it had never existed in her son. She pressed her fingers to her temple, with the memory of the superb specimen he had been.

"Your play, Edna," Sarah reminded her, then looked up at her bloodless face. "Why, whatever is the matter?"

Edna drew herself erect. "Not a thing," she said, and boldly playing the queen of spades, won trick and game.

Up in the cockpit Roland was busy inspecting the instrument panel. "How fast can this thing go?" he asked.

"Cruising speed's two hundred. In a pinch we could do two-forty. That is, if you got out and pushed," Keri answered.

A jagged mountain range began to take shape. "How tall's the highest peak?" Roland asked, checking the altimeter.

"Kilimanjaro's 19,000 feet. Mount Kenya is 17,000. But don't worry, I've learned to go around them."

"Could we crash? Say if we got hit by lightning?"

"How is it you're not humming *Dies Irae* with all those jolly questions? We do get a fair share of electrical storms. One could conceivably burn out the radio, bollix the compass. But very remote that it would knock us out of the sky."

Sarah's voice drifted to the cockpit. "Farragut, I don't mean to tell you how to play—"

"But, Sarah," Farragut answered, "it was you who reneged on that last trick."

Roland lost himself in the puffs of foliage following the meander of a river. "Ever get lost?" he asked.

"On occasion," Keri said. "Though not since Nairobi installed modern equipment." He switched the radio on long enough for a garbled voice to announce weather conditions.

"But planes do go down," Roland insisted.

Keri nodded. "There's Grzimek, crashed in the Serengeti. Never could explain that one." Then Keri's eyes narrowed. "Wait a second—you're not planning an encore to that railroad caper, are you?"

"Gee, let up, will you? You're the one who said to forget it."

"You're right, and I apologize," Keri said.

Roland cracked his knuckles. "It's just that I get these premonitions."

Far to the north a column of fair weather cumulus billowed up, above it a layer of thin altocirrus and barely discernible above that, wisps of altostratus. There was a whoop and scramble for the cards as the *Solar Bark* plummeted in a sudden downdraft.

"What's happening?" Roland gulped. "Hey, look." He pointed to the plane's shadow, which had just plunged off a cliff to be lost thousands of feet below.

"The Great Rift Valley," Keri said as he fought to keep the plane level. An enormous gash in the earth stretched to the horizon like a huge bolt of lightning burned into the ground. Keri adjusted course to follow it. "About a third of the earth's surface is affected by the fault, from Siberia all the way down through East Africa's plateau country. The oil companies are convinced there are vast deposits all along it, particularly in the Northern Frontier District.

"There's been fighting in the N.F.D. for more than a century. It's still going on. Last week, the Shifta, that's what these bandits are called, massacred an entire village and then melted back over the borders."

"You mean all that's happening now?" Roland said. "Look, I'm your simple garden variety nonviolent coward. Catch them!"

"Bit more complex than that," Keri said. "As long as the area's in upheaval it gives the various governments room to negotiate. Whichever country gets final claim—"

"Gets the oil," Roland finished. "These Shifta are meanies?"

"Oh, very. When they're feeling especially fond of their prisoners, they get high on a weed called *bhang*, a stronger version of marijuana, and while away the hours with the Torture of the Joints."

Roland stuck his fingers in his ears. Curiosity got the better of him and he pulled one finger out. "Well?"

"Starting with your wrists and ankles, they lop off a joint a day. Cauterize it so you don't bleed to death and spoil their fun. By the twelfth day they've worked themselves up to the you-know-what."

Roland counted on his body. "Ouch. You're not putting me on, are you? Any chance of our running into them?"

"Not a chance. We've cut out all the game parks in the N.F.D. Pity, too, because those barren reaches have some of the most exotic game."

"Say, you wouldn't happen to know where a guy could get a little of this—what did you call it?"

"*Bhang*," Keri said, spelling it. "Matter of fact, I do."

Roland leaned toward him. "Yeah?"

"I believe that Edna is the pusher on this trip."

"Roland, what are you so hysterical about?" Edna called out. "Share it with us."

They'd been flying for almost three hours when Keri said, "We'll be over my ranch soon. If we're lucky, perhaps the missus will flap her apron at us. She runs the place now that I'm off safariing, and a cracking good job she does of it."

"How long have you been changing dirty silk diapers for tourists?" Roland asked.

"Touché," Keri said. "Three years. And for a farthing I'd chuck the whole mess and land in time for dinner."

Roland laughed. "Were you born here?"

"Second generation. Granddad fell in love with these highlands, said they reminded him of Kent. He hewed a ranch out of the wilderness and cross-bred cattle, English and native stock, until he had a superb herd. Then my dad devoted his life to it. But when I was called to serve with the R.A.F., in the early fifties, we began having our troubles." Keri's eyes glinted like agates. "I came home to find he'd been killed in a Mau-Mau uprising. Some of our own servants ..."

Roland scrambled to say something consoling, but Keri's mind was elsewhere.

Dinner ... then night would roll down the mountains, bringing the frost that made the library fire such a delight and the warmth of Livvie in their four-poster such a luxury. In this bed Keri discovered he truly loved the rather plain girl he'd met during service in London, who'd cheerfully transplanted herself and struck roots in alien soil. In this bed their first child was delivered, stillborn, and the others had come squalling into the world.

Roland's voice broke through. "If you own a ranch, then what makes you do this chicken kind of a job?"

"A chicken kind of fate," Keri said. "You've seen what's just happened to the Asian settlers? Well, now the government's trying to placate every native by giving him a patch of land. Soon most of the white settlers will be stripped of their holdings."

"Didn't it belong to the natives to begin with?"

"Rot!" Keri exclaimed. "By that reasoning, why don't you give America back to the Indians? This land was wilderness, lying unused for centuries. Why didn't the natives claim it then? No, only *after* it had been developed. Oh, to be sure, there's old Jomo Kenyatta's mollifying *'Harambee'*! Let's all work together," Keri translated. "Black and white. Fine. Except we must renounce British citizenship or lose everything."

"I don't get it. Why didn't you become a Kenyan?"

Keri shot him a disgruntled look. "Oh, act your age, boy. Would you give up your American citizenship?"

Roland mulled that over while Keri fell into a mood. Each time they discussed it, he and Livvie had come to the same helpless conclusion. Habit, sentiment and "for the children's sake" won, and they remained loyal to England. Livvie and the kids would run the ranch until it was confiscated. Keri would find work in the fiercely competitive international market and try to save enough money for a new stake.

Keri had plodded down to Nairobi's work mart, only to discover that this was not the white man's moment. Certainly not for a farmer in his late thirties. He declined shopkeeping and other desk jobs offered by friends, recognizing them as a slow wasting away. However, he was still a crack flier, and pilots were much in demand for the burgeoning tourist industry. His first tours were comic disasters. He couldn't quite believe the helplessness of most people. Or the stupidity. But, as he'd told the boy, as long as you didn't lose any of them in the bush it all worked out.

Adaptability seemed to be the prime requisite in this new world. And, having adapted, Keri daily convinced himself that his choice had been correct.

"So that's why I ran away from home," Keri finished with a touch of rancor. "Left my dullard existence to mingle with the rich, famous and successful, like you."

"You want me to cluck a few times, right?" Roland asked. "Look, I'm sorry about your parents and the farm. Honest. But there's a bigger truth to this than just you. Nobody asked the English to colonize. You came with a gun and you stayed with a gun. So now when the worm turns, you complain? If the land really meant so much to you, then why *not* become a citizen? Know why? Because you're trying to hold onto both worlds at the same time."

Keri swallowed a retort and tried a more jocular vein. "You *have* been talking to my eldest son! Sounds like much the same balderdash he plagues me with. You pups rant and rave against conformity, yet you listen to the same music, wear the same clothes, think the same thoughts—Lord!"

Keri banked the plane over the Rift wall. Trees flashed by, then a clearing of neat furrowed patterns, and suddenly a house revealed itself. A woman rushed out, three children scrambling after, waving frantically. Feeling an ache in his groin, Keri blew the toy family a kiss.

From out of nowhere he was overcome with a wave of guilt for all the women he'd bedded these past years. Some who'd crept into his bed. Others into whose bed he'd climbed. He tried to console himself with the fact that he'd never have strayed had he remained home. But when a man was away from his mate for so long...

Volunteering to pilot this safari with no break between had been a mistake, he realized now. It was unfair to himself, Livvie and the kids. Still, there had been the extra money. And the rumored possibility of a junior partnership with the firm.

For a split second the silver props whirled with spiraling sunlight and Keri thought, I'll never see them again.

He dug his fingers into his eyes. Easy now, he warned himself. Or, you'll be getting as daft as the boy.

"What was all that circling about?" Edna asked. "Aren't we late enough as is?"

"Keri, what exactly happens at Treetops?" Roland asked.

"Nothing like anything you've ever done in your life before," Keri answered. "You'll see."

10

They piled into the car waiting for them at the Nyeri airport and tore along the mountain curves. Bouncing, complaining, they raced the sinking sun through the highlands and reached the Treetops enclave with only minutes to spare.

An armed, agitated white hunter met them at the base of the hill and rushed them upslope toward a plateau fringed with ancient Cape chestnut trees.

"Inconsiderate Americans," the hunter said. "Over a hundred buffalo are at the waterhole. If they get wind of us and panic, the jackals will be dining on us."

But they reached the grove without stampeding the herd and climbed a narrow wooden staircase high into the tree hotel.

"Ever seen anything like it?" Roland asked Apple, whose swaying form preceding him up the ladder made him stumble more than once.

Tree limbs fragrant with buds grew through the corridors and the tiny rooms. Edna could not quite hide a grimace when she discovered she'd been assigned the room next to Apple and Angus.

The structure had three levels, each with an outside deck facing the waterhole. Every seat was occupied: Europeans, Asians, Africans, some sketching, others taking photographs. Animals were lined up around the waterhole, which glowed like a sheet of burnished copper in the setting sun. The buffalo had given way to duiker, bushbuck, waterbuck and other assorted game that kept Edna in a frenzy leafing through her books.

"Why, we're like Swiss Family Robinson," Sarah said as they reached the top deck.

Sarah scored points for that one, Roland thought. It was the treehouse of everybody's dreams. Smack in the middle of danger, yet safe above it all.

"Look—there at ten o'clock!" Simeon cried.

"Giant forest hog," Keri said. "Both male, three hundred pounds apiece, easily. There'll be trouble."

The other game scampered away, leaving a wide arena for the two hogs who were pawing the earth. With a piercing squeal they charged, tusks clashing. When the dust and grunts of rage subsided, one boar was kneeling on its front legs; blood coursed from a gash in its shoulder.

Angus took a long swallow of his drink. "Go on, finish him," he said.

Edna hit the rail with her fist and repeated in a barely audible voice, "Yes, finish him."

Keri looked at her in mild surprise. "No, they'll separate. Edna, I should like to see you at a boxing match."

Edna flushed but quickly recovered. "No point leaving an adversary around who'll eventually try to get revenge, is there?"

Keri smiled wryly, " 'To the death' and 'for revenge' are human refinements, I'm afraid."

Apple, slightly nauseated by the battle and the blood, pointed beyond the immediate hills. "What is that mountain?"

"Mount Kenya," Keri answered.

A turmoil of sullen blue and gray clouds obscured the summit. The mountain itself was the color of a ripe frosted grape, and the ice cap flamed with the sunset.

"Native legend has it that Mount Kenya is the seat of God," Keri said. "He envelops himself in that constant cloud cover to hide His face from man."

"Don't tell the lamas," Roland said. "They think they've got that market cornered in the Himalayas."

Apple laughed. "And my pope believes He is a permanent house guest at St. Peter's."

Whereupon Simeon launched into a sermon of how God was everywhere, in every human heart, in every—

I love you, Roland said to Apple with his eyes, but she paid no attention to him.

The last of the game had their fill and began to drift from the waterhole into the surrounding twilight.

Roland leaned over the rail. "I can't get over how they lined up and waited their turn. No pushing, sharing it all."

Sarah snagged his belt loop and pulled him back from the rail. "I declare, child, you're enough to give a body heart failure."

Keri was saying to Edna, "Most animals have a sense of live and let live. We've lost that, more's the pity. We're too hellbent on refining our killer instincts."

"Killer instincts?" Edna repeated slowly. "What can you mean?"

Keri cracked his fingers, a habit that he was, oddly, picking up from Roland. "Let's save it for some dark night around a campfire." He opened his eyes wide as though telling a horror story. "Man—the instinctive, dedicated killer."

Apple asked hurriedly, "Will we see any giraffes? I have a passion for them."

"How come, honey?" Angus asked, his arm on her shoulder.

Her mouth pursed. "I don't know. Maybe because they are such comic misfits in a world of comic misfits."

"Apple?" Roland said eagerly, "you really missed something back in Nairobi. Two males and this female? Before our very eyes—"

"Roland!"

Keri cocked his head. "There's the dinner gong." He offered his arm to Edna. "Madame, may I have the honor?"

Edna would not take his arm until she'd herded Roland safely in front of her.

After a gourmet dinner, most of the group went back to the top veranda. Apple and Angus bought a bottle of vodka and retired to their room.

The quart was half gone before Angus began to get a buzz on. Directly below their window Apple, in her nightgown, watched two sable antelope sparring with their horns. A female waited patiently for the winner. The defeated buck scampered away; the doe presented her hindquarters to the champion. He gently nosed his way down to her loins, then nimbly mounted her.

"What do you say to a little of that?" Angus said, kissing Apple's fingers.

Apple pulled her hand away.

Angus poured them another round of drinks. He got undressed slowly. Pity there were no mirrors in the room. The lamp behind projected his shadow on the pine wall and he watched it change shape. A simple lay tonight, he decided. Missionary position, the way he'd first learned to do it back in Michigan.

The suddenness of his move caught Apple by surprise. Without a caress, without a kiss, he bullied his way into her, the dryness and friction exciting him even more. Her cry of pain only spurred him on.

Christ, he thought, reveling in his performance, technique was everything. Then, for no reason, no reason at all! Oh, God, not again! The panic gripped him. With an oath he rolled off her and lay panting.

Apple looked at him with a mixture of compassion and loathing. She wanted to help him. But how? She could not help herself. She slipped from the bed, threw on some clothes, and was out of the room before Angus had fully recovered.

Angus sat up, started to make himself another drink, and then smashed his fist against the wall. *She's* doing this to me! Yes, that's it, he thought.

He hustled into pants and a jacket and went after her. She wasn't going to get away. Not this time.

11

From the top deck Roland looked out at the mountain mists stealing across the waterhole. Shifting shadows made the landscape more surreal than any he'd ever dreamed. The swirling fog drew denser, more elusive, and Roland felt a million light-years away from the bounded life he'd led with Edna.

Iron or gold, chains are chains, he thought. He hugged himself, excited by the brief stirrings of freedom.

Farragut, loaded down with camera cases and a telescoping tripod, came out on the deck. Roland went over to help him set up his equipment. "Wow, this has got to be the most expensive flashgun made," Roland said. "In fact, everything you've got is the best."

Farragut smiled at him. "I did shop around quite a bit before I decided."

"Say, Farragut, why did you pick a safari like this anyway?" Roland asked. "You don't seem like the rest of those—dinosaurs."

Farragut slapped his leg and laughed. "Oh, I had my

reasons. And the way it's working out couldn't be more perfect.''

"You've got something big going for you, don't you?" asked Roland. "Come on, Farragut, level."

Farragut seemed about to confide in Roland, but then his eyes got a cornered look. "All in good time," he said. "Right now I've got to work."

Roland got the message. He squared his shoulders and walked off in a determined stride. Though there aren't exactly a lot of places to go, he told himself. He leaned over the fence railing. Three stories below, two sable deer were putting on a show. The buck made it look so easy, so different from the bumbling attempts Roland had made.

He felt his own body tense in a contact high. Too dark to film it. He jammed his hands in his pockets and watched until they were finished. When he'd calmed down enough he wandered around and finally wound up at the huge spotlight that lit the waterhole.

Hordes of insects swam suspended in the beam of the artificial moon. Bats dipped and swooped, throwing their webbed shadows on the night, their barely audible ping-ping like the squeak of mice.

Roland spotted Apple and Angus at the top of the staircase. It looked as though they were arguing. Faking nonchalance, he ambled over.

Angus whirled at the interruption. About to boot the kid the hell away, he pulled himself up short. A way-out liquor-fogged idea began to form in his mind.

He squeezed Roland's shoulder. "Say, guy? What was it you were telling us about those giraffes?"

Roland's tongue stuck to the roof of his mouth.

Apple yanked free of Angus's hand. "Forgive me," she said, "but I am very tired." She quickly started down the stairs.

Roland looked after her, crestfallen. "Doesn't dig me much, does she?" he said.

"You're way off, guy," Angus said. "In fact, she was just telling me how much she liked you, wished she could get to know you better."

Roland gave him a doubtful look.

"Okay, I'll prove it to you," Angus said, his charm working at top power. "Give us fifteen, maybe twenty minutes to clean up and things. Then stop by the room and have a drink with us. See for yourself." Angus's crooked grin got broader. Slapping Roland on the butt, he went downstairs after Apple.

Roland stood nailed to the spot, mouth slightly open.

Out of the night Edna's voice was calling. He went to the row of deck chairs where she sat, wrapped in a blanket against the mountain chill.

"Roland, what did that couple want?" Edna asked.

"Well, they—nothing," Roland said.

"Of course, I wouldn't dream of telling you what to do, Roland. That's why we have such a good relationship." Her fingers never stopped kneading the brittle skin of her carryall. "But at best," she said, enunciating every word, "those people are just not our sort, dear."

Roland toed the planks with his sneakers.

"I know I don't have to remind you how right I was about your friend, what was his name? Oh, Howie."

"Yes, ma'am."

"Excellent, then. I knew I could count on your good sense. Now Roland, it's been a fierce twenty-four hours. Promise me you'll go right to bed? Get a good night's sleep."

She took his silence for a promise.

"Sweet dreams, then. Why don't you wake me an hour

before dawn? We'll watch the sunrise together. They say the birds are at their most magnificent then. You won't forget?"

"I won't," he called over his shoulder. Taking the steps two at a time, he raced through the narrow corridors to his room. Checked his wristwatch. Changed into a fresh shirt. Sat down on the bed. Jumped up and put on fresh underwear. Then he sprawled out on the narrow cot, folded his hands behind his head, and let his imagination run wild.

Minutes after Roland left, Edna experienced a wave of dizziness and went down to her room. It's only the altitude, she told herself, fighting to keep the room in perspective. She sank onto the narrow bed, taking her bag with her, and pressed her forehead to the leather until the spell passed. Where am I, she wondered. She looked into the caldron of her carry-all; then with a sigh dumped its contents onto the counterpane. As she carefully put each item back in the bag, she saw the jigsaw puzzle of time and place take a more definite form.

Binoculars, insect bomb, sunglasses. Credit cards good for anything anywhere in the world. Twenty-thousand dollars in travelers' checks for incidentals in places that might not know her name. Passport, driver's license, social security card, library card, luggage claim check, travel insurance and the return tickets home.

Oh, yes, I'm in Africa.

Keys for the country house, keys for the co-op in the city. A cosmetics case, a small black-framed photograph of her son, which she put on the night table, a pharmacopoeia with ointments, antibiotics, sleeping pills, water purifiers, amyl nitrate, salt tablets, malaria pills, and vitamins that ran the gamut of the alphabet. Though her health was excellent, Edna believed in being prepared.

Only two items were left. A slide rule on which she calculated percentage returns on principal. And, in a gold-tipped leather case, a small straight razor.

Everything safely back in the carry-all, Edna breathed another long sigh. She devoured the brochure on where they would be flying next, said a prayer for Roland, and turned off the light.

A sudden scream made Edna sit bolt upright. It had sounded so human. She listened, her heart thumping, but only the silence answered her. Edna stared at the photograph of her son until her eyes blurred. Her arm began to ache. She massaged it, trying to rub the pain away.

The night sounds made her aware of the growing turmoil within her. She closed her eyes, knowing all the while that sleep would not bless her. This would be another night of endless recrimination. Years would telescope, despairs long buried would parade past her closed lids—the husband who had failed her, the son who had failed her, the way of life which was fast failing her. Till at last, her thoughts would flee down the twisted corridors of her past . . .

To the hospital where she traded her naval captain husband, dead of influenza, for a tiny, pink baby just born to her, and the unholy feeling that she'd gotten the best of the trade.

Widowed, with an infant son, Edna set about the business of living. With her wealth and handsomeness she had many chances to remarry, but chose none. Physical contact had been an obligation, never a pleasure, and any need for love was fulfilled by her son, a handsome child, who under her slavish attention grew to a rococo beauty.

At twenty-five, he married the debutante Edna chose, divorced her a year later, remarried at twenty-eight, divorced again, each time returning to Edna's understanding bosom.

By the time he was thirty-six, Edna grew alarmed. He had not yet discharged his responsibility. The line ended with him. Daily she increased her pressure; reasoning, cajoling, finally threatening excommunication from the family fortune. At forty he slipped from her grasp and sought salvation by living in quick succession with an Eurasian entertainer, a sometime B-girl, and a career diplomat with an unsavory reputation. Finally he shocked the family by eloping with a robust girl from the Midwest whom he'd met by chance in a hotel lobby. In a desperate effort to qualify as Edna's heir, Roland impregnated the girl quickly. They named the boy Roland, Jr. Mother and grandmother loathed each other. Edna's refusal to receive the family in her home proved the final blow for Roland, Sr. His excesses grew. His wife divorced him, taking the baby with her. Roland, Sr., had a breakdown.

Edna fought his dissipations with her love, determined to pull him back to sanity. On the verge of this accomplishment, she discovered him one night in a cheap hotel, alone and dead.

Family influence was brought to bear. The coroner listed the death as due to natural causes, though the combination of alcohol and barbiturates and the note written to his mother hinted in a different direction.

"Mother, you are contemptuous of weakness, but you are drawn to it like a scavenger to carrion. Without an inner life of your own, you are condemned to feed on others. For forty years you have fed on mine, and all your good and charitable deeds cannot mask the black instinct in you. Mother, you are a killer. And your weapon is love."

For two years Edna wandered from doctors to spas to rest homes, existing with a quiet desperation that verged on madness. She came home with a new plan. It was not a simple task to get custody of the child, and a bitter legal fight ensued. Edna did everything possible to persuade the mother. She reasoned. She offered a ransom. She prayed.

The matter was suddenly resolved when her daughter-in-law died of a ruptured appendix, a pain she'd neglected because she'd been so harassed by the court battle.

Edna accepted this death as a sign of higher intervention. Appointed legal guardian, she grasped at the new chance given her, determined to fill the void left by one Roland with another.

A dream spasm contorted Edna's face. She thought of Roland, Jr., and felt her heart contract. Was his every act, every word, to be an attack against her? Terror tore open her eyes. With her pulse pounding she hurried out of bed and down the hallway to Roland's room. She knocked, then threw the door open.

Roland sat up and stared at her dumbly, rubbing the sleep from his eyes.

Edna drew herself erect. "I just wanted to see if you were all right, dear," she said. "Wouldn't you be more comfortable if you weren't in your clothes? Remember, I love you."

After Edna had gone it took Roland some minutes to figure out what had happened. He looked at his watch. Nuts! Almost two hours had gone by. He would have slept till morning if she hadn't wakened him.

He waited five minutes, then crept down the deserted corridor. No other way, he'd have to sneak past Edna's room. Somehow he did it. With a silent prayer that he wouldn't make too much of an ass of himself, he knocked on Angus's door.

12

"Thought you'd never get here, guy," Angus greeted him. His undershirt showed his massive neck and arms. "Apple, make—what's your name?—yeah, make Roland a drink."

Apple, clad only in a bra and half-slip, crouched on the bed, staring out the window. Below, ponderous rhinos rooted at the salt licks.

Roland tore his eyes from her and swallowed. "Edna says they've been around longer than man," he stammered. "Sixty million years."

"That a fact," Angus commented flatly. Apple didn't turn or speak. "Don't mind her," Angus said. "She popped a couple of pills a while ago. Made her dopey in the head."

"Maybe I'd better split then," Roland said, reaching for the doorknob.

Angus put his arm around Roland's shoulder. "After waiting for you this long? Listen, guy, you know the way women are. She'll come around in a couple of minutes."

"Sure," Roland nodded, not knowing the way women were at all. Jesus, what a build Angus had. And the smell of booze in the room was enough to pickle you.

"Vodka okay?" Angus asked, reaching for the near-empty bottle.

"Thanks but I don't drink much," Roland said.

"What do you do?" Angus grinned. "Say, wait. I made a score in Nairobi. Local weed, guaranteed to blow your mind."

"Grass?" Roland asked eagerly. He opened the envelope Angus handed him.

"Yes, but they don't call it that here," Angus said. "Hey, Apple, I knew this kid would turn out to swing. Come on, guy, roll us a couple."

Roland squeezed in beside Angus on the bed. He rolled a joint, lit up, took a long drag, and almost choked. It was the strongest stuff he'd ever had. He passed the stick to Apple, who pushed it away. Angus joined him, though.

Silent minutes ticked by as the roach burned down to Roland's fingers. The cube of the room lost its sharp outlines. "You know, this could turn out to be not such a bad trip after all," Roland said to the friendlier, more attentive furniture.

Somehow, Apple was moving across the bed.

Angus shoved her back down. "You don't actually want to go anywhere, now do you?"

Roland watched with amused detachment as the undershirt lifted itself off Angus's head and floated across the room. Roland got up to leave. "Looks like you want—"

"Yes, go quickly," Apple said hoarsely.

Angus's finger poked his chest and pinned him to the bed. "Stick around, guy. You've got time for another joint, right? Hey, you know how to work a Polaroid?"

"I'll be so whacked out of my skull if I have another stick, and there's Edna to wake at dawn—"

That did it. He lit a second joint. About two weeks later he finished it and went on the nod.

When he opened his eyes it didn't seem at all strange that the vodka bottle was lying empty on the floor, that Angus was in his jockey shorts, and that Apple's bra had disappeared.

At the waterhole the artificial light freed the animals from gravity. The man-made moonlight cast underwater shadows in the room and gleamed off the beautiful blue bodies moving languorously.

"Awake now?" Angus's voice called through a conch shell. In one slow stride he was at the door. The bolt slammed loud enough to be heard in Edna's room, Roland thought.

Angus grabbed Roland under the arms and propped him against the wall. "Listen, guy, better get with it. Isn't it about time you got a divorce from your hand?"

All Roland could make out were the jockey shorts bursting with Angus and the husky voice that breathed, "Come on, Apple. Let's show the joys of living to our young stud here."

They were in some kind of a dance, Roland decided, and now she was using the bed as a trampoline but Angus grabbed her and kept her from floating away.

"I'm not hurting her, guy. It's just a little game we play, like punching up a pillow to make it more comfortable. That's the way you get your kicks these days, dear, right? Or have you popped too many downers to even remember that?"

Angus peeled off the restraining cloth. His white haunches floated between the suntanned parts of his body.

Roland looked, looked again. Either it was the distortion from the grass—no, it was real. He felt himself shrivel.

Roland saw Angus's tousled head roll to Apple's thighs, watched her legs melt apart and her body arch upward with an involuntary shudder.

He stared at the swell of breast, the dark hair that cascaded off the bed to the floor. You'll never see anything this beautiful again, he thought. His trembling fingers reached out to weave through the strands.

Angus reached through the marijuana haze and pulled Roland closer. "Don't just sit there, dummy, strip," he commanded.

Hands that were attached to Roland's arms but curiously didn't belong to him shucked off his chinos.

Angus's hoarse voice was telling him what he had to do to be a man, and the strong fingers on his neck guided him.

"I love you," Roland whispered.

Her body was a garden, and her sweet smell engulfed him. Rough hands roamed over him, violent, pressing him tighter against Apple while the husky instructions spurred him to a dizzy frenzy.

Roland caught a glimpse of Apple's sweat-beaded face. "Are you all right?" he asked anxiously.

"She's never been better," Angus said, grinning. "And, guy, you're the one who's doing it."

Roland swelled with the praise. But now something was happening that he couldn't figure out. A jumble of bodies moving in three separate directions. Indiscriminate mouths seeking and finding, flesh sliding against flesh, caresses tightening until they blurred into pure sensation.

Roland reached to kiss Apple's mouth but her face was hidden under her hair.

He felt the tender, pliant body beneath him, felt his energy building and for a wild second wished he hadn't turned on so much—nuts, Angus was in his way again. The three of them rocked in their disparate rhythms, the energy building until Roland had no control, pounding hard, driving faster, deeper. Roland felt his world slipping away while Apple gripped his body with her own. "Live," she whispered frantically. "Live!"

He sank his teeth into her shoulder to throttle his scream, shooting himself into manhood.

When Roland woke a block of concrete was pinning him down. Only Angus's leg. Apple lay pressed against the window. Roland shook his head, fighting his stupor. He'd have given anything for a pint of ice cream.

He looked to Apple to thank her. Or whatever it was you said afterwards. Like, I love you. Wasn't that always in it somewhere? Or a kiss? There sure had been a lot of mouth work, but not one kiss.

He traced his finger along her chin and turned her face to him. She looked at him, wide-eyed, unseeing. He realized she'd been awake all this time, her lips moving in endless litany. "Pray for us . . . now and in the hour. . ."

Who are you, Roland wondered, staring at her. Who did I share my moment with?

"Apple?" Roland whispered.

Her blank eyes went straight through him. She doesn't know who I am, he thought. She never even saw me.

He scrambled out of the bed.

Angus rubbed his eyes. "What's up? Why are you getting dressed?" He gave Roland a sharp, playful slap on the ass. "We're ready to go another round. You going to let an old man like me put you to shame, guy?"

"The name's Roland!" he barked.

"What?" Angus grinned crookedly and reached out to grab him, but Roland had already zipped up.

He fumbled with the latch and lurched out of the room. Angus's laughter followed him down the corridor.

13

Roland couldn't get to sleep. Always he came back to the same sad place. He could have been *anybody* to them. He sat up to stop thinking. Almost dawn. He straightened out his wrinkled clothes and went to Edna's room. It was empty.

He found her on the top deck, talking to Keri. The sharp air jabbed into Roland's lungs and made him lightheaded again.

Edna was leafing through her *Book of the Heavens* as Keri pointed out the constellations.

"See there in the east? That's Spica in the Virgin. And Sirius, the Dog Star, brightest of them all," he said. "They're especially brilliant during the last hour."

"Extraordinary, how it takes one out of oneself," Edna murmured.

Roland came up behind them and Edna cried out with fright. "Don't *ever* do that!" Her face tightened. "Roland, where have you been? I went to your room—"

Roland blinked to keep her in focus.

Edna looked at him closely "What *is* the matter with you? Why do your eyes look so strange? And what's that odor?"

Keri's nose wrinkled. *Bhang*. Where in the world had the boy gotten the weed?

Roland looked back at Keri defiantly. Go screw, he thought.

From the dense bush across the waterhole came the simpering cry of a hyena, answered by another and another until at least a dozen had joined in, their mournful howls rising to the galleon moon.

Every hair on Roland's body prickled. "That a pack of them?"

Keri nodded. "Out for the last murder of the night. Or to steal a soul before dawn. Whichever appeals to you more."

The wailing grew distant. Roland hung his head back and slowly lifted his hand to grasp the stars. With a noiseless scream a shooting star blazed through his fingers and was gone. Roland stared at his empty hand.

Keri looked at him levelly. "My old Kikuyu nanny once told me that shooting stars were God's tears. For the evil that man brings on himself."

"Sure they are," Roland said. "But you know what else they are? Compressed hydrogen burning itself out."

Keri shrugged. "Perhaps that's the form God's tears take."

Edna interrupted irritably. "Roland, I asked you a question."

"If you'll forgive me," Keri said, getting to his feet, "I've some alternate routing to plan. The Northern Frontier's definitely been closed." He left Edna and Roland alone on the veranda.

After a silence she repeated stiffly, "Where were you?"

Roland weighed what his answer would be. In his mind he heard the Iron Maiden creaking shut.

"Tell me!" she said.

With a sinking feeling Roland answered, "Why? I don't ask you where you go, do I?"

Edna's face registered shock and then disbelief. He had been a trial before, but this was the first time he'd deliberately disobeyed her. A dull pain radiated through her left arm and shoulder.

"How dare you?" she whispered.

Roland clenched his fists to keep from shaking. "All right," he said, his voice trembling. "Apple and Angus invited me to have a couple of drinks with them."

Her fingers tightened on the carry-all. "After I expressly forbade you?" she said.

Roland heard his heart pounding throughout his body. "Yes," he said. "What's more, the minute they invite me I'll do it again. Anything else you want spelled out?"

Edna took in his disheveled clothes, the blood-swollen lips, the crooked grin. Once more she shut her mind to the moans that had come from the room adjoining hers and had driven her to the top deck.

No, she did not need to know anything more.

Roland went down to his room.

Edna did something she had not done for many years. She started to cry.

14

The travelers flew to three game parks in as many days, as they made their way toward Paraa in Uganda. There they were to take an excursion boat to the headwaters of the Nile, a much touted highlight of the safari.

The morning started with calamity and progressed to disaster. Farragut left a camera behind. Sarah cut her leg shaving. Simeon came down with *turista*. By the time they were on their way they were running almost two hours late.

During the flight Roland reviewed the night at Treetops as he'd done a hundred times before. Had it really happened? The way Apple was avoiding him, he could have hallucinated the whole thing. The only proof was Edna. She was being too damned nice.

For her part, Edna was still in a state of profound confusion. Besides feeling revulsion at Roland's behavior, she felt as though her sanity was at stake. She was frightened, and for once in her life, she didn't know what to do.

"Look sharp," Keri said over the intercom, "that's the Nile below."

The cutthroat bridge tournament stopped long enough for a few snapshots as they streaked low over the purling cataract. A heavy mist spumed from Murchison Falls, painting a perpetual rainbow across the banks. The sky stood on end as they circled sharply, then flew under the rainbow.

Crocodiles lay scattered over the banks like gray matchsticks.

"Must be thousands of them," Roland said, shuddering.

"Make an awful lot of handbags," Sarah called out.

Simeon informed them that ugly as they were, they were God's creatures too.

"The crocs are particularly vicious this season," Keri said. "The river's overpopulated, and the beasts have gotten quite brazen. Dragged a fisherman right out of his dugout last month."

"Just what I needed to hear," Roland groaned. Whatever you do, don't get on that boat, he told himself.

When they arrived at the motel overlooking the Nile, the manager told them they were too late to charter a boat. Certainly not during the noon-to-three siesta with its brain-roasting sun. All the river excursions were booked for the next day also. Roland sagged with relief.

Edna, agitated at this new crisis, had a few whispered words with Keri. "Certainly not" turned out to be a few more minutes of bargaining, a sizable bribe to the boat captain, and a warning that they proceeded at their own risk.

That gave Sarah and Simeon second thoughts.

"Nonsense," Edna chided them. "You proceed through *life* at your own risk."

"Mad dogs and Englishmen, maybe," Angus said to

Apple. "You'll find me wrapped around a Tom Collins at the bar when you get back."

"Think I'll skip this one, too," Roland said nonchalantly.

Edna's eyes flicked from Angus to Roland. "This may be your only opportunity to go to the headwaters of the Nile," she said. "Would you miss such an adventure because of a little sun?"

Even the prospect of time alone with Apple could not calm Roland. When the others trekked up the gangplank he threw up his hands.

"I feel faint!"

"Roland!" Edna dug her knuckles into his spine and pushed him on board.

The flat-bottomed, forty-foot boat was diesel-powered, open on all sides. They had the craft to themselves. Keri unhitched the hawser, slammed the gate shut and yelled to the captain to cast off.

"Captain, what a laugh," Roland muttered. "His last assignment was the *Titanic*." He sat down close to Apple. "There isn't a lifeboat in sight. What do we do when we start sinking?"

"It's too hot," Apple said and got up and moved away.

The heat clobbered them as the boat moved to midstream. The brittle strip of river broke into shards at the touch of the advancing prow. This whole thing's a mistake, Roland thought, his mind scurrying for a survival plan.

Unable to find a way out, he gave up and watched the tendrils of color snake through the water. Where the current ran fast it was murky blue, but near the banks it turned red-brown with slimy green algae floating among the lily pads and stands of papyrus. A goliath heron balancing on one leg looked like a living hieroglyph against an outcropping of striated stone. A white-hooded fish eagle hung suspended in the air, then plummeted into the water and emerged with a squirming perch in its beak.

River, shore, and sky teemed with life, and Roland drank it all in. He came up to Apple again. "There's so much going on in this place God must've spent at least five of his six days here."

Once again she turned from him; then she clapped her hands delightedly. "See? A unicorn!"

Near the bank an impala stood in the shade of a thorn bush. In profile only one horn twisted up from its forehead, but when it turned for signs of danger both horns showed, curving upward like the arms of a lyre. The animal bent to drink; the nose tentatively touched its water twin.

Keri came up and put his hand casually on Apple's shoulder. "Legend says the oryx was once mistaken for the unicorn. But if any deer deserves to be fabled it's the impala. Natives believe it's surrounded by a veil of magic, that its very beauty protects it from evil."

Roland stared at Keri's hand on Apple's shoulder.

Keri went on. "But I've come to believe that beauty often attracts evil. In some instances—"

Edna's stricken cry cut the air. "My carry-all! Where's my bag? Has anybody seen it?" She hunted frantically along the rows of wooden benches. "Roland, I gave it to you to hold. Where is it?"

Roland, bewildered by her outburst, insisted that she hadn't given it to him.

The blood had drained from Edna's face and her fingers were trembling.

"Well, look at her!" Sarah hissed at Simeon. "I don't

care how many foundations she's got, she's nothing but an old lady. Why, she'll crack into a million pieces if the going ever gets rough.''

Apple hovered around Edna, trying to soothe her. "You must have left it in the plane or at the motel. Surely it will be safe until we get back.''

Edna couldn't be consoled. "My passport. Identification. Pharmacopoeia. My absolutely everything! Keri, we must go back. I must have left it at Treetops when—''

"That was *days* ago,'' Roland said. "You've had it since then.''

She lashed out at him. "Your fault! The constant tension. Forever late. Consorting with scum. A menace to everything decent, that's all you've ever been!''

Roland rocked back on his heels. "What did I do? You *didn't* give it to me!'' He stared at her ashen face. It was frightening, like seeing Gibraltar go under.

"Now, be sensible, Edna,'' Sarah said. "Maybe you haven't noticed, but there's more than one person aboard this safari. And to go back for a pharmacopoeia—''

Edna hurried to the captain. He listened to her demands with a toothless grin, nodded eagerly, and kept to his upriver course. Finally, she collapsed on the seat nearest the wooden gate, to be first off when they landed. Cradling her left arm in her right, she stared at the rushing currents.

"Doesn't anybody understand?'' Edna whimpered. "I'm *lost* without it!''

Her fingers roamed nervously over the gate rail. Keri offered her some water, but an impatient shake of her head made him retreat.

The boat zigzagged to both shores, lacing its way upstream. Farragut clicked telephoto shots of sleek red-gold

Uganda kob, giraffe-necked gerenuk. They moved through an oppressive stillness. The overhead sky was a searing white, and the heat beat through the boat's canopy.

Roland stripped to his undershirt. Edna still sat hunched over. How could he make it easier for her? When he offered to lend her his binoculars, she turned away.

Apple tied her hair back with a yellow ribbon. Her throat felt parched. She thought of Angus at the bar with a drink, imagined his mouth giving her the icy liquid till none was left, only his thick tongue in her mouth, the powerful body ready—Apple's hand flew to her throat.

"Water?" she said, turning to Keri. He handed her the canteen.

She drank greedily, letting it spill out of her mouth to stain the yellow blouse. As she handed the canteen back, their fingers touched.

Then Roland was between, chattering. "Say, when am I going to meet this chick, Sadly?" he asked.

Apple retreated to the far rail, heat and shame pulsing through her till she thought she would throw up. That peculiar nausea had lurked just below the surface all this week.

The boat skirted sandbars, distressing hundreds of nesting skimmers. The air grew fetid with jungle-river smells and every breath burned in the lungs.

"I believe we shall all broil," Keri said, trying to be humorous. He should not have let himself be talked into a midday outing. He knew better; it was too much even for the natives who lived on the river. Well, nothing to do but make the best of it. "Anybody have any salt tablets?"

"Pharmacopoeia," Edna coughed.

"I think it would make sense to head back now," Keri said. "That all right with everybody?"

But hard and fast positions had been taken by Farragut

and the Shallotts. The headwaters, or nothing. Even though Sarah had cursed herself a hundred times over for a fool. It would have been the *perfect* chance. There was Angus, alone at the bar . . .

Then Simeon cried, "Yonder—at two o'clock!"

They followed his finger up a gentle hill toward the saffron sky. Over the rise they came, a heraldry of elephants moving in majestic slow motion. Huge bulls, graceful cows, adolescents clashing tusks in play, *totos* hanging on to their mother's tails. As they advanced with implacable dignity, the scene took on a flow that spanned eons.

The boat hove to for a closer look. "Another species dying off," Keri told them. "Pity, too. They've a highly developed social structure. Each herd has only one leader, but when a bull matures he's allowed to challenge him. They battle—never to the death, only to establish who's best for the herd. Should the leader be deposed, two males accompany him to the jungle and stay until he dies."

Roland's head was churning. "Supposing the old leader won't go?"

"No such thing," Keri said. "In every species save one, the old make way for the young. They give up territory, their lives if necessary. Only in our species do the seed carriers destroy themselves.

"Throughout history," Keri continued, "at some secret signal from nature—overpopulation, famine, whatever—the young almost willingly killed themselves off. I've often wondered if that might have been the underlying reason for the Children's Crusade, or the flagrant abuse of child labor during the Industrial Revolution. And it would certainly go a long way toward explaining why young men go to war again and again, willingly."

Roland was so excited he could barely organize his

thoughts. "Wait a minute," he said, holding up his hands. "Part of what you're saying is right. But there's something just as important." He shut his eyes, trying to visualize his feelings.

Sarah nudged Simeon. "I do believe that boy is not quite · all there."

Roland moved off and tried to write what he wanted to say in his journal. But everything seemed to melt away in the heat. Don't worry, he told himself. It will all fit into place someday, just remember that in every species the old make way for the young. *Except*.

The craft labored upstream, water boiling from its stern in a lugubrious wake. Keri passed the canteen around, but it barely quenched anybody's thirst. Roland began to get the bad vibrations again. He threw a pebble at a tangle of liana vines on the bank.

Half submerged in the brackish slime lay the creature of his nightmares. Gray-tan-green, a no-color like Edna's dining room. Armored ridges ran from its flat head down the fifteen-foot body and ended in the serpentine tail. The eyes sat in bubble tops on its skull. Ripples from the chugging craft reached the lizard and it slithered underwater.

"Crocodiles do for the river what hyenas do for the land," Keri said. "Superb garbage collectors. They'll eat anything from eggs to logs to man. Once they clamp onto something, their jaws lock in place. Even if they're killed, the victim has to be pried loose. And Roland, if I were you, I wouldn't trail my hand in the water."

As if beckoned a croc broke the surface not twenty feet away and kept abreast of the plowing craft.

"You're disgusting," Roland yelled. "I'm not even going to take your picture, what do you think of that?"

A sandbank jutting into the current was alive with the

reptiles, sunning themselves, webbed feet splayed, some with mouths open revealing rows of spiked teeth. Roland gave up counting at thirty.

Apple flicked the perspiration from her eyes. "On the surface it all seems so peaceful. Fish swim, my unicorn drinks. But underneath is death, waiting with the patience that only evil has."

"Evil?" Keri said. "I don't think of death and evil as being the same. It's just the way things are, the true cycle made more recognizable under the African sun."

The boat plowed to a bend in the river. A mile away Murchison Falls gushed through a gap in the cliff, a thousand tons a second falling in a thunderous spray. The craft rocked in the turbulence as the captain maneuvered them around. They photographed the cataracts from every angle.

The source of the Nile, Farragut thought. Mother to all Africans. This is where he might start his project. He was changing lenses to a wide-angle one when he cursed. In his excitement he'd stripped the threads. He hurried to Keri.

Completely about now, the boat strained for home. Roland put his camera down. They passed the tangle of crocs still basking on the sandbar.

"Not this time," Roland called, thumbing his nose.

Suddenly, Edna slipped off the seat and landed on the floor. Roland looked at her incredulously. She did not try to get up. Her mouth worked in tremors, and her fingers scratched at the collar of her safari jacket.

Apple darted from her seat, recognizing that this was no joke. Heat prostration, sunstroke, perhaps even something more serious. She ran astern to get Keri, who was still trying to fix Farragut's camera.

Roland dropped to his knees to help Edna up. She was unyielding. He wedged his body against the rail for leverage.

Why it was so important to get her back on the seat he didn't know. But *her*, sitting like *that*—he just had to get her up.

He managed to struggle her to her knees. From the corner of his eye he glimpsed Keri coming toward them and saw Edna's fingers groping for a hold on the gate rail.

The next instant Roland swung out on an incline, not really believing that the gate had opened. His body hit the rushing river with a wallop, and in the seconds that followed, the roiling waters closed over his head.

15

Keri had turned in time to see Roland hit the water. Impossible! It couldn't have happened! He shouted to the captain to stop the boat, and stretched over the rail waiting for Roland to bob up. If only he'd surface! He could throw him a line, dive overboard, whatever. Keri's peripheral vision took in the sandbars crawling by as the boat shuddered to a halt.

Five hundred yards upstream the shock of a body hitting water roused the reptiles. With a speed that denied their lethargic look, they slithered into the river.

A continuous scream stretched from the circle of horror that was Edna's mouth. Simeon, Sarah and Farragut rushed to where Edna knelt at the open gate, arms stretching toward the concentric circles where Roland had disappeared.

Apple struggled with the life preserver hanging on the cabin wall. Keri kicked off his boots. The distant sandbar emptied; the crocodiles headed in a widening fan toward the boat. The captain reversed engines against the current. The propellers would mangle the boy if he got caught, but there was no alternative. Props or crocs, unless they spotted him fast it would be all over.

For Roland, somewhere in his dim awareness, the whole thing had a roundness, a perfection like a circle. His recurrent dream. The fear he'd felt when he first stepped on board. Instinctively he fought to surface. The putrid waters grew brighter and exploded with brilliance. The current and his flailing arms carried him toward a sandbar in the center of the river. He swam as though he'd never learned, arms and legs out of sync, swallowing water in his desperation.

At the very end of the sandbar his feet scraped against the slimy bottom. He dragged his way up the incline and collapsed.

"There! On the island!" Apple screamed.

Distances clicked off in Keri's mind. The sandbar was perhaps thirty feet wide. Roland lay on the shore farthest from the approaching crocodiles. Keri knew he could swim to the boy before them, but then what? The reptiles would be dining on both of them before they could ever get back to the boat.

He cursed the boy. Cursed the demons stalking this group. Cursed the regulations that prohibited him from carrying a gun. But curses were a waste of time. The water boiled with the oncoming beasts.

There was the slimmest chance. It could get them all killed, but . . .

He charged into the cabin and elbowed the captain aside. Opening the throttle to full forward, he drove the boat onto the sandbar between Roland and the approaching lizards. The hull ground noisily as they beached.

"We're sinking!" Sarah screamed and threw her arms around Simeon.

Keri vaulted the rail, running before his feet hit the sand. He reached Roland and slung the limp body over his shoulder just as the first of the reptiles nosed onto the sand.

Bowed by the boy's weight, Keri stumbled back toward the boat.

Roland, barely conscious, lived the scene upside-down. Two crocodiles had skirted the prow and were coming at them with awkward speed, tails snaking violent patterns in the sand.

Then Apple was somehow on the beach beside Keri, yelling and jabbing with the long boathook. The steel pike bounced off the snout of the nearest crocodile. Its tail swept in a wide arc, knocking the pole aside. But the distraction was long enough to allow Keri to heave Roland through the boat gate.

Keri caught Apple under the arms and threw her on board. He leaped for the rail and hoisted himself up, then slammed the gate and bolted it shut.

Now the shelf of sand writhed with the reptiles, snapping at each other in the frenzy of the lost prey. They scraped against the hull, jaws straining upward at the screaming people. The captain tried frantically to get the boat off the spit.

"To the far rail, fast," Keri shouted, shoving everybody to the water side. He ran to the cabin and shot the boat into forward, reverse, forward again. The screw raked up weeds and mud. The craft rocked violently and with a heave tore free and spun into the current.

Keri pushed the captain back to the controls and raced out on deck. Edna had Roland cradled in her lap and was trying to apply artificial respiration. Keri lifted Roland away and jammed his mouth against his, forcing his own breath into the boy's lungs. Imperceptibly the rhythm caught and Roland began breathing with short, choking gasps.

Roland opened his eyes to stare at the hazel eyes owling at his, his mouth locked against a mouth that tasted of tobacco and maleness. He gave in to the luxury of the throbbing floorboards against his spine, the press of lips, and began to spin down and down into something beautiful, protective and—

Keri slapped him hard across the face. "Snap out of it!" He slapped him again.

Apple caught Keri's arm.

Roland's head jerked to the side. Out spewed the river and his terror.

16

That night at the Paraa motel Keri paced the length of his terrace. The dark Nile stretched before him.

Incredible! The boy had almost been killed, yet he insisted on going on. One would imagine that his grandmother or guardian or whatever she was would have more sense.

"If I thought it would do the slightest good, *of course* Roland and I would go home," Edna had explained to him earlier. "But I'm convinced that leaving now would scar Roland for the rest of his life. Naturally, though, I'll let him make the final decision."

Roland had pleaded with Keri not to cancel them out. "I promise, I *swear*, I'll do anything you say. But please don't spoil it for her."

The final determinant had been the main office in Nairobi. Keri had rung them up and explained the situation, demanding that they scratch the entire group. The office was shocked, of course, and relieved that nobody had been hurt—but even more relieved that everybody wanted to go on. Contracts had been signed, money had changed hands, civilization's laws must be honored.

Keri's instincts warned him that to go on with this group was to court disaster. If Roland kept having accidents at his present rate, sooner or later—and Keri would be held responsible. He thought of the vice presidency almost in his grasp, security for Livvie and the kids.

Exhausted, Keri dropped off to sleep and dreamed he was chasing an impala across the plain. When he caught her she turned into a young girl, beautiful, naked. He ran his fingers through her long, sable hair and found that he had woven a snare around himself.

Lake Manyara Reserve, where the lions live in the trees, lies deep in Tanzania's Rift Valley, some four hundred miles southeast of Paraa. The group arrived without incident. By an unspoken agreement, no one mentioned what had happened on the Nile. After all, as Sarah had said, this was a pleasure trip.

Edna had recovered from her heat prostration. Finding her carry-all in the plane had proven the final tonic. It was with her constantly now, looped over her arm or lying in her lap like a pet.

Roland thought he must be imagining things. Edna was acting nicer to him than she ever had in his life.

Lying on her bed after the second day's game run, Apple sipped her martini. She'd taken a Dexedrine earlier, another when the first hadn't worked. Angus was in the bathroom.

"Never seen such a bunch of deadheads in my life," he said. "Get ready for me, huh, I'm shaving real close."

The night at Treetops had been a great rejuvenator for

Angus. For days things couldn't have been better. Then, for no reason at all, he'd started to get edgy again.

Apple slid open the window wall and went out onto the balcony. The hotel buildings sprawled in a semicircle to the brink of the escarpment. Near the cliff's edge the oval swimming pool shone like a giant aquamarine in the twilight haze. Thousands of feet below, the lake, pink in patches with a million roosting flamingos, filled the valley.

Apple stood, captivated by the terrain. A rainbow rose from the lake to the sky, linking heaven and earth. "Beautiful," she whispered and realized how little she had been aware of her surroundings for the past year.

"Couple more seconds," Angus called.

Apple felt she had to get out of the room. She slipped into a bathing suit and ran down the hewn steps to the pool area.

Roland appeared out of nowhere and startled her.

"I've been trying to get you alone," he said, rapid-fire. "This is the first chance—could we sit for a second? I want to thank you for what happened." His face turned red. "I mean on the river."

"I'm sorry, but I am—" Apple began, then shrugged. Perhaps if she gave him a moment now he would leave her in peace. She followed him across the lawn to a secluded hollow fringed with frangipani and fire bush. Roland threw himself down on the springy grass.

Looking down with detachment Apple considered the boy. In these few weeks there had been a subtle change in his face—his jaw line more defined, his eyes brighter and more responsive. He will be a fine-looking man, she thought, if that woman gives him a chance.

"I dig the name Apple," Roland began lamely.

"It is Mela, really," she said, sitting. "But I have always preferred the English."

"You're Italian, right?"

She nodded. "Florence."

"How come you speak English better than me?" he asked.

Apple told him that her mother was American, a nurse stationed at the Italian front during World War II. There she had met Apple's father, a doctor. English was the second language at home. "Also," she said, "I studied it at the convent."

"You? In a convent?" Roland said.

Apple looked at him intently. "You have a kind expression. *Simpatico*. Will you help me?"

"Sure," Roland said.

"I must leave this place. I am not well. But Angus will not believe me, he won't let me out of his sight. If you could help me get a driver—"

Roland picked a white bud of frangipani and drew it absently along his chin. "Gee, I had no idea, I mean, I kind of think of Angus as a friend."

"You are right," she said hastily. "Forgive me, I should not ask you to become involved in something I should take care of myself."

Roland reached out and slipped the flower behind her ear. "Besides, I don't want you to go. You and Angus are the only live things on this trip." He jerked his head at the flagstone terrace where the others sat intent on their cocktails and the marathon bridge tournament. "You've got to save me from the mummies."

Sarah's voice floated to them. "Course, this is a very

·98·

nice pool. Ours is a mite bigger, though, wouldn't you say, Sim?"

Apple got up to leave but Roland grabbed her hand. "You're too young and pretty to look so sad. What's bugging you? Come on, maybe I can help."

Apple sat down again and reclined on an elbow. Her hair fell to the grass. Perhaps it was the pills taking effect, perhaps it was Roland's wide, eager eyes, but she felt like talking.

"Have you ever felt that you've trained like a gladiator for years?" she said. "Then without warning you are told that your moment in the arena has come?"

Roland hand't expected that at all. "Not unless you call a swimming meet—no, wait," he snapped his fingers, "I know *exactly* what you mean. Like studying for the SAT's."

"What?"

"Scholastic Aptitude Test. To get into college. You can't cram for it because it's everything you've ever learned in your life. So there you are in a panic, knowing your future is on the line."

"Ah," Apple murmured, "but surely your future—"

Roland snorted. "Oh, I know Edna would *buy* me a college. That's why it's so important to make it on my own. Boy, I'd sell my soul to get a scholarship the way Howie did. That's a friend of mine," he added. "Never mind about me, though. A gladiator, huh? Who's the enemy?"

Who was, she wondered. Angus? From the first night of the safari she knew she'd made a mistake coming with him. And though she had not spared herself the punishment—drowning beneath his thighs, clinging to his pounding buttocks—that debasement had not freed her from her guilt. Even this innocent sitting beside her like a puppy had not helped. Forgive me for using you, she said silently.

Apple shook her head. "No, it is not Angus. It is me. You see, I killed my husband."

17

"You what?" Roland croaked.

"I killed my husband," Apple said again.

Roland squirmed. Pure case of flip-out, he thought. First she's got to get away from Angus who's tailing her, now this? Better change the subject, fast.

He rolled over onto his stomach. "I just can't imagine you in a convent."

Apple tilted her head to the sky. "Matins and vespers," she murmured, remembering the tolling bells, "vespers and matins. In those days my eyes were turned to Our Lord. I dreamed only of devoting my life to Him. I would perform miracles, become a saint, rise straight to heaven."

Roland didn't know what to make of this new Apple.

"Then one day I told Mother Superior of a dream I had about the delivery boy from the village. *Dio mio*, the punishment! And I was threatened with eternal damnation just because of one little dream! That was my first hint that sainthood was a long and tedious road."

"The biggest drag," Roland interrupted, "is that the

church hasn't worked it out to have it happen while you're still alive. If they did I bet more people would work harder at it. Then what happened?''

"I left the convent when I was eighteen," Apple went on, "only to find that my home was another prison, with a morality even more stultifying. At the convent at least the nuns *believed*, but my parents, they only followed blindly.

"At the university I met my gentle soul, my Guido. He was working for his doctorate in geology. So thin, a little like you, Roland. I convinced myself I was in love with him and I moved into his apartment. It was a way out of my house. My father nearly had apoplexy.''

Roland felt a twinge of jealousy. "How long did that go on?''

"About six months. Then Guido graduated and was offered a job with an oil company looking for new fields in Africa. It meant that he would be gone for more than a year, but it was an opportunity he couldn't turn down. He asked me to wait for him. I told him I would not. A year was a lifetime. If *he* was worth waiting for, then *I* was worth marrying.''

Apple raked her fingers through her hair. "After the wedding we moved to Dar es Salaam. Guido was away a lot. When he did come home he was so exhausted, all he wanted to do was stay in our apartment. I began to fret. How many times can you wash your hair? How many letters can you write? In Africa there is not much a woman, especially a white woman, can do alone.

"One night I persuaded Guido to go to a cocktail party at our embassy in Dar es Salaam. Angus was there, too, for some Pan African business conference. He was very high and very charming. He flirted with me. I flirted back. We talked about having lunch, perhaps dinner when Guido was away. I meant no harm by it, I swear.

"Guido came up and took my arm. He told me we were leaving the party. I did not want to, it was the first time I had been out in months. Guido threatened. I got mad. I said that marrying him had not made me his slave. If he wanted to go, then he could go. I could find my way later. Perhaps somebody else would escort me.

"Guido slapped me. In all my life I had never been hit. Not in the convent, not even at home. And this in front of a hundred people.

"I got my wrap and asked Angus to drive me home. He grinned and said sure, let's get out of here, have a nightcap at my hotel."

Apple broke off and stared beyond Roland at the jagged precipice that disappeared into the gathering darkness.

"Angus drove with one hand. With the other he . . ." Apple shook her head. "He started to tell me what he was going to do with me—words not fit for a girl to hear. And with my cheek still stinging with Guido's slap, how I thrilled to hear them.

"Angus kept looking in the rear-view mirror. Then he said, somebody's following us. I recognized the car. Angus drove like one possessed. I thanked God that there was no traffic. In minutes we would be at his hotel. I prayed only to get out of the car, to be back with Guido again. I would beg forgiveness. I would never leave his side. I—"

Apple sat up and hugged her knees. "Angus saw the boy on the bicycle in time to swerve. But Guido could not see him until it was too late. To save the boy's life he went off the embankment. His head went through the windshield."

Roland put his hand on her shoulder.

Apple remembered how she had wandered through those weeks, unable to feel, filled with such shame she could not face Guido's family or hers. They would be kind, and that would only make her feel worse.

·103·

Angus, genuinely saddened by what had happened, had tried to help. He persuaded her to eat, took her on long walks. God knows what she would have done had she been alone. They became inseparable, drifted into bed. Sex became the hub of their existence.

Apple massaged her neck. "If I could have one wish ... if giving my own life would make a difference ..."

Roland moved closer and put his arm around her shoulder. "You poor kid. It's okay, go ahead and cry."

She looked up. "Strange," she said, "in all these months, that is the one thing I cannot do."

"How awful for you," Roland said.

"For me? What about—?"

"For him, too," Roland said. "But he's dead. And if there's a heaven then he's got to know that it wasn't your fault."

"Ah, but it was. Because if I hadn't been so intent on my sinful desires he would still be alive."

"Come on Apple, you weren't even driving."

Her voice was barely audible. "In my heart I was."

Roland stared at his hand, remembering a night long ago, the rails vibrating through his shoes. He fought to control his voice. "Apple, if you believe in balancing the books—without you, who knows what would have happened to me on the river."

Apple felt a rush of hope. With a slender finger she lifted a droplet from the corner of Roland's eye, looked at it, and put it in her mouth.

Roland cleared his throat. "I'll do whatever you say. When do you want to leave?"

Apple reached over and stroked his cheek. "Thank you. But now it does not seem so important. Angus and I," she shrugged, "well, perhaps there is still more to be worked out between us."

"Apple, you mustn't blame yourself," Roland said, "you've got to—"

Apple got up, walked to the pool, and floated into the water. Her fatigue seemed to melt away, and she felt her body aglow with moonlight. She knew her ordeal was not over, but for the first time in months she felt peace.

Her reverie was interrupted by a series of dull thwacks. She opened her eyes to see Angus bouncing on the diving board. Roland and two airline hostesses came over to watch his exhibition. The bridge players barely glanced their way.

Apple treaded water and looked up at the square pectorals, the pelvic girdle as well defined as a Praxiteles. With a final spring Angus jackknifed into the water. Apple felt the waves reach her skin and shatter. As Angus swam toward her underwater she no longer saw his perfect body, only a reminder of her own grief.

"I am going mad!" she laughed. How simple, how luxurious, to leave the battlefield to madness. But Apple knew that God had denied her this crutch.

Angus's hands were tunneling between her legs. Tendrils of his hair brushed her thighs as his head passed through. With a shudder of revulsion she clamped her legs around his neck, trapping him. His hands signaled for her to let go. She took a breath and held him tighter as they sank. Pain shot through her pelvis as his fists punched and then his shoulders heaved her out of the water. Her halter came undone. Roland's flower fell out of her hair and drifted off.

Apple came up for air, her hair clinging to the stalk of her neck.

Angus lunged at her, his face working with fury. Apple heard the stewardesses squeal at their roughhousing, and from the corner of her eye she saw Roland start toward her.

"Get the hell away, guy," Angus shouted.

Angus's fist was drawn back for the next punch. Looking at him calmly, Apple retied her halter. When he realized the extent of her challenge, Angus roared with laughter. Yes, there'd be some excitement after all before this one was broken.

Still laughing, Angus turned and hoisted himself from the pool, brushed past Roland and went over to the two stewardesses. Greeting them broadly, he promised himself he'd stab both of them before the night was over. And though he was to try mightily, fortifying himself with more than enough liquor, he couldn't quite make it with either of them.

Apple scooped Roland's flower out of the water and held it lightly in her hand. She floated onto her back, her mermaid hair a fan on the moonlit water.

I will never sleep with Angus again, she swore. Never.

18

"We'll be using this camp as our base for the next week," Keri told the group. "We're within motoring distance of the Olduvai digs, the Ngorongoro Crater, and hopefully, we should catch a glimpse of the Great Migration."

They'd flown in that afternoon to the tented camp in the Serengeti Plains. A native boy secured the *Solar Bark* at the edge of the compound. Maurice and Jen Siebert, the English couple who ran the camp, led them on a tour. Two more old people, Roland thought, lagging behind. They must be at *least* forty.

Seven two-man tents of thick, green canvas were strung out in a neat row, their roofs protected by latticed palm fronds. Tall Cape chestnut trees shaded the camp and hummingbirds looped streamers of color through the site. The settlement fronted a river about fifty feet wide which turned into a torrent with every cloudburst. At the moment it was shallow but swift-running. No crocodiles, Roland was relieved to hear.

Across the river baboons drank at the water's edge,

groomed each other, chattered in the trees. A ring of lookouts guarded the colony against attack.

Sarah rummaged in her bag and threw bits of crackers toward them. A few started across the shallows, but the Sieberts and the natives shooed them back.

"We never feed the little nasties," Keri told Sarah. "They're apt to nip you out of sheer malice. And since they attract leopard, let's keep them on *that* side of the river."

"Hey!" Roland cried. "What's going on?"

An oryx had fallen into step behind him, playfully butting him as he walked.

"Meet Sadly, our camp mascot," Keri said, slapping her flank. "I'm furious that she's taken such a fancy to you. Pull the fringe on her ears, Roland, and you'll have a friend for life."

Roland laughed nervously as the four-hundred-pound Sadly nuzzled his neck. He stroked the white muzzle tentatively, then ran his hands up her two-foot, saber-sharp horns. "Glad you're on our side," Roland said.

Keri explained that Maurice and Jen had found the antelope in the savannah when she was a few days old. "With those black stripes running from her eyes she looked like she was constantly crying, hence the name."

"You permit her to just wander about?" Edna asked.

"Oh, she's quite harmless," Keri said. "We've tried to get her to rejoin a herd, but outside of some clandestine lovemaking she prefers our easy life. We're terribly excited that she's about to become a mother. And at any moment, as you can see."

Keri assigned the tents. The first was permanently occupied by the Sieberts. Edna chose tent Two, since it was closest to the center of things. Sarah and Simeon took Three;

Farragut, Four; Apple and Angus, Five. Which positively thrilled Roland, who was in Six. Keri occupied the last, closest to the bush. At the other end of camp near the rude garage that housed two Land Rovers, four native workers—a Waheehee, two Luos and a Kikuyu—bedded down in a branch and frond lean-to.

Sarah scurried into her tent, unzipping flaps, poking her head through the windows. "That hotel at Manyara was grand," she announced. "But this is *my* idea of Africa. Where's the little girls' room at?"

Keri pointed to an outhouse some hundred feet behind each tent. "That bucket contraption to your left is the shower. If you have any kind of faucet control, do use the loo before you retire. Remember, with baboon about, leopard won't be far behind."

In her tent Edna sniffed the water carafe, peeled back the linen on the cot. She couldn't fault the cleanliness. She hunted vainly for a safe place; would she have to carry her bag wherever they went?

A moment of fatigue gripped her and she clung to the tent pole. Then with a vague awareness of something terribly important still pending, she fought off the sinking spell and thought back to that day on the Nile. What had Roland tried to do with the gate?

"Not much room, is there?" Angus complained, his head creasing the canvas. Apple sat cross-legged on the cot to be out of his way. He kicked off his clothes and handed Apple a bottle of cologne. "Do me, baby, will you?"

Apple's eyes darted to the tent flap but Angus blocked the way. She forced herself to reach up and lave his shoulders. His body contracted with the shock of cold, and then the astringent aroused him. He looked down at himself, surprised and pleased. "Look, baby, let's take advantage of this." He guided her head to him.

The combination of fumes and naked closeness was too much. Apple gagged and buried her face in her hands. Angus grabbed her hair and jerked her head back.

"What the hell's the matter with you these past couple of days?" he breathed hoarsely. "I didn't bring you here as an ornament."

He forced her lips to him, quick, before he died.

"Leave me alone," she choked. "I'm pregnant."

Angus collared Keri as the Sieberts raised the cocktail flag. "Come on," he said, "I'll buy you a drink."

Nobody else had come into the bar yet. It was a homey affair, neat as a ship's cabin, with thick-planked flooring and bamboo walls hung with skins and trophy heads.

"What I wouldn't give to be stalking leopard right this minute," Angus said, bolting his drink. "Must be a bloody bore for you, ferrying these old farts around."

Keri raised his eyebrows. He didn't much care for Angus, but since the tourist was always right he said, "I notice you don't photograph much. I hope you're enjoying the trip anyway."

Angus shrugged. "I had to kill a few weeks before a big business deal. I was sort of stuck with the *figlia*," he said. "Say, I know this is going to sound tacky, but do you know any of the local remedies for being knocked up?"

It took Keri some seconds to decipher what Angus meant. He felt the blood rush to his face. "You'll find most Africans want their children. Fact is, we've quite a flourishing market in potions to increase fertility."

"Nothing to get in a sweat about. Plenty of time to take care of it. She says she's only about six weeks gone." His hearty smile was man-to-man. "Sure is cutting down on performance, though."

Keri got to his feet. "I'd better get cleaned up for dinner. Thanks for the gin."

He strode toward his tent. Angus reminded him of an onion; peel off layer after layer and there still wouldn't be any core. He'd known men like him in the R.A.F., lamenting that there were no more dogfights and happiest in a locker room, swapping raunchy experiences.

Apple was just coming out of her tent. Keri turned to look as she walked toward the shower. Her pink shift swung with her and that hair—extraordinary. He pulled his eyes away. What kind of woman would be involved with a man like Angus? Still, she had acted superbly on the river. All at once he was aware of a bulge in his pants. Why, you gamy old bird, he thought. "Well," he said aloud, "she is an extraordinary specimen. Oh, objectively, of course."

"Objectively of course *what*?" Roland asked, coming up from the river bank with Sadly. He wagged a finger at Keri. "You know what Edna says, if you talk to yourself God knows what people will think."

Keri grinned and waved. The closeness between the lad and the antelope delighted him. Roland was acting like a normal seventeen-year-old. Though what *that* was, Keri thought, reflecting on his own teenager, was anybody's guess.

Around the campfire after dinner Sarah sipped her crème de menthe and extolled the virtues of the Sieberts. "I declare if Jen doesn't have the guts of a pioneering lady," Sarah said.

·111·

Keri nodded. "The Sieberts take pride in their job. It makes all the difference."

Edna said thoughtfully, "That, of course, is the basic flaw in believing that all people are created equal. We aren't born equal, nor do we die equal. And so we institute programs that kill initiative, trapping men into remaining indolent."

"Edna, if you run for office I promise you at least two votes, 'n'at right, Sim?"

Edna warmed to the topic. "Do you realize that twenty per cent of the American population is supported by a dole? And we wonder about moral decay."

"The way to solve everything," Roland cut in, "is to let them eat cake."

"Roland! You are so rude that—" Edna composed herself. "Youth is a disease that lasts such a *long* time." She got to her feet. "I'm for bed. Roland, if you were smart—the Olduvai excavation is bound to be exhausting."

"Soon as I say good night to Sadly," Roland called after her.

"In my time children jumped when spoken to," Sarah said.

"Yes, Miss Scarlett," Roland said with a grin.

"Why, of all the impertinent—"

Farragut chuckled, "Oh, come on, Sarah, he was only joking."

"I am perfectly capable of doing my own interpreting, thank you." Sarah got up and stalked off.

Simeon faked a yawn and sauntered after her. Inside their tent, Sarah bustled into a frilly gown and clicked off the battery lamp, leaving Simeon to grope around in the dark.

"Now, Sim, this bed's too small for that. Why you suddenly decided ... well, all right. We did vow for better or for worse, though lately you're finished before I even—move a little lower there.

"Aren't you glad I used my alimony money for this trip? Not so rough! Let's take pictures ... tomorrow before we get all sweated up. Maybe that Farragut person ... will oblige us. Don't you think he's the oddest ... getting *mighty* dark from the sun...."

Sarah lost all sense of what she was saying. Her inner eye saw through rows of canvas to where Angus lay, naked. Sim's mousy hair turned wavy and dark, his flaccid limbs became a rugged body—those thighs!—that made her respond with a passion that confounded her partner.

As for Simeon, the body he now lay beneath had turned into Apple's.

19

"Surely this is the most fascinating spot I've ever seen," Edna exclaimed. She clambered behind the native research assistant who led them deep into the barren cleft of Olduvai Gorge.

"Roland, pay attention," Edna said, pulling him away from Apple. "You're walking on ground that saw the dawn of mankind."

Though it was only midmorning, the heat had already turned the site into a rock oven. Edna felt her head churning. Part of her responded to the guide's spirited lecture. But another part reviewed again what had happened on the boat.

She did remember resisting . . . Roland pulling at her. But was he trying to pull her into her chair, or toward the gate? Don't even *think* such things! she warned herself. She gripped her carry-all tighter. I will have to remain alert to every possibility, she thought.

Keri helped Sarah over terrain that sent up puffs of red dust with every step. "How are you feeling now?" he asked.

"Couldn't be better," Sarah said through gritted teeth. She'd wakened with the trots ("What can you expect from a country that fertilizes everything with night soil?") and had decided to stay behind. Until she interpreted Farragut's expression as being unbearably smug. Popping two Lomotils in her mouth she'd announced, "We don't spring from pioneering stock for nothing!" And had suffered the long drive tight-lipped and -legged.

The guide stopped at the marker of the famous anthropological find. "In 1933 the major diggings were begun by Dr. Leakey and were subsequently financed by the National Geographic Foundation."

"We have a subscription," Sarah said. Farragut shushed her.

"It was Mrs. Leakey," the guide continued, "who first discovered the bones of *Zinjanthropus*, an ancestor of man's estimated to be about two million years old. His life expectancy was eighteen."

"I should be getting ready to kick off just about now," Roland joked.

"Bite your tongue!" Apple scolded.

The guide was saying, ". . . adding to the already strong evidence that this area of Africa is the true cradle of mankind."

Farragut jotted down a string of titles. Roland leaned over his shoulder. "*Dark cradle? Black genesis?* What's that all about?"

"Don't you see?" Farragut said excitedly, "They'll have to rewrite the history of man—the way it *really* happened."

Sarah tugged at the guide's sleeve. "Where's the little girls' room?"

Farragut snapped frame after frame of the four strata of Pleistocene rock; bone fragments of wild pig bigger than hippos; crude artifacts which *Zinjanthropus* had fashioned to dig his way up from the primordial slime. It was unbearably hot. Sweat ran into Farragut's eyes, but he couldn't stop. The gamble he'd taken on this safari seemed to be paying off at last.

"Farragut, can't you hurry?" Sarah said, shifting from leg to leg. "I can't see what's so interesting about a lot of rocks and bones."

Farragut turned on her. "Of course you can't! Not after centuries of twisting the truth. You heard the guide. It was the black man who developed first, the black man who—"

Apple's hand flew out to steady him. "Do not upset yourself any more. This awful sun—"

Farragut jerked away from her. "It's only the truth, Sarah. Go on, admit it!"

Sarah rallied shrilly. "Even if it was the cradle, then how come it took a *white* scientist to discover it? It's one thing to be top caveman a million years ago. But you'd better smarten up, Farragut, it's *this* year that counts!"

Blessed are the peacemakers, Keri thought as he stepped between them and began chatting about the next attraction.

"On to Ngorongoro," Roland yodeled out the car window. The name resounded like a drum roll down the volcano's slope.

The air was heady with fresh cedar and juniper as the Rover strained the last of the 8,000 feet to the crater's rim. In the distance, massive faulted mountains, some still spewing smoke and ash, made the land look like it was still in the throes of creation.

Keri broke the hush. "Once this was an enormous volcano, perhaps the tallest in the world. Can you imagine the inferno when it erupted?"

What remained was a crater twenty-five miles in circumference. Millions of years of beneficent rains had covered its scars with running streams, an ash-white soda lake, and stands of giant lobelia and senecio.

They began the hair-raising ride to the floor 2,000 feet below, bumping past huge boulders, towering cactus and wind-carved trees. Twice the car seemed to plunge into space, but Keri, humming a native tune, swerved in time.

Sarah and Simeon clutched at each other. Farragut cushioned his camera cases. Apple and Angus looked carsick. Only Edna remained vibrant, delighting in the fright on Roland's face, punctuating each hairpin turn with her laughter.

When they reached the bottom their relief gave way to unease. The caldera rim high above, the mountain's drifting shades, and a breeze that stirred the astringent air, gave the place a feeling of unnatural isolation.

"It is like Dante," Apple murmured.

Here the game was less shy than any they'd previously seen. Herds of zebra loped by followed by shaggy wildebeest. The Rover cruised past eight-foot anthills, red as lung tissue, tunneled with airholes the size of an arm.

Keri maneuvered through a civilization of hills. "Curious beast, the ant, the only form of life that practices slavery."

"Besides man," Farragut interrupted.

Keri nodded. "One queen can lay an egg a minute for years. God knows how many cultures have been crushed between their mandibles."

Farragut ticked them off on his fingers. "Nok, Mali, Ife, Songhai, Kanem, Benim, Ghana, Timbuktu, Jenne, Kano."

"Never heard of them," Sarah said.

"If you had would you admit it?" Farragut said. "Nok and Ife culture had no equal when white men were still foraging like animals."

Sarah's eyes twinkled. "Nok, Nok. Who's there? Ife. Ife who? Ife hollers let him go!" Laughing uncontrollably, she was delighted to find her cramps cured.

They forded a shallow *donga* lined with exuberant growth. Within the crater fires still burned, warming underground streams and creating a jungle of trees and lianas. In the chiaroscuro three elephants contemplated the Rover's approach, their ears waving like great sails in the gloom.

The Rover moved into a small clearing where two lions played in a dreamlike rhythm. The female crouched while a majestic black-maned lion mounted her. Roland, watching the lions pumping away, got weak in the head. *Why* was he sitting next to Edna instead of Apple?

Edna put her carry-all on the floor to focus her binoculars. About two hundred feet away, a second older lion lay licking his wounds under a copper-leaf bush. Keri grew intent.

"No noise," he cautioned them. "The males must have just fought. I've known them for years and that's not her usual mate."

"Then why is she letting him?" Sarah asked.

"That's the way it goes," Angus chuckled. "If you can't hold onto her, you don't deserve her."

Once more Keri warned them to be quiet.

Disturbed by the noise, the male dismounted. He stood over the lioness, licking her face while she rolled over and nibbled at any part of him she could reach. With a swipe of his paw he flipped her onto her stomach and mounted again, sinking his teeth into her neck to keep her positioned. His haunches drove in a relentless rhythm.

"When they go into heat they're inexhaustible," Keri whispered. "They'll be at it for days."

"Always did like lions," Angus grinned. He noticed Simeon, lips puckered, staring at Apple. What do you know about that, Angus thought.

Apple cringed. Angus's sweaty hand was rubbing one thigh, Simeon's tentative knee touching the other. She watched intently as the beasts approached climax. Such uncomplicated passion. If only I could stretch out like that lioness—she shuddered with a stab of self-hate. Tomorrow, she resolved, I must get Keri to fly me back to Nairobi.

Talk in the Land Rover grew more raucous. The lion glared balefully at them, amber eyes burning.

Suddenly Keri slammed his window, yelling, "Shut them all around!"

In a blur the cat sprang onto the hood, its roaring jaws filling the windshield. Everybody in the car nearly lost muscular control.

"Don't make a sound," Keri whispered hoarsely. "The hatches—Roland, when I give the word reach up and close yours. I'll do the front. Ready? Now!"

Keri's hatch slammed shut.

Roland jumped up and stumbled over Edna's carry-all. Thrown off-balance, he fell back onto the seat.

"What the hell are you waiting for, boy?" Keri shouted.

The lion had his front paws over the windshield. Edna screamed. Roland leaped up on the seat and slammed the hatch shut as the lion bounded onto the roof.

With a deafening roar the lion jumped down and sank his teeth into the fender. He bit through the metal, regarded the dead car with royal disdain, and padded back to the lioness.

Every nerve in Roland was twitching. He turned to Edna, who was holding smelling salts to her nose.

"Are you okay?" he asked.

Edna didn't dare look at him. She couldn't be mistaken,

·119·

not this time. If she hadn't screamed—and it was she who was sitting directly below the opening. She *must* devise a plan!

Keri tried not to show his fright. Was he slipping? His reflexes going haywire?

"Roland, can't you even close a little hatch?" Sarah exclaimed.

Angus was rocking with laughter. "If somebody barged in on me while I was in the saddle, I'd be out for murder too. But listen, guy," he leaned back toward Roland. "You'd better get your marbles together. You could have gotten us all killed."

20

From Sadly's pen late that night, Roland watched the moon turn the river phosphorescent. He listened to the buzz of insects, the rumble of distant hippo, and some animal cry he didn't recognize.

Roland leaned against Sadly, who had her legs tucked beneath her. He stroked her warm fur. "I know you're scared, but don't worry. I'm here."

She twisted her head to lick his hand.

Roland had never had a pet—Edna despised them. "But Sadly, you make up for it all. When you come to visit me back home, you're going to be the biggest dog on the block." He threw his arms around her neck. "You're my unicorn," he whispered.

They sat together for over an hour. Finally Roland croaked a chorus of "Rockabye Baby" to Sadly, who somehow endured it, her fringed ears flat against her head. Then he walked back toward the line of tents.

Outside Angus's and Apple's tent, he cleared his throat prodigiously, but it stayed dark.

A wave of loneliness passed over him. He looked around. The only light still on was Farragut's. Roland poked his head into the tent. "Knock, knock. Just wanted to tell you I thought you were great this morning, Farragut. Hey, what've you got there?"

Farragut scrambled to get a pile of pictures off the cot, but Roland was already inspecting them.

"You take these? Wow." His honest enthusiasm made Farragut relax a little, and he sat back.

Roland picked up a sheaf of papers and read the title page aloud. *"A Black Returns to His Ancestral Land for His Heritage."* He slapped the papers. "I knew you had something going for you!"

Before Farragut could object Roland was leafing through the pages. Some had writing, others, photos with captions. The first picture showed a large family, wearing rags and somber expressions, standing in front of a clapboard house.

"Your folks?" Roland asked. "Whereabouts?"

"Mississippi. All dead now. I'm the youngest," Farragut pointed. Opposite the photo was a yellowed newspaper clipping about a lynching. Roland looked at Farragut.

"My oldest brother," he said. "I was eight. I remember thinking that they were ghosts with pointed heads. Yelling, 'Come on out, nigger. Move that ass or we'll burn the shack down.'" Farragut took a deep breath. "He kissed us goodbye and went out. I saw them grab him. 'This'll fix the nigger,' they laughed. They hanged him from the limb of a tree, then castrated him. And the worst of it, nobody ever really knowing why." Farragut looked at Roland and repeated softly, "Why?"

Roland couldn't answer. He turned the page to a candid shot of Farragut as a grinning, teenage redcap. The caption read, "My own underground railroad to Washington, D.C."

Farragut said, "Took a lot of correspondence courses while I was riding the rails. Then the army. Almost got in trouble there, tried to brain my sergeant. He called me nigger." Farragut shrugged.

"Afterward I used the G.I. Bill for some more courses. Worked at the post office and saved for years to buy the franchise to a camera store.

"Even that was never right. Can you ever satisfy a customer? 'These prints have a double image.' I watched other people's lives emerge in the developing pans while I spent my life in a darkroom. Twenty years! And for this?"

Farragut flipped the page angrily. A fire-gutted store, its 'soul brother' sign no protection against the indiscriminate flames that took the entire block.

"I'd have flipped out," Roland breathed.

Farragut clenched his jaw, remembering.

"No," he said. "I'd come too far for anything to stop me. I took the insurance money and went to the best photography school I could find. Remember these?"

The next two pages were a photo-essay of black children playing in the riot rubble with the dome of the Capitol gleaming in the distance.

Roland didn't recognize them, and Farragut seemed hurt.

"They won honorable mention in our newspaper contest," he said. "I knew I could never own a store again." He tapped the title page. "I got this idea and wrote away to a dozen magazines."

"Then you're here on assignment?" Roland asked, impressed.

"Not exactly. Everybody liked the idea, but said their own staff handled such things. Two magazines, though, and you understand that I can't mention names, well, they both said they were *very* interested. And to come see them when I got back.

"I took all the money I had left, borrowed the rest, and signed up for the most expensive safari I could find. I thought it would give the project another dimension, contrasting the slave trade and a white luxury safari."

"Far out," Roland said.

"I *was* pretty smart. I did everything by mail. Used a post office box in a fancy neighborhood. No sense risking a last-minute 'We're terribly sorry, Mr. Nigger, but we find we're all booked!'"

Roland nodded. "Think you'll pull it off?"

"Like I said, nothing's stopped me yet. I found one of the keys at Olduvai today. But I was stupid to antagonize Sarah that way. Now, Roland, you've got to promise me—"

"Aw, come on, Farragut. Whose side do you think I'm on?"

Roland turned to the last page. Sentences had been crossed out, paragraphs transposed. He turned it every which way, trying to read it.

Farragut took the booklet from him. "It's how I plan to wind the whole thing up. Of course, it needs a lot of polishing."

"Go ahead, Farragut, read it," Roland said.

He cleared his throat and began, his voice low and urgent. "And so I have retraced the road, one of many roads my people have traveled from this very land, bent under the master's whip, Sarah's whip, down through the centuries of Sarahs.

"Columbus opened a New World and the slave trade went on. Bach thundered his paean to the Lord and the slave trade went on. Marx cried out for a classless society, Einstein grappled with the mysteries of the universe, and—

"How many more centuries, O Lord, before the light of equality transfigures the heart of Sarah Shallott? Or must she be dragged screaming to the bar of justice while millions of castrated brothers—"

Farragut put the book down, unable to go on.

Roland whispered, "It's beautiful, Farragut. They're going to be falling all over themselves to buy it. Only . . ."

"What?" Farragut asked, on guard.

"I didn't know you hated her that much."

21

The following day Keri drove his group twenty miles east and five thousand years back to a Masai village. For ten shillings apiece they could take all the pictures they wanted.

"For the most part the Masai are untouched by our civilization," Keri told them as the village came in view. "They're a warrior tribe, fierce and quick to take insult. Don't do anything to provoke them. Roland, that goes double for you."

Edna gave him a searching look. Roland turned red.

Keri contrived to approach the village downwind but even so—

"Why, this place is nothing but one big cow pie," Sarah exclaimed.

The loaf-shaped huts, made of a mixture of mud and cow dung, stood in a circle. Thorn bush barriers connecting them formed a corral, or *shamba,* for the scrawny cattle. Flies, gnats, and mosquitoes swarmed everywhere. The natives made no move to kill them or even brush them away, since they believed, Keri explained, that any living thing except the lion might house the spirit of an ancestor.

A mahogany-colored man with cicatriced skin met them at the *boma* gate. Greeting Keri somberly in Swahili, he gave the group permission to wander about.

"Who's that?" Simeon asked.

"The elder of the tribe," Keri said. "In the old days he would have been the witch doctor. I wouldn't be a bit surprised if he still dabbled a bit."

"You don't mean it," Edna said, turning to stare at the ancient man.

"Witch doctor, huh?" Angus said. "Say, is there any truth to the rumor that powdered rhino horn is an aphrodisiac?"

"Not the slightest," Keri said, grinning. "What's more, the taste is *awful*."

The older natives were as wrinkled as prunes. But the young girls, Roland decided, once he got past the perky boobs, looked like reincarnations of Nefretete. High cheekbones, slanted eyes, shaven heads. Copper necklaces banded their slender necks.

"Aren't the children a*dor*able?" Sarah exclaimed, then said in a low voice to Sim, " 'N'it a pity that kittens grow into cats?"

A willowy young warrior in a rust-colored robe came over to meet them. His hair had been plaited into elaborate pigtails and dressed with ochre-colored mud. This *moran* was about Roland's age, Keri told them, and had just killed his first lion.

"Alone?" Roland asked.

Keri nodded.

Roland shook his head in amazement. "Listen, man,"

he said to the warrior, "whatever you do, don't let them cut your hair."

Keri interpreted and the *moran* grinned, revealing teeth filed to a point.

"Welcome to Transylvania," Roland said under his breath. "Don't translate that, Keri," he added hastily.

"Walk around," Keri urged them. "Crawl into one of the *shambas* if you like."

Sarah eyed the crawlspace leading into a hut and pinched her nose against the oppressive odor. "Far as I'm concerned, I'm ready to leave right now."

For once Farragut agreed.

On the way out they passed a cow pen. The elder was about to draw blood from a steer. He tied a thong tightly around the beast's neck, popping a vein. Then he got up close, drew an arrow, and deftly severed the vein. He placed a gourd under the running blood, all the while whispering endearments to the animal.

"The Masai have a symbiotic relationship with their cattle," Keri said. "They use their dung for building, hides for clothing, and a gruel of milk and blood for food. That the smell of blood draws every predator in the vicinity disturbs them not one whit."

Edna stared at the gourd slowly filling with thick, red liquid. "Surely the smell of blood can't be *that* potent?"

"Oh, absolutely," Keri told her. "The most potent draw known."

"But to run the risk from lion and leopard?" Simeon asked, shaking his head. "Well, they're nothing but children."

Keri hunched his shoulders. "The Masai look at it another way. They made a covenant with God. He would give them all the cattle in the world, provided they were willing to live with the horror of the jungle. So, whatever happens, they attribute to fate."

Apple listened intently. She envied them this simple belief.

The elder undid the thong and sealed the steer's vein with a mud poultice. Keri said, "Lest you think the Masai aren't gourmets, they do spice their gruel with a dash of cow pee. But we needn't stay on to see that."

Ordinarily, Edna would have reacted strongly to the crude language, but this time she shrugged it aside. More important things occupied her mind. As they made their way back to the Land Rover she reached into her carry-all, cataloguing its contents. Yes, it was still there. Her fingers closed around the gold-tipped leather case sheathing the cold steel.

The group picnicked near a grove of gnidia trees. Keri picked a shaded spot for a siesta and the others followed his lead. Keri put his hat over his face. He wondered how he could ease the squabbling. Not that he was too concerned, this kind of bickering erupted midway in any trip. In a few days they'd be flying to Samburu, this side of the Northern Frontier District. Rugged terrain, no time to do anything except take care of oneself. Tempers would cool as the safari drew to its close, and by the last week they'd all be swearing undying love for each other.

Keri was startled awake by Simeon's yowls. Lord, what next, he thought, scrambling to his feet. Simeon had turned in his sleep and rolled into a thorn bush. He was hopping about in a mad dance. Keri ordered Simeon out of his clothes. At first Simeon resisted, but the pain proved too much and he squirmed out of his trousers. He was wearing scarlet underwear dotted with pink hearts.

Angus waggled his eyebrows. "Wow, Sarah, better watch out for this dude."

Keri sprayed Simeon with antiseptic. "These spines can cause a bad infection," he said.

Simeon spent the next hour digging out the thorns while Sarah sniped at him. "Fine outdoorsman you turned out to be. Why didn't you look before you laid down?"

Simeon gave her a hard stare. "Why didn't I indeed?"

They returned to the tented camp to discover that baboons had stolen Simeon's Bible, smashed the flashgun Farragut had left on his cot, and otherwise wreaked havoc before the Sieberts and the natives drove them off.

Farragut flew into a tantrum. "It's all your fault, Sarah! You were warned, but you kept feeding them anyway. I saw you throwing crackers across the river."

"Gentlemen do not scream at ladies," Sarah said, and walked away.

The raid made the camp seem very vulnerable, and it was an uneasy group that retired early that evening.

22

Apple's nightmare of being sick brought her awake. For a moment she was back in Florence, her fingers lingering over her body, taut with desire.

A nun slapped her hand. Her father shook his finger. The priest behind the confessional screen warned her against hell-inspired appetites. All the while her rebelling body told her that to deny that part of life was a greater sin.

The tent slowly came into focus. Apple's hand moved with a will of its own toward Angus.

"Wake me when you're ready," had been his last words before passing out.

Her fingers trembled as her battle of vow and need raged. If only she could experience the release without the guilt!

Nausea won. She searched in the dark for the basin, but could not find it. Throwing on her cotton robe she stealthily unzipped the flap. Angus groaned and rolled over. She held her breath. Before ducking out she took the water jug.

The expanse of cool air gave her momentary relief as she made her way toward the outhouse. Somebody coughed, and she froze. It didn't sound like Angus. It didn't sound like anybody. A feeling that something lay waiting in the darkness made her heart thump. She hesitated and then pushed on.

When she got to the loo the smell of lye and formaldehyde was so overpowering she couldn't go in. A few more feet into the bush, she told herself, and nobody would hear. Some thirty feet beyond the camp clearing Apple leaned against a baobab and retched up the sour taste of dinner.

Just as she finished rinsing her mouth somebody seized her arm. Before she could scream Keri clamped his hand over her mouth.

"Don't move. Not a word."

She struggled against his grip.

"Idiot!" he hissed, "there's a leopard prowling about."

Apple nodded that she understood. Gripping her wrist Keri inched back toward the clearing. Apple imagined dark forms lurking everywhere, the sudden spring.

When they reached the shower stall she began to tremble. Keri held her arms. "It's all right. The cat won't follow us here. But what in God's name were you doing out in the bush?"

She started back toward the tents and her robe snagged on a thorny bush. Keri stiffened at the sight of her white thigh. He reached to stop her from going and then held her close.

Apple flinched from his touch. "You are a married man," she said.

"Angus is married too," Keri answered, pressing his head into her neck.

"You are married in your heart," Apple whispered, her clenched fist before her lips to keep him from kissing her.

"She's not here," Keri said. "Confess, we both knew this would happen."

She tried to fight him, but he forced her to the ground.

"Forgive me," Apple whispered, her eyes staring up at the blackness. "I am not strong enough."

After a few moments her reluctance gave way before his sensitive searchings. Through some tangent in time Apple remembered the others . . . Guido . . . Angus, whose violations had not scoured her soul. Now this one. Strong, but with a delicate heart. A heart that urged her to admit that their closeness was beautiful.

Her fingers raked his broad back, rested in the hollow of his waist. Rising to meet him, she expanded from slow motion to quick, finally giving herself up to exultation as though after a long sojourn in the desert she had come home to the sea.

Whorls of stars witnessed their ageless motion. Spent, his weight between her thighs was warmth and comfort, a peace she had never known—

A stab of fear for Keri's safety. In one of his drunken rages Angus was capable of anything. Though Keri urged her to remain quiet, she resisted with such force that he helped her to her feet.

"What?" He jerked his head toward Angus's tent. "You don't have to go back there."

"Where would I go?" she asked, choking on the tears that would not come. "Oh, it is difficult to explain. We should not have done this. I am not free. I may never be."

"Angus, then?"

She placed her finger on his lips. "I have not slept with him for a long time. Nor will I ever again. We must not see each other this way. It will be better for all of us. Will you take me back to Nairobi?"

His lips brushed her eyelids. "I can't," he murmured. "Not after tonight."

·133·

"You must! I cannot stay here any longer. Will you arrange it when we move on to the next place? I will say that I am ill, anything."

"All right," he said, fighting for time. "But at least let's have these last days."

"No," she whispered fiercely. "I will not see you again."

"Tomorrow night. Same time. I'll be waiting here."

She shook her head, reached up and touched his lips with hers—their first kiss—then broke away.

Keri watched her run back to her tent. His senses returned and he almost hated himself. Stupid to have chanced it with a leopard about. Even more stupid to have added complication to his already overcomplicated life. And all for a momentary sensation.

Apple was right. Better for them not to meet again.

Keri made his way back to his tent. The moon, half-alive, appeared from its cloud covering. Once more rational judgment faded before his deeper feelings. As sex, it had been extraordinary. And for that he somehow felt sorry for his wife.

Keri started with the realization of what he had seen in Apple tonight. A need more desperate than sex, more compelling than love. What had he said to Roland? There was nothing more powerful than the urge to live.

23

Monday

Well, they're never going to appoint me Keeper of the Journals, this being my first entry since we got here. But I guess I better jot down the high spots before I forget.

After that baptism in the Nile I feel born again. But these past three weeks so many weird things have happened! And now there's this mystery about the killing—whoa, don't get ahead of yourself.

Got to spend more time on my stomach. No meat left on my behind from bouncing around in the Rover. The vibration sets up what Henry Miller calls "a personal hard-on." I wonder what an impersonal one is?

Sadly came to call this morning. Unzipped the tent flap with her horns. "Do you love me, Sadly?" A butt with her head. "How much?" She gave me a generous lick that smelled of grass. Keri said she likes the salt on my skin, but Sadly and I know it's something else. Ah, Sadly, if only I was an oryx, or you were an Apple.

Anybody can see this thing she's got with Angus is only temporary. So what if she is a couple of years older than me? Eleanor of Aquitaine was more than twenty years older than Henry II, and that didn't stop them from five children and a dynasty.

For the past couple of days I've been worried about Edna. Why does she keep telling me that appendicitis strikes suddenly and once it's burst you can't do anything about it?

Gave Apple a big "Hi!" at breakfast. When I clocked that form I got that Land Rover vibration. *Very* personal. I repeated my offer to help her get to Nairobi, but she smiled and said she'd taken care of it. This morning she was even humming over her fresh pineapple.

Angus is so damned good-looking I wonder if anybody has ever said no to him. Little friction going on between him and Keri. I think we're all beginning to bug each other.

Simeon announced he'd heard a lion during the night, and Sarah chimed in, "Keri, I surely hope you'll show us the Great Migration today, because that's why we're here."

Come on, Keri, whistle for the animals so Sarah can pet them. Keri said it wasn't a lion. He took us to the edge of camp and showed us the spoor of the leopard. While everybody else was getting ready for the game run, I followed the cat's pug marks. Got to a baobab and found a water jug with the number five painted on it.

So I went to their tent to return it. Inside, Angus was swearing, "I won't take this crap. Who the hell do you think—?" Not wanting to interrupt True Love, I beat it. What else could I do? Tell Keri? What the hell, she turned down my offer.

Back to Edna for a second. I don't know what's coming off. Yesterday she asked me about a guy I never heard of.

Said he'd been a classmate of mine, and mentioned a school I'd never heard of. When I didn't answer she smiled kind of sad, and went on checking her bird book.

Then all of a sudden people were yelling and running around down by the livestock pen. Sadly! I raced over. There was a lamb lying near the gate, throat slashed from ear to ear.

"That leopard, huh?" I said to Keri.

He shook his head. "This was no cat. All the blood's been drained from the carcass. The liver's been neatly cut out. With a panga, no, a very sharp knife, or a razor, I'd say." He turned in disgust. "The natives must have used it for one of their bloody rituals."

He spotted a footprint near the pen and said to me, "Lift your sneaker." The imprints were the same.

"Not me," I yelled. "I didn't do it." I told him I must have made the print when I said good night to Sadly.

Maurice spent an hour questioning the natives. Even promised them he wouldn't do anything if they confessed. They swore they were innocent and looked so scared that I believed them. It sure put a pall on the day.

Tuesday

Farragut is a fuck-up! Worse than me, if that's possible. He spent an hour before the game run posing the natives. Finally Keri told him that unless they finished their chores everything would fall apart with sun rot.

What intrigues Farragut most are your more cheerful things. Dead trees. Black clouds. Bleached bones. Loading some new film he didn't get the perforations onto the spool sprocket and the film advanced cockeyed. When Mother's Little Helper told him, Farragut went right through the hatch.

Didn't I know he was a professional? That he'd won an

·137·

honorable mention? And if there had really been equality it would have been a first prize? He'd listen to criticism as soon as *I* won—okay, okay, Farragut.

To sweeten the whole scene Sarah's on a new tack, so pleasant that I wonder if Farragut's getting her kill-by-kindness message. Listen, I am *not* antiblack. I am anti-fuck-up.

Are those baboons across the river really my ancestors? So much of what they do does look human. What about those bubble-gum-pink asses and purple balls? Ugh, Secondary sexual characteristics, Keri told us, designed to focus attention on the mating zones. That's what lipstick is all about.

Bouncing along in the Rover, Keri pointed out Mount Kilimanjaro. A fruitless hot morning then, searching for the Great Migration. Where the hell are those million animals? We headed into the savannah. Soon there were no trees, no bushes, nothing but the endless plain reaching for a sky without limit.

We came to islands of boulders rising hundreds of feet from the waving grass. Trees grew from clefts in the rock. We circled in figure eights searching for game.

Sunning himself on a boulder lay a horny lizard. His tongue would flick through his jaws and zap! An insect would meet his end. Nothing seemed to disturb the lizard. With his cold blood warming in the sun, maybe he was remembering the good old days when his dinosaur ancestors roamed the earth, throwing their weight around. How fickle of Mother Nature to reduce him to this pygmy through overspecialization.

I watched the trees and wild flowers stirring in the hot breeze, and got this urge to climb the very highest boulder and look down at these tiny people in this small car on this continent of a minor planet of an insignificant star in a mysterious universe, and roar! So that one and all would know I was alive!

I woke up from the noon siesta in a cold sweat. Talk about nightmares?

In my dream the lizard talked to the reptile part of my brain. "Fret not for me, my time will come again. After the fire withers all other life, our cold blood will once again make us the inheritors of the earth. For we are the true children of The Bomb."

Okay, so one insane bloodbath is over. But what about the next one they've got on their drawing boards? Oh, they're planning one, they're *always* planning one!

Politicians bullshit, and I see my generation slaughtered. Wait, what did Keri say about elephants? That in every species the old make way for the young? Except us, we invented war. Name any war. What's it been about? I mean once you get past the flag-waving.

War is old people sending young people off to die to protect the things that old people own. They all belong to the PTA—the Protect Things Association.

Great. So I understand the problem. But what can I do about it? Guess I was just born dumb. Or has every guy in every time wanted answers as desperately as me?

24

Journal

Wednesday, Two A.M.

So wound up I can't sleep. I'm going to be a father! Well, a godfather. The Sieberts told me they were going to name Sadly's calf Roland or Rolanda. Angus sang out that I probably didn't know the difference myself. Real pal. I should have doped out what he had in mind then.

Maybe I was ready, maybe it was fate but this afternoon's game run completely changed my life. We'd all broken out in a diaper rash about the no-migration. Sarah was taking it personally. *Why* were all those animals hiding from her?

Keri radioed the game warden at Seronera. Herds were on the move about fifty miles from us. It meant a lot of butt-punishing motoring, but guess who insisted?

"Animals are what this exercise is in aid of," Edna said, so off we went.

After an hour of nothing your eyes start playing tricks.

Are those spots? Or are they heads and legs you see in the binoculars? Everybody got very tense. Another small herd or—then all at once we were surrounded by herds of zebra followed by wildebeeste, gazelle, bushbuck, kongoni, lesser kudu, so many everywhere it's enough to blow your mind. Right smack in the middle of Serengeti's Great Migration!

A spontaneous cheer went up from the car. There was a lot of hugging and handshaking and at that minute I think we all loved each other. Edna even patted my arm.

"How many do you think there are?" Sarah asked, her arm sweeping out to include the whole world.

Keri estimated fifty thousand.

Sarah gasped, "Why none of my bridge girls will believe—how did you arrive at that figure?"

"You count the legs and divide by four," Simeon said, and laughed a lot at his funny.

Sarah didn't laugh at all. I think she's a little nervous about Simeon's showing signs of a backbone.

Edna lifted her arm slowly toward specks wheeling in the sky. "Birds of prey?"

Keri's field glasses dropped against his chest. "Vultures. Not worth watching."

Simeon said hopefully, "There's a zebra walking kind of funny. Maybe it's about to die?"

Well, you would have thought the car was full of ambulance-chasers. Nothing would calm us down except that Keri drive straight to it. The zebra had been caught in a poacher's snare and was struggling to stay with its herd. But with hobbled legs it couldn't keep up, and the others left it a lone speck in the savannah. Impossible to guess how much blood it had lost. It had this terrible look in its eyes.

Keri swore about the bureaucratic stupidity that prevented

him from carrying a gun. He could have put the beast out of its misery. The zebra stumbled, got up, then collapsed on its side, its ribcage heaving.

"Is there nothing we can do?" Apple cried.

"We can get the blazes out of here. Before those birds," Keri pointed toward the bull's-eye of vultures circling above. But when he gunned the engine to leave, you should have heard the howl that went up. Me? You couldn't have dragged me away.

A dozen birds zeroed in on the prey. A vulture's wing-spread is easily the length of a zebra. Even when their talons touch the ground, they keep their wings open. They've got wide, white stockings, their red necks arch forward so they're hunched over like worried businessmen.

They jockeyed for position, flapping forward in a dance of death. With the last of its strength the zebra kicked, and the birds danced back, screaming. Now the zebra wasn't moving at all. Fright alone should have done it in. Keri said it was dead. That made everybody feel better. But I had my doubts. Not with all that skin quivering.

A buzzard swooped down and hooked its talons into the zebra's head. Its beak struck repeatedly at the zebra's eyelid, ripped it off, and then plucked out the eye. Down it went like a soft marble. Without a pause the vulture tore into the skull trying to get at the brain.

One bird attacked a nipple. The skin stretched but wouldn't give. Keri said that was why the birds went for the soft parts first.

Most of the flock gathered at the zebra's hindquarters. One hopped close and wiggled its beak between the striped half-moons of its ass. More and more of the beak disappeared. Finally the whole head was inside. You could see the zebra's back legs trembling.

Angus laughed, "My God, instant hepatitis!"

The vulture dug its talons into the ground and jerked its head free. Out came a length of purple intestine. The other birds fought over it like starved kids at a mess of spaghetti. A second and a third bird attacked.

Would you guess that everybody in the car was throwing up? Not at all. For once, nobody made a sound.

Every couple of minutes a few vultures would fight over some tidbit, beating their wings and screaming. Then they'd settle down again to their victim. It all looked so frightening and somehow, sexy.

I caught Simeon staring hard at Apple. Sarah noticed it too, because she clamped her arm tight around his. Angus had that crooked grin plastered all over his face. He caught my eye and the grin got bigger. I shouldn't have grinned back.

"Perfectly shocking," Edna murmured. Everybody took off about the cruelty of animals until Keri cut them short. "First, one of *our* kind is responsible for the poaching. Second, it's nature's way of disposing of the carcass, otherwise it would contaminate the land. So, the vultures are fulfilling their function as carrion eaters. But what are *we* doing, watching?"

I wasn't really clear on his point. Guess it's something like, Cruelty is in the eyes of the beholder?

Keri went on, "Biologically, the important thing is the propagation of the species. The loss of one or even a thousand is insignificant when you consider the millions."

"Maybe there are 999,999 others," I said. "But there's still that particular one. And he's got to be somebody's relative or child."

Keri said I was reacting like a typical primate. "We're the most successful species in history, yet we insist on assigning individuality to every offspring, making him special, giving him a name."

Apple came to my rescue. "In my country we call that love," she said. "And perhaps that very quality is *why* we have been so successful."

Out of nowhere the hyenas came loping across the plain.

They had no problem tearing through the leathery skin. In seconds the carcass was covered with a rippling cape of fur and feathers. When we heard bones crunching we knew it was time to go.

Back at camp there was that scene between Angus and me. Gross! But I can't face putting that one on paper tonight.

25

Wednesday, continued.

Nuts! I can't sleep. An insomniac at seventeen! Okay, I'd better face that blow-up with Angus.

About an hour before dinner Angus dropped by my tent and said he and Apple were going for a walk. If I wanted, meet them about a quarter mile upstream. Did I want to? I'd only been holding my breath for two weeks. I even took a fast shower.

Edna saw me coming out of my tent. "Roland? Where are you going? I want to talk to you!" I kept right on going. Trudged upstream and found Angus swimming. He yelled for me to jump in. The Sieberts had told us that this part of the river was safe, but the only water I ever wanted to get into again was in a bathtub. I yelled back that I didn't have a suit.

Angus jerked his knees to his chest, squirmed out of his trunks and tossed them to me.

So there it was. I knew if I didn't jump in I'd never get

over my hangup. His trunks were so big I had to knot the waist.

I dove in, panicked, drowned. But once I got past that it was okay. I swam toward him, came up on his right. He ducked me down around his thighs. Just when I thought my lungs would collapse, he hauled me up.

"You're not a bad swimmer," he said. The booze on his breath almost knocked me over.

I choked a lot and managed to say, "I was on the swimming team at school. The 200-yard freestyle is my event, but it's a lot easier when you don't have to hold onto the suit."

"For chrissakes, take it off then," he said, and yanked it below my hips.

We dived and ducked and swam around for a while. It felt great after spending days in that cramped Rover. And even better knowing that I'd licked my fear.

Then Angus said, "Race you to the far bank. Loser gets a task."

"Like what?"

"If I tell you beforehand, you'll lose on purpose. Ready? Go!"

Every time I'm in a race the other guy's halfway there before I even get started. It was only around twenty yards, and I knew I could cover that with only one or two breaths. At first Angus was churning the water in front of me, but stroke by stroke I caught up, came abreast, and in the final sprint beat him out by an arm's length.

"Damnation!" He grabbed me in a bear hug that made my eyeballs pop. "It's all those cigarettes. But you beat me fair and square."

We flaked out in the water, current lapping around our waists, our butts on the sandy bottom. When I got my breath back I thought I heard something on the far bank.

·146·

"Angus? You hear anything over there?" I should have realized he was too drunk.

Angus turned and listened. "Nope, only a croc," he said and made a grab for me.

I toppled back, laughing and fighting off his hand.

He looked at me funny, almost pathetic. "Reminds me of the time I was at this party?" he said. "Everybody in the buff. A couple of chippies getting plowed in the pool. People going down on each other."

"When's Apple getting here?" I asked. "Hey, maybe that's who I heard?"

"Apple chickened out at the last minute. But don't worry, guy, before this trip's over, the three of us—" He made a circle with his forefinger and thumb.

The current washed us together till our shoulders touched. Angus leaned back on his arms and with a great yawn arched his back.

"Hey, guy?" he said, "did you see the way those vultures got at that zebra? I swear I almost got my rocks off watching them."

It took me a while to stop stuttering. "You too? At least I'm not the only sex maniac. I sure hope that zebra was dead."

Angus laughed out loud. "Oh, I don't know. There are a lot of people who dig it that way. Take a word of advice, guy. The more you use it the better. Now, listen, you won fair and square. Which is it going to be? Zebra or vulture?" He reached out and grabbed hold of me.

"Hey, wait a minute, Angus," I yelped. "*I* won."

There were tears in my eyes by the time I managed to jab him in the stomach and tear free. I stood up. "Angus, I would if I could, honest. But this isn't my scene. Anyway, I keep hearing something."

"There's nothing there, guy. Come on, only take a couple minutes. I'll scratch your back, you scratch mine."

He stood up and his bulk loomed against the dark skyline. I might have done it if only to get him off me, I was so scared of him. It was like I'd never known him before.

Then we heard Keri's voice calling from downriver. "Angus . . . Ro-land . . . Ed-na . . ."

I dug my feet into the sand, did a side dive into deep water, swam like hell, and scrambled up the bank. I could feel him coming up behind me. I scooped up my clothes where I'd left them, but my sneakers were gone. Some animal must have made off with them. I raced back to camp and threw on my clothes at the edge of the clearing.

Well, I just reread that whole scene. Why did I get so turned off? Especially since I dug that first night with Apple?

There's no other way around it, I'm just plain scared of Angus.

Maybe the who of who you're making it with is what finally matters? If I had a choice, I'd rather spend a couple of hours just kissing Apple.

Wait! About secondary sexual etc., and all that lipstick means? So *that's* what kissing is all about? Kissing is going *up* on somebody!

26

Two more days of game-viewing and everybody fell into a mood of mellow exhaustion. After dinner, a barbecued suckling pig, the group sat around the campfire.

Sadly, head lowered to succulent shoots, grazed nearby. In the glow of the fire her outline looked like a cave drawing scratched against the night.

"Don't go too far," Roland called to her.

Edna sighed, "If only you showed the same consideration to human beings as you do to that beast—"

Sarah hugged her knees. "When I was little I loved the dark. Lay awake and wondered how my life would turn out. Feel that way tonight, thinking what might've happened if I'd gone to veterinarian school like I wanted. Now, Sim, I still love you, but it's fun to think of alternatives."

Apple had washed her hair earlier. She undid her kerchief and bent toward the fire, combing out the last of the dampness with her fingers. She'd lost her tense look and in unguarded moments had even caught herself singing.

Shadowy native boys moved among the tents, securing stakes, turning down beds.

Edna broke the stillness. "This experience has made me believe that though much of life's design is hidden from us...." With surprising clarity she began to sing an old camp song.

> Father Time is a crafty man
> And he's set in his ways
> And we know that we never can
> Ever bring back past days.

Roland, feeling a surge of affection for her, sang along.

> So, campers, while we are here
> Let's be friends firm and true
> We'll have a gay time, a happy playtime
> For we all love to be with you.

Edna finished to extravagant applause and Apple's delighted *"Brava!"*

"I don't know what got into me," Edna protested, but she was obviously pleased.

Watching Apple, Keri saw his own fingers in her hair and could barely restrain himself. When she hadn't appeared that second night he'd gone to her tent. Apple, terrified that he'd waken Angus, had slipped out. They argued until there were no words, only the hard ground and a passion that grew with each night.

I will not fall in love with her, Keri told himself. Yet during the day he contrived to touch her, waited for the moments to press against her. He didn't care if Angus suspected.

Suddenly screams tore the night, and there was a thrashing of branches. Mingled with the baboon shrieks was a low cough that sounded almost human. Sadly bounded up the bank and lingered close to the fire.

"That leopard again," Keri said. "The baboons have spotted him, though, so he'll go off. If the tribe ever cornered him they'd tear him to pieces, no matter how many of them were killed."

Everybody edged closer to the fire. Once more the night grew silent. Sadly began to graze off.

"Shouldn't I put her in her pen?" Roland asked.

"Good idea," Keri agreed. "Better bolt the gate, too. She'll be at her most vulnerable when she goes into labor."

As Roland led Sadly away, Edna followed him with her eyes into the darkness. She coddled her brandy and took a sip. "Keri, do you remember at Treetops when you said a murderer lived in all of us?"

"Nonsense!" Sarah exclaimed. "Why, it pains me to even cut flowers."

Keri smiled at Edna. "I don't think this is the moment to bore you with my theories."

"Oh, but there's nothing I like better than a good horror story," Sarah said. " 'N' with that poor lamb murdered and its liver torn out for some heathen rite—" her eyes flicked to Farragut.

Roland came back and sat between Keri and Apple.

Angus got up. "Come on, Apple, let's go to bed."

She shook her head. "Go, if you like, I want to hear this."

Angus started to object but sat down.

Keri tried to hide his satisfaction. "All right, then, it has to do with our schizophrenic personalities, the planter and the killer."

"What?" Sarah cried.

"Sarah, a moment ago you were horrified about the murder of the lamb," Keri said. "Yet earlier, you ate your meat with gusto."

A chorus of objections swept around the fire. "But that's not the same thing," Angus said.

Keri cracked his fingers. "For all our so-called civilized achievements, there still lurks in every one of us that killer instinct we so gorgeously developed in order to survive."

"I've just had the most curious thought," Edna said. "Wouldn't that help explain why women wear nail polish and lipstick? The atavistic memory of blood on the claws and mouth signaling that a kill has been made, that there would be food that night?"

"I've never come across that theory," Keri said, "but you could make a case for it. Particularly in regard to the great carnivores, where the females do the killing."

Roland liked his "going up" theory better, but decided to keep his peace.

"You believe that this instinct is evil?" Edna asked.

Keri stoked the fire and a shower of sparks flew up. "Only man systematically kills his own kind."

Sarah pointed a manicured finger at Keri. "Hey, I'm surprised at you! I came here to get away from that kind of godless talk and all the troubles back home."

"You came to *Africa* to get away from trouble? In South Africa they've still got slave labor. Do you know how many millions of Africans are starving right now?" Farragut was livid.

"Oh, stuff!" Sarah exploded. "There's always one in every group who's the prophet of doom. Boy, didn't your mammy ever tell you—?"

"My *mother* told me that most folks are born stupid and prefer to remain—"

"And *my* mother," Sarah said, rising, "taught me to walk away from a scene rather than lower myself to common folk. Come along, Sim."

The others listened to their departing footsteps, the whirr of zippers and Sarah's voice. "Now don't you start too!

What's his kind doing on a trip like this anyway? 'N' if you were any kind of a man instead of a spineless—"

A slap cut the air. Stay put, Keri warned himself, or they'll both turn on you. But he couldn't help wondering who had slapped whom.

After some uncomfortable minutes Edna, Apple, and Angus retired. Roland stared into the fire, deep in thought.

Keri watched the shadows on the canvas walls. Edna, hanging her bag on the tent pole, then taking it with her when she came out and headed toward the loo. Farragut, hunched over a table, checking his cameras, probably. Apple and Angus . . . blackness. The three-quarter moon began to rise. Minutes dragged by.

Was Angus having her now? Keri nearly strangled with the idea. Even if he was, what can I do about it? he thought.

Edna went back into her tent, humming.

Shadowed people, Keri thought, nothing but brief shadows. Now I understand why I've allowed their antagonisms to come to a head. This life of shadows will never be enough for me, this is my last safari. The hell with being vice president of anything.

"Know what?" Roland asked. "Ever since man first came on the scene, we've managed to find what we needed to get by. Keri, you say it's the killer instinct. But remember Apple's reason? She said it was—"

Roland's comment was cut off by sinister laughter, answered by a second and a third hair-raising cry from downstream.

Roland gulped.

Keri said, "Those hyenas have been hunting this area all week. If you have any pity, Roland, pray that their victim dies quickly."

Roland jumped as Maurice Siebert stepped into the circle

of light. "Has anybody seen Sadly? I just checked her pen and she's not there. The straw's stained. She must have come to her time."

"But I locked the pen," Roland exclaimed.

Keri stood up. "Relax, Maurice. Probably wants her privacy. She'll be back in the morning with a little Roland in tow."

Except for the fire's crackle there was no sound. Then came the undulating laughter again. But this time, threaded through it was a barely audible moan.

Keri ran toward the Land Rovers.

"Maurice," he yelled, "you take one car. Stay on this side of the river. I'll take the other and cross over. Sound your horn if you find her."

Before Keri realized what was happening, Roland scrambled into the seat beside him.

"I know I locked her pen, I *know* it!" Roland cried as Keri gunned the car forward.

27

A fan of water sprayed up as the Rover plunged into the river. "Keep your eyes and ears open," Keri shouted. "Try to gauge the direction."

When they bounced onto the far bank, the troop of baboons rent the darkness with their warning screech.

Keri swung left over the rudimentary path and headed downriver. "If it is Sadly, she'll try to head for deeper water. Submerge to her neck. It's about the only chance she'd have. The river forms a sort of pool downstream."

"Could she have opened the gate latch with her horns?" Roland asked.

"No time to worry about that now," Keri said. The headlights picked out shapes. From the camp side of the river they could hear Maurice's car and see the intermittent flash of headlights breaking through the dense bush.

Roland gripped the dashboard. "What if they cut her off from water? Could she outrun them?"

Keri shook his head grimly. "Two hyenas will race after her at top speed. The rest of the clan will jog behind. When the front runners tire two more will move up. Besides, she's in no condition to do any serious running. She's about to calve."

"I hear something," Roland yelled. "Over in that direction."

Keri turned off the path to crash inland through clumps of thorn bush. Three hyenas materialized out of the darkness, loping close together.

Keri eased the car behind them. "They've got the scent. They'll lead us to the rest of the clan."

Roland checked the speedometer. Twenty miles per hour, and they were running without effort. One of the beasts turned, and the reflected headlights made his eyes look like a ghost's. Startled by the light he broke his stride and shied away.

The Rover broke clear of the bush, bumping over the savannah which spread before them under the three-quarter moon. Suddenly the hyenas disappeared down into one of the dry wadis that ran perpendicular to the river. Keri braked and backtracked until he found a passable spot. The speedometer crept up to thirty-five before he caught up with the hyenas. Once more he settled behind them.

Insects splattered against the windshield. Roland and Keri were more than a half mile from the river now and the ground rose and dipped sharply.

"Hang on," Keri warned.

Roland braced himself.

With a thunder of hooves a herd of zebra peeled away in front of them. The hyenas paid no attention to the herd.

"No," Keri muttered, "they're not interested in zebra tonight. The bastards are after the easy mark."

The Rover hit a tussock, leaped into the air, then smacked down on two wheels. Keri fought to keep from overturning.

"That would have been pretty," he said. "The

murderers would have been dining on our stringy flesh."

"They go after people too?" Roland gulped.

"Hyena will go after anything at—there she is!" Keri shouted. He jammed his fist on the horn to alert Maurice.

In the drifting moonlight they could see some twenty spotted animals running in an arc behind the galloping Sadly. The pack converged, snapped at her flanks, and Sadly leaped from side to side. She wheeled to kick, and her swinging horns cut a wide swath through the air.

"A few more seconds, girl," Keri yelled, jamming his foot down on the gas pedal. He twisted the wheel and tried to run down a hyena racing alongside the Rover. The beast dodged. Keri sped closer, flashing his lights on and off. The pack hesitated. Their eyes glowed like white-hot cinders. A few slunk off, blinded by the light.

But the flashing headlights only further bewildered Sadly. Tormented by the bristling pack she plunged into a steep wadi.

"Don't" Keri yelled. "I can't get the car—"

But Sadly heard only the snapping of jaws as she fled deeper into the ravine. The hyenas spilled over the top. The Land Rover screeched to a halt at the edge, its front wheels spinning over the brink; its back wheels lifted from the ground, leaving them hanging over the gully.

Below, the pack had Sadly circled.

Roland lunged to get out of the car but Keri yanked him back. "You can't do any good now. You'd only get yourself killed."

"Can't we do something?" Roland screamed. He began crying, shouting Sadly's name over and over. He rummaged through the tool chest, grabbed a wrench, threw it, grabbed a hammer, and threw that. The pack took no notice. The smell of blood, the culminating moment of the chase, had whipped them into a frenzy.

·157·

One after another the hyenas went for Sadly's legs, ripping a tendon, splintering a bone, until the laboring antelope hobbled to a stop.

Sadly moaned as the pack closed in. Foam flew from her mouth and her body heaved with involuntary contractions. Swinging her horns in a vicious arc, she speared one animal through the neck; her flailing hooves crushed the skull of a second. The clan turned on its wounded and tore them to bits.

Sadly, her white tear-marked face staring up, stopped for an instant of birth. As the calf emerged the hyenas ripped its glistening form from the womb, tearing it to pieces.

One hyena darted between Sadly's hind legs and clamped his jaws onto her bloodied loins. Another tore at her soft underbelly, ripping it open and devouring her before her eyes. Sadly, trembling in massive shock, turned toward the Rover and made a pitiful sound.

Roland sobbed hysterically. "Im-ag-ine?" he stammered. "Being born like that? Eaten alive before—before you even took your first breath? Oh, God! Why Sadly?" he pounded his head against the dashboard. "May God strike me dead if I didn't close that gate!"

Keri grabbed Roland and held him close, telling him it wasn't his fault. He put his hands over Roland's eyes and ears, to block the sounds, until Sadly had no life left, until Roland had no tears.

They hung over the gully until Maurice found them. By then there was nothing recognizable left of Sadly. Maurice pulled their Rover free, and they started toward camp.

Through his swollen eyes Roland stared at the speeding plain. "I hate it here," he hiccoughed. "It's too fucking cruel."

"That it is," Keri said, rubbing his pounding temples.

"If she had calved a half hour earlier she might have made it. The calf would have been on its feet and running with her." He clutched the wheel to fight off his fatigue. "But— damn! The darling did put up a good fight, didn't she?"

"Lot of good that does her," Roland muttered.

"The good fight is all any of us have."

"Bullshit!"

"That too," Keri said gently. "But if there is something else, I wish somebody would tell me."

Back at camp Maurice went off to break the news to his wife. Everybody else was asleep. Roland dragged his way toward his tent.

Keri fell into step beside him. "Are you all right, then?"

Roland nodded. Keri handed him his bandana to dry his eyes and waited until Roland controlled himself.

Roland choked, "Remember when I told you I was scared? See? I don't mean only tonight. I mean this whole damned trip. Whatever I touch—"

Keri took the boy's arm and led him away from the cluster of tents. "You should be frightened," he said, thinking aloud. "I don't know what it is but you seem to be one of those people who draw the lightning." Keri shook his head. "That day on the Nile? I'm positive that *I* shut *that* gate before we shoved off. I still can't fathom it."

Roland hung his head. "I know I've been a mess," he said. "If it's any help at all, I'm sorry."

"Apologies aren't necessary," Keri said. "Roland, listen, I know you're going through a difficult period. I've a lad a year or two younger than you, and I'll tell you something I told him."

Roland waited.

"Don't settle for anything less than your big dream," Keri said. "Time enough to compromise when you get to be

·159·

an old man like me." Keri paused. "You see, I don't want my son to follow in my footsteps. Decide what you want to be. And that's what you will be. I promise you. And Roland, from what I saw tonight ... you've already taken the first steps."

The lad looked so forlorn that Keri reached out and hugged him.

"Now, good night. Tea's at dawn."

Keri watched Roland disappear into his tent, then ducked into his own, stripped to his shorts, and sank to the cot. Sadly ... his stomach knotted with misery. But before he could fall asleep another, unbidden feeling came over him.

The boy in Keri had responded to the boy, Roland. And in so doing Keri suspected he might have found a path to his own children. Rocky, but a path all the same.

Odd, he reflected, to be given this understanding by a stranger. And he'd never really told his son those things. "But when I get home," he promised himself, "I'll take him into the mountains. Camp out for a week, perhaps two. Just talk. Find out who we are."

Keri checked his watch. Three more hours. He fell into a fitful sleep where long fingers combed firelit sable hair, while his third ear listened to the warnings of the night.

28

On their last night at the Sieberts' tented camp everybody retired early, exhausted with game runs and the makeshift accommodations. Edna would have traded the family crest for a bathtub. Sarah pined for a beauty salon.

Dark dreams chased Roland as he lay asleep in his tent. Fingernails were clawing against the canvas near his head. There was a low cough as of somebody clearing his throat, and Roland catapulted awake. "Who?"

Beyond his thudding heart he heard the rustle of wind, the animal sounds he thought he'd gotten used to. Then came a flash of light, answered by a distant mournful rumble, and he slumped with relief. Only a thunderstorm.

He lay back, only to discover he had to go to the bathroom. "No you don't," he told himself. "Count sheep." But all the sheep had to go too.

When he unzipped the flap he could have sworn he heard something moving behind his tent. But once he got outside, there was no sound. A fiery bolt shattered the sky. "You're not kidding around up there," he thought. He heard branches thrashing. The heavy air forecast rain any minute.

Turning the tent corner, he stopped into a puddle of something wet and sticky. He jerked his foot away, then told himself it was probably just some dumped basin water.

Again the silent lightning lingered under the massed clouds. No, it wasn't a trick of the night, or his imagination. There were two people on the ground about thirty feet away. And they were going at it hot and heavy.

Roland held his breath and waited for the next flash. Wouldn't you know! Not even a flicker. He groped his way along the shower structure. Finding out who they were was almost as exciting as watching the action.

He was so aroused he ached. Who? Not Edna, her carry-all wasn't in sight. Simeon and Sarah? Hardly passion-under-the-stars material. That left Apple and Angus—of course! Though why anybody in his right mind would leave his tent to get rained on . . .

A thorn branch snapped under his bare foot. He bent to pull out the spines and saw his whole foot was smeared with red sticky—what had he stepped in? It looked like blood.

Bolts of lightning lit up the area. Straining his eyes, Roland could see the dark hair fanned out on the ground. Above, pale in the intermittent flashes, he made out a shock of blond hair.

Roland felt a monumental sense of betrayal. What an idiot he'd been! Apple and Angus always fighting. The water jug he'd found by the shower. Keri must have been making it with her since the very first day.

And he'd listened to that crap Keri had handed out about the good fight, about his kid. Be what you want to be. When what it really boiled down to was a fast screw on the ground. Roland laughed bitterly.

Keri sprang to his feet, body crouched, his hands reaching toward the intruder.

Roland didn't move.

Now Keri was beside him, one hand groping to fasten his shorts, the other gouging into Roland's shoulders. "You little bastard," he whispered. "Get back to your tent."

Keri raised his hand to slap the boy, but Apple caught him. He jerked his head toward her tent. Seeing that he had control of himself, she slipped away.

Keri gripped Roland's arm. A roll of thunder nearly drowned out his words. "Look, boy," he began. "It's not what it seems. What are you laughing at? I tell you, you don't understand!"

"I don't want to understand," Roland choked.

"Then cut your laughing." He shook Roland's shoulders. "You'll wake everybody in camp. Then she'll be in one hell of a mess."

"Why didn't you think of that before?" Roland cried.

Keri caught sight of the splotches on Roland's foot. "What is that all over you? Is it blood? Are you all right?"

"I'm okay. Just get your hands off me."

The ground trembled with a roll of thunder, and suddenly torrents were falling, drops bigger than coins battering the leaves and shrubs.

Roland and Keri stood staring at each other. Rain matted Roland's hair and mingled with his tears.

Keri led Roland like a sleepwalker back to his tent.

When they were within five feet Keri stopped. The entire back of the tent was stained dark, and in a lightning flash he saw that the rain trickling off the canvas ran red. "What is this?" he whispered. He looked at Roland. "What have you done?"

"Nothing," Roland said.

Keri picked up something from the ground. "Is this yours?"

Roland reached for it then jerked his fingers back. "My sneaker! I lost that pair when I went swimming. But it's all chewed up! And what's that gook all over it?"

Keri lit a match and cupped it against the rain. He ran his hand over the tent wall. Blood had been poured all over it, and the canvas was clawed in parallel slashes. Keri reached into the bloody shoe and pulled out—

"What's that?" Roland asked, hugging himself against the downpour.

Keri's voice was flat and ominous. "Part of the lamb's liver. I don't know what you've been up to, Roland, but if you slaughtered that animal just to indulge yourself in some cheap sensation—"

"Are you crazy?" Roland cried. "I told you I didn't do it. Even if I did, would I be dumb enough to hide it in my own shoe? And slash my own tent?"

That made sense, Keri decided. Cautiously, he went to the front of the tent and lifted the flap. Roland followed him inside. Keri took the flashlight off the table and played it around. The head of the cot was stained red where the water had run in through the slashes.

Roland clutched his neck. "I thought I heard something. But what is all that? And what happened to my shoe?"

"Get some clothes on, before we lose you to pneumonia," Keri ordered. "You'll sleep with me tonight."

Roland pulled on his pants. "Nothing doing," he said.

"Don't argue," Keri said. He poked his hand through the rips in the canvas. "If you stay here it may be the last night's sleep you'll ever have. As it is, the only thing that saved you was the lightning."

"Saved me from what?"

Keri shook his head. "I don't know. We'll try to track the spoor tomorrow. But right now, get cracking."

In his own tent Keri spent an hour questioning Roland. Either the boy was a psychopathic liar, or he knew nothing. Both were distinct possibilities, Keri told himself, but at the moment he inclined toward the latter. Confounded, Keri went to bed at last.

Long after Keri had dropped off, Roland lay motionless on the next cot. The questions about the blood, the ripped tent, and the shoe faded from his mind, and he thought about Apple and Keri. What are you so unhinged about? Roland asked himself. It's not your bag if two people want to make out, so why the hell are you—I mean, what the hell?

29

Dawn never came. The dark hours gave way to gray, and the birds that normally greeted daybreak were silent. The wind howled through the camp, sending palm leaves crashing to the ground.

The rain had swollen the river over its banks. The Sieberts and their native helpers worked furiously to strike the tents, flushing out the occupants before the rampaging waters swept everything away. Everybody sought shelter in the bar.

No time for Keri to investigate the previous night's mystery. He scrambled over the *Solar Bark*, securing the engine tarpaulins, wedging the chocks tighter under the wheels. The rise of airstrip hadn't yet turned into mud, but the stakes securing the plane couldn't take much more strain.

Keri slogged back to the bar. A sorry sight the group made in their plastic raincoats, huddled to avoid the leaks in the ceiling.

Sarah hurried to Keri. "Has it let up any? I declare, this surely is Ark weather, 'n'at right, Sim?"

Simeon ignored her and said to Keri, "What's the plan of the day?"

Sarah's mouth pinched shut. And he'd been so ornery these past nights. Well, two could play that game.

"About all we can do is wait," Keri said. "This weather is unseasonable. Ought to blow over shortly."

Sarah perched on a bar stool. "An hour or so, do you think?"

"A day would be more like it."

"A day?" Angus blurted. "Cooped up like this? We'll go ape. Now if we'd gotten the hell out of here days ago when I wanted—"

"I don't know, Angus," Roland interrupted. "If we'd left earlier, think of all the fun some of us would have missed."

"What the hell's that supposed to mean?" Angus asked.

Roland turned to Apple and tried to stare her down, but her gaze went through him to the teeming rain. An hour, a day, she could bear anything now. For last night, before Roland had discovered them, Keri had sworn he would drop her in Nairobi as soon as possible.

"What a shame about Sadly," Edna said, touching Roland's arm. "How terribly sad."

Sarah's eyes sparked. "Knock, knock. Who's there. Oryx. Oryx who? Alas poor oryx, I knew him well."

Simeon studiously avoided laughing. "Weather's made me forget where we're headed," he said.

"Samburu," Keri answered. "About a four-hour flight north."

"But we stop in Nairobi first, no?" Apple asked.

"Nairobi? Why?" Angus asked.

"Pick up accumulated mail," Keri said. "Also, we run a routine maintenance check at this point," he lied.

·167·

"Oh, good," Farragut said, "I can buy another automatic flashgun instead of these flashcubes. I only have four cubes left. Of course, if some people hadn't fed the baboons . . ."

Keri's eyes met Apple's, but dropped when he saw Roland glaring at them. The boy had given him quite a turn a moment ago. Keri knew Roland longed to tell all. And what about the business with the blood? Yes, a leopard had clawed the tent. But it had been drawn there by the smell of blood on the sneaker. And how had the sneaker gotten there?

"Say, there," Simeon said, "Samburu's in the wrong order according to this itinerary."

"Hate to admit it, but Sim's right," Sarah said. "Says right here we're supposed to be at Lake Rudolph today." She read from the guidebook. "Nestled in the Rift Valley in the Northern Frontier District, the lake is savagely beautiful, shimmering blue in the midst of a stark desert. Nile perch have been caught weighing up to 340 pounds!" Then Sarah's eyes narrowed. "Why, Edna, you've been repeating things right out of this here book. And all the time I thought you were *Information Please!* Aren't you our clever puss?"

"I am not anybody's clever puss," Edna said coldly.

"Lake Rudolph's out," Keri told them. He spread out a map and pointed to the northern borders. "The whole area's in upheaval," he said, and explained about the recent attacks by the Shifta.

"First the rain and now this?" Sarah declared. "I hope we'll get some kind of refund. Why can't these Shifties behave?"

"Most of the population is Somali," Keri said. "In their last election they voted overwhelmingly to ally themselves with Somalia. Kenya, however, stated, 'The blood of our last man will be shed before an inch of sacred soil is surrendered.' Even though the territory is mostly wasteland."

"Then why?" Edna asked.

"Oil," Roland said and Apple added, "My husband believed—" She broke off.

Keri said, "The major petroleum companies won't risk their millions as long as there's unrest."

"More proof of colonial exploitation," Farragut muttered.

Sarah yawned.

A violent gust caught the palm roof, and as they watched, sailed it away like a giant coolie hat.

"Lord, what next?" Sarah shrieked into the pelting rain.

Edna gripped her carry-all. "Whatever happens, it will be an adventure!" she sang out lightheartedly.

With the rain pinging off her plastic babushka, Sarah scurried about for a dry spot, the lee of a wall, the cramped space beneath the bar counter. "Simeon, *do* something!" she cried.

Farragut stripped off his raincoat and wrapped it around his camera cases.

The wind peeled away one of the walls and it was Edna's turn to cry, "We've got to do something!"

Roland yelled, "What about the plane?"

The others stared at him as though he'd just invented the wheel. The affirmative shout went up. They grabbed their luggage and headed for the *Solar Bark*. Angus swiped two bottles of scotch from the bar. Bodies bent into the driving rain, they plodded through the mire. Simeon lugged both his and Sarah's suitcases. Halfway there his foot caught on an exposed root, and he slid to a graceful halt in the mud. On impact, Sarah's bag snapped open and the contents popped out.

Sarah screeched and shoved her clothes back in. "Stupid oaf!" she cried. "A porter could handle things better. How could I have—?"

Simeon regarded her with intense concentration. Very slowly, he picked up a clod of mud and flung it at her. Sarah stopped, mouth agape. A second mud ball hit her. When she saw him kneading a third, she fled toward the plane.

"Splendid!" Apple cried.

With more dignity than he'd shown on the entire trip, Simeon got up, retrieved his suitcase, and walked to the plane.

"My bag," Sarah wailed.

"It's right there, waiting for you," Simeon said, pointing. "Get yourself another porter."

Sarah clenched her teeth, "You just better get that bag, Simeon. If you know what's good for you." Her mouth gulped air as Simeon walked by her. "Keri?" she called in an aggrieved voice, "Simeon's dropped my suitcase and he won't—"

But Keri was struggling to open the luggage compartment.

"Angus?" Sarah said.

"Learned a long time ago to stay out of family spats."

"Now, Farragut, be a nice—"

"Why, Sarah," Farragut responded. "Would I deprive a pioneering woman like you of—?"

Sarah whirled from him, eyes blazing. "Here, you, Roland, get my bag? Hurry! Before everything gets soaked."

Roland moved to help her. What could be more pathetic than throwing down the gauntlet over a stupid valise?

But hard on Sarah's demand came Edna's "*Roland!* Not a word of backtalk. Go and get her suitcase."

He stopped dead in his tracks. "A 'please' would have done it. Without that, no."

A quiet, simple no. A no he was proud of.

With her mind plotting intricate tortures, Sarah got her valise.

As Keri loaded the gear the rain stopped. He studied the lowering clouds and the river swirling toward the airstrip. Not a bird chirped. Not a baboon to be seen. "It's not over," he said. "The animals are still hiding."

Angus wrestled the cabin door open. "Let them! But let's get us the hell out of here."

They elbowed into the plane. Sarah deliberately plopped into the forward seat, knowing that Simeon's head would be cramped by the fuselage. Simeon motioned for her to move. When she didn't he stepped down hard on her foot. Sarah managed to swallow her yowl. It would be worth it, to see him miserable for four hours.

Keri radioed Nairobi. The static was so bad he could barely make out the report. An electrical storm was driving in from the west, picking up additional force over Lake Victoria. All airports in Uganda were shut. Nairobi and Mombasa on the coast were still open. The storm hadn't reached Samburu, and Keri asked Nairobi Air Control for clearance.

They advised him not to risk it.

The wind came up again, rippling the plane's wing. A ground stake ripped free and splashed into the river.

Edna called out, "That's where we'll wind up unless we get into the air and outrun this."

A distinct possibility, Keri admitted to himself.

Edna grasped her carry-all. "It's all very well for Nairobi to give advice when they're in no danger of drowning."

"Move this crate!" Angus yelled.

Everybody was equally vociferous. Edna, a strange excitement glinting her eyes, spurred them on.

Keri explained the danger to the passengers and the aircraft to Nairobi, and finally they gave him permission.

Except for occasional gusts the wind was steady. The takeoff path would carry them across the river and over the line of trees. With a bit of luck we'll make it, Keri thought.

Damn! The rain had started again.

Keri gauged the floodwaters curling around the rim of the airstrip, hesitated an instant, then flipped the starter switch. A high whine, the slow prop revolutions, then the engines caught and flames shot from the exhausts. Keri checked the panel. All instruments working.

"Job for you now," Keri said to Roland. "Think you can release the ropes anchoring the wing? Then kick away the chocks. Make sure you walk around the *tail* of the plane. Stay away from the props!"

Roland looked at him suspiciously.

Keri snapped his fingers. "Remind me when we've a minute alone. I've got to talk to you about that shoe business last night. I have some theories that only you can verify. But off you go now before we get dunked."

A double half-hitch secured the line. It should have been a cinch to loosen, but the rope had swelled. A penknife, anything with a blade, Roland thought, scrounging around for a sharp twig. He tore at the knot with his teeth and managed to free it.

The prop wash plastered the skin against his skull. He kicked the right chock free, raced around the tail, and attacked the other. It wouldn't budge. The plane had shifted so part of the wheel rested on the wooden triangle. He'd have to get Angus or Simeon to help.

"No, goddamn it," he shouted. "Adapt!"

He dug furiously at the muddy earth. Keri, realizing the difficulty, alternately released and jammed on the brakes, forcing the chock to shift slightly. With a final lurch the wheel rolled free.

Roland climbed back into the copilot's seat.

"Good show," Keri said, slapping him on the shoulder. "Couldn't have done it without you."

Now why should that make me feel like I've just won the Olympic freestyle? Roland wondered. Especially coming from him?

"All strapped in, then?" Keri called over his shoulder.

Through the arcs of the windshield wipers Keri peered at the river and the wall of trees beyond. He had a sudden vision of branches reaching up to snag the wing and a burst of flame. Don't try it! reason shouted. But his blood was charged with the battle against the odds.

More important, if he waited for the storm to pass he'd have to land in Nairobi, as he'd promised Apple. Leaving now, there was a chance that Nairobi would be closed and he'd have to fly on to Samburu. Once there he knew he could persuade her to stay till the end of the safari.

Thinking back to their interrupted night, he shot Roland a quick glance. Damned kid. Not his fault, really. Just one of those accidents. He hadn't realized until this moment how much Apple had— Maddening! He just couldn't get enough of her.

I'll leave Livvie and the kids! he decided suddenly, and as quickly killed the idea. That would solve nothing. Not his own feelings of rootlessness, nor his despair over the sterile turn his life had taken. Fighting against circumstances that would soon leave him without a ranch, without a country.

No, best to remain in harness and trust that the next seven days would burn out this passion. But the next seven days he must have.

Keri revved the engines to full r.p.m. and waited for a lull in the wind.

"Now!" he yelled and raced the *Solar Bark* down the strip. Almost at once he knew they were in trouble.

30

The wheels were losing traction on the slick turf. Keri watched the speedometer anxiously. Takeoff should have been at 110 m.p.h.; the needle oscillated at the 78 mark. The end of the runway sped toward them and Keri knew he must either take off or plow into the river.

Keri pulled back, retracted the wheels and banked sharply to clear the trees. A sickening *carrumph!* shook the plane as the topmost branches caught the wingtip and momentarily fouled the right propeller. But they were airborne, and the engine seemed to be functioning properly. Relief lit Keri's face. He circled, climbing for altitude.

Below, the cresting waters had covered all but the tops of the Land Rovers. The Sieberts and the natives sat huddled on the roofs of the cars, waving to the plane.

"Will they be all right?" Roland asked.

"Sure," Keri said. "They'll rebuild as soon as the flood recedes. Compared to the rainy season this is child's play to them."

The *Solar Bark* angled into the black clouds. Keri

switched on the cabin lights. The intrepid bridge players attempted a rubber, but turbulence soon made them give up. Despite Keri's advice Simeon loosened his seat belt; moments later his head conked against the ceiling as the plane plummeted in a downdraft.

Sarah stretched her legs luxuriously into the aisle.

Keri tuned in the radio. The storm was closing in faster than expected. He did a fast estimate of the flying time. He might *just* squeak through to Nairobi if he pushed the speed to maximum. He glanced at the blur of prop. Strong chance that it had been damaged. He used that excuse to hold the plane steady at 160.

He flipped on the intercom. "Nairobi's just closed their field. They've advised us to fly straight on to Samburu."

Apple fought her way up the aisle and stuck her head into the cockpit. "But you promised," she said.

Keri said over his shoulder, "We've no other choice. Don't worry, I'll arrange something. Tomorrow, the day after. Now *please*. Strap yourself in or you'll get too knocked about to go anywhere."

With a sigh of exasperation, Apple retreated to her seat.

Roland stared into the dense clouds. "Could we have made it to Nairobi?"

Keri didn't answer. The airspeed crept up to 170. The altimeter read 7,000 feet. Keri had to keep compensating for the bucking winds driving them off course. Up to 11,000 now, and still the storm tossed them like a balsa glider. He climbed to 14,000. If anything, it was rougher and everybody began to wheeze, so he dropped back to 10,000 and held it steady.

Lightning blazed all around them. A bolt hit the fuselage and zigzagged through the cabin touching every metal object with blue light. The ceiling bulbs blacked out.

"No reason to be frightened," Keri called to the passengers. "We're built to withstand the severest hit. Still it would be wise to take off any metal jewelry, steel-rimmed glasses, and the like."

The *Solar Bark* fought the storm for another half hour. Simeon's knuckles, braced against the ceiling, turned white. Even Sarah was too miserable to complain. Only Edna seemed unperturbed, as though drawing energy from the maelstrom.

Keri veered toward a break in the cloud cover to check his ground bearings. In the momentary clearing his heart dropped. Mountains surrounded them on all sides, mountains which shouldn't have been there! He jerked the nose up sharply and climbed to 13,000 feet. That could only mean the Abedarre Range. But how? According to the charts his course should have taken him along the north-south trench between the Abedarres and Mt. Kenya.

Obviously I am lost, Keri told himself. By at least 60 to 90 miles.

Roland began humming through his teeth,

We are poor little lambs
Who have gone astray

"Not quite," Keri cut in cheerfully. "The compass is off-kilter and the wind's blown us off course, but it's nothing we can't remedy as long as we've got radio contact."

His voice sounded reassuring, but he knew the situation was serious. The world might be well lost for love, but not if they all wound up in their graves. He made up his mind. Radio Nairobi for a fix and for clearance to land there. He reached for the transmitter. His fingers recoiled from the deadness. The radio had been knocked out by the lightning too.

Shaken, Keri reassessed their predicament. Too risky now to backtrack through the mountains. They did have plenty of fuel. The safest plan then was to outrun the storm and land at Samburu. Fortunately, he knew the terrain well.

He'd have to hope that luck would hold and that he'd be able to find the occasional break in the cloud cover to get his bearings.

The plane tossed for another hour. The muscles in Keri's neck and shoulders began to knot. Ahead, the churning clouds seemed to lighten. All at once the relentless drumming on the metal ceased.

They'd broken free. Keri slumped with relief. Below, flocks of maribou stork, geese and other fowl winged northward before the storm. Mount Kenya took shape, the peak obscured by its perpetual cloud cover.

"The seat of God, right?" Roland asked. "Good thing we broke free or we'd have knocked Him on His ass. Or vice versa."

Keri grinned and passed on the left of the mountain, making sure to give it a wide berth to avoid being sucked into its downdrafts. Samburu lay to the northeast, perhaps another 80 miles. "At present airspeed we'll be there in a little more than half an hour," he said to Roland.

The mountain gradually receded as the plane droned on. Without a compass, Keri planned to fly directly north using Mount Kenya as a guidepost. When he'd gone about 60 miles he would make an abrupt ninety-degree turn, then fly east until he ran into the Samburu Preserve. Once there he could find the airstrip blindfolded. A bit longer, to be sure, but he'd taken far too many risks already.

Banking the plane into the tight ninety-degree turn, Keri never saw the vulture. The vulture probably never saw the plane. The right engine exploded as the propeller sucked the bird in, and its chewed pieces hit the fuselage like shrapnel. A wing rocketed into the tail, destroying the aileron controls. The bulk of the bird hurtled into the windshield and smashed it into a spiderweb. As shards of glass slashed Keri's forehead and streams of blood ran into his eyes, he reexperienced the moment of flying over his ranch and the voice that said, I'll never see them again.

Everybody was shouting at once. If only they'd stop long enough for him to wipe his eyes. Then he heard a more piercing sound—the plane screaming toward the ground.

Keri fought the unresponsive controls, fought to keep from losing consciousness. Automatically he groped for the radio. Must give Nairobi our position, speed—then he remembered.

He heard the rip of cloth and felt Roland's fingers on his forehead trying to stem the blood. Keri fought off the waves of dizziness. He squinted through the pain and blur of blood.

A plume of smoke trailed from the right engine. They'd pulled far to the left, away from Samburu. The flat whine warned him they were spiraling down fast. Unless he broke the tailspin, they'd grind into the ground like a cigarette stub.

"Altitude," he barked at Roland. "It's the biggest dial on the panel."

"Eight thousand feet," Roland replied, his hand still pressed against Keri's forehead.

"Give me a reading every hundred feet. Keep talking. Don't let me pass out. Tell everybody to stay in his seat or we'll lose more control."

"Seventy-eight hundred. You're going to be okay," Roland panted. "Everybody's sitting. Is there glass in your eyes? What can I do? Tell me! I didn't mean anything I said last night, I—"

Keri grated, "Pull back on the wheel with me, *now*!"

Straining every muscle, they pulled the plane out of its spin. The wings shuddered violently. The ailerons wouldn't respond, and the craft veered off to the left again.

Angus bolted from his seat. "For God's sake, man, land! This has gone far enough!"

"Angus, can you fly?" Keri shouted.

He couldn't. Neither could anybody else.

"Strap yourselves in *tight*!" Keri shouted. "Or you'll be dead when we crash."

The Matthews Range should be straight ahead, Keri thought. Or had they strayed farther north? Were they approaching the N'doto Range? Good Lord, where were they?

"Roland? Are there any mountains in sight?"

"A big one over to the left. We're headed back toward the storm. It's just started to rain again."

"Airspeed. The little dial to the left of—"

"One-ten. Dropping. Just over a hundred."

"Keep wiping away the blood, that's it, boy."

Blood—

"Roland!" Keri exclaimed urgently, "that business about your shoe—"

With a screech the engine cowling ripped away.

Keri yelled above the din, "Tell them to put their heads on their knees—clasp their legs with their arms. And not to look up when we crash!"

Roland repeated Keri's instructions. Simeon kept struggling to his feet, Sarah screamed continually, and Edna was very white. Roland took an instant to wave to her.

Roland cinched his seat belt until it dug into his hip bones, then checked Keri's belt. "Airspeed's just *under* a hundred," he said. "Altitude, six thousand."

"Where's that mountain now? Have we passed it?"

"Can't see. Too many clouds. No, there it is. Coming up on our left. We're dropping faster."

"There's a red lever on the right side of the control panel. Push it down hard. It will jettison the gas tanks."

The plane jerked as the wing tanks fell away.

"Good boy," Keri said. "Now for the inboard fuel tank. Make sure it's the right one, not doing the dead engine much good. Find it? Open the stopcock."

Roland saw the gasoline trail behind them like a silver rope.

"We're clear of the mountain, aren't we?" Keri mumbled, just as the clouds broke enough for him to glimpse the peak looming straight ahead. He tried everything to get them off the collision course. But the controls were dead. The plane acted as if it had a life of its own.

A forest began to take form. Keri knew if they crashed there it would be all over. Please, God, let there be a bamboo grove on the mountain. The plane would cut a swath through that, but the reeds would slow them down enough so there might be a chance.

"What about the landing gear?" Roland asked, his voice quavering.

Keri shook his head. "If the wheels snagged on anything we'd flip over." He reduced airspeed as much as he could.

"Heads down, everybody!" Roland shouted as the mountain flew toward them.

They passed over a deep green forest, the banshee wind in their ears, and now the softer green of the bamboo belt was on them. The wings cut through like a giant scythe as they plowed into it. The right wing sheared off and flew away, while the fuselage raked across the ground striking huge sparks. The plane shuddered to a halt.

The storm closed over them.

31

Roland opened his eyes to row on row of dials. Through the windshield the boulder-strewn terrain came into focus. He was alive!

"Edna! Keri!" he shouted.

Keri's head was turned away, his fingers still on the controls. The fuselage ceiling was ripped open in a jagged can-opener line. Rain was falling steadily.

Moans came from the cabin.

"Edna?" Roland shouted again. "Apple? Is everybody okay?" He squirmed out of his seat, wincing with the ache in his bones. And he was scared out of his head.

He gripped Keri's shoulder. "You did it. You got us down." Then he saw Keri's blood-streaked face and drew in his breath. He pressed his ear to Keri's chest; he was still breathing. Roland grabbed Keri's head and kissed him. He unfastened Keri's seat belt, but couldn't budge him. A dot of crimson bubbled at the corner of Keri's lips. Then Roland's nostrils contracted at an acrid odor.

"Something's burning!" he yelled, and looked around

wildly. The props were twisted like paper clips, the engines were smoldering.

The burning smell was growing stronger. A wisp of smoke curled up from the buckled floorboards. Tears sprang to Roland's eyes. "Don't cry," he commanded himself. "Don't!"

He did cry, but he also grabbed the fire extinguisher. A shot of foam blanketed the floor, smothering the flames. But there's no telling if other fires are burning in the wreck, Roland thought, yanking at Keri frantically. "Keri, unless we get out—" No use. He'd need help to move him. Edna, he thought. Yeah, she'll know what to do.

Squeezing into the cabin, Roland heard Sarah's voice. "Now, Sim, you help me, hear? Sim! Pay attention." Then her piercing wail, "Oh, merciful Jesus! He's dead!"

Roland fought through the debris in the aisle. Opposite the Shallots, Farragut and Edna were still unconscious. Farragut writhed as if he were having a nightmare; Edna looked serene. Roland saw a network of veins pulsing at her temple and almost collapsed with happiness; she was alive.

Sarah was sobbing uncontrollably. Roland unbuckled her seat belt and said, "Don't worry, Sarah, Simeon's just conked on the head. There's a fire in the cockpit. We've got to get out of here before we blow up."

Sarah paid no attention. Roland shook Simeon, but his "no-bones" feel made him jerk his hands away. The seat-belted body lurched forward. Behind his head the ceiling had been crushed. No more than six inches, but six inches too many.

Sarah leaned over him, kissing his fingers, making entreating sounds.

Roland couldn't tear his eyes away. His first dead man.

A day ago he'd been saying, "Look yonder, a vulture at four o'clock, a jackal at ten." Look there at twelve o'clock. Death.

Edna surfaced slowly. The instant her eyes were open, she sat up straight and reached for her carry-all.

"Are you all right?" Roland asked her.

She waved his questions away, already unhooking her seat belt. "Tell me," she ordered.

"Fire in the cockpit. I used the extinguisher, but I think it's still burning."

Her nose wrinkled. "I smell it," she said and rose on trembling legs. "Keri?"

Roland gripped her elbow to steady her. "He's too big to handle alone. I'll need help."

Edna's eyes turned from the unconscious Farragut to Simeon. "He'll help you."

"Simeon's dead," Roland whispered.

"Then get Angus," Edna said without hesitation. She looked behind the rear partition, where Angus had begun to groan. Apple had her head on her knees like a child napping. Edna took the smelling salts from her pharmacopoeia and moved it under Angus's nose, shaking him to consciousness. Except for some bruises he was uninjured.

"The bicycle!" Apple screamed, reaching out in a gesture of warning.

Edna slapped her across the face.

Apple's eyes registered recognition. "How? What—Keri?"

Angus glared at her.

Edna started for the exit. "Roland, see what you can do with this door."

He lunged against it a few times. No use, the crash had

·183·

jammed it. He yanked the emergency lever and blew out the hatch. The wing had sheared away from the fuselage, leaving a six-foot drop to the ground.

Edna thrust the spirits of ammonia at Apple. "See to Farragut." She turned to Angus. "We must get Keri out. He's the only one who knows where we are. Quickly—the plane may explode any minute."

Apple managed to rouse Farragut. He struggled to his feet, screamed, and fell back. His right leg was broken.

Supporting Farragut under the arms, Apple and Edna inched to the emergency exit. Farragut sat carefully, swung his left leg out, and was about to hoist his right when he yelled, "My camera bags!"

Grinding his teeth against the pain, he tried to crawl back to his seat. Edna blocked his way, shouting, "Are you insane? You must get out!" They pushed back and forth.

Angus and Roland shoved past Sarah, who knelt in the aisle rocking Simeon's body, and squirmed into the cockpit.

"Go easy," Roland cautioned Angus. "The wheel must have jammed into his chest. Broke some ribs, maybe."

They dragged Keri out of the seat. He opened his eyes for an instant of pain and collapsed again.

"I told you, easy!" Roland cried. "You want to kill him?"

Angus grunted. "He'll be dead soon enough unless we move him."

They jockeyed Keri up the aisle, once more stumbling over Sarah. Apple was on her knees reaching under Farragut's seat. Farragut was still frozen at the hatch, fighting off Edna's jabs and pushes.

"Farragut, you must jump," she cried. "What good are your cameras if you're dead?" She clouted him with her carry-all. Farragut pitched forward and landed on the wet ground.

Edna eased herself down, followed by Apple with the camera case. Farragut clutched it to his chest. "Apple, where's the other one?" he cried. "The one with all my film?"

But the women were already reaching up to help Roland and Angus lower Keri's limp body. They collapsed under his weight. "Never mind," Edna called from the tangle of bodies, "we'll manage. Get Sarah."

Sarah wouldn't leave without Sim.

Cursing her, Angus motioned to Roland. Together they lifted Simeon and dumped his long body through the exit. Sarah pummeled their backs, yelling, "Don't bump him like that!"

Edna was again on her feet directing the group. "Roland, take one of Keri's legs, Apple, the other. Angus, you get him under the arms. Try not to jostle him too much. We *must* protect him."

"What about Sim?" Sarah shrilled.

"I'll help you with him," Edna said. "Farragut, can you make it on your own?" Without waiting for an answer she helped Sarah pull Simeon across the rough scree to a small clearing in the thorn bush where the others had carried Keri. Farragut, camera bag looped over his shoulder, crawled after.

Heaving with exhaustion, they collapsed on the ground. Edna alone remained standing, tall and straight, watching for the plane to explode.

32

Minutes dragged by. Roland glanced around. The clearing ended at a rocky escarpment about fifty feet away. Carefully, he made his way to the edge and peered over. Hundreds of feet below, the valley was obscured by rain. Small blessing, he thought. Nothing could climb up behind them.

With each breath Apple felt a pain inside her. But there was no time to worry about herself. She took some hurried gulps of air and began tending Keri.

Farragut got his breath and begged Roland to get his other bag. "Please! I'll give you anything. It's got my outline in it!"

Roland was busy helping Apple with Keri. "What do you think?" he asked.

"Shock," she said. "We must keep him warm and the circulation going." She began rubbing Keri's hand and motioned for Roland to do the same.

Roland looked at her anxiously. Without Keri they wouldn't have a chance! He was the only one who knew anything about anything! Roland rubbed harder.

Edna took her binoculars out of her carry-all and peered at the plane. "There isn't a sign of fire anywhere," she said. "Roland, are you sure?"

"Yes, I saw it. And you smelled it yourself."

"Well, there's no fire now. Even if there was, the rain has surely put it out. We ought to salvage everything we can."

"Blankets," Apple said. "And see if there is a first-aid kit."

"There ought to be a tool chest someplace," Roland said.

Edna took his arm. "Roland, you're the quickest. Strip everything out of the cabin. Make sure you get the radio, that's the *most* important. Angus, you unload the luggage compartment."

"Hell, I'm not going back into that trap," Angus exclaimed. "Think I'm nuts?"

Edna's lips thinned. "All living is dangerous. It's dying that's easy. I've no intention of doing that. Not just yet."

Angus kicked at the rocky earth.

Edna went on solemnly, "Angus, I make you this promise, and the others can bear witness. When we're found, as we most certainly shall be, I will be honest with the press. You understand how that will look? How your company will react to your behavior? Now, which shall it be?"

"Where will *you* be?" Angus asked belligerently.

"Right beside you. We've got to form a sort of bucket brigade. Get all of the salvageable things from the plane. Roland, remember, take everything, maps, manuals, any utensils. And we *must* have the radio."

"My other camera bag," Farragut pleaded.

Apple said to Farragut, "Keep massaging Keri's hands and feet until we get back."

·187·

Warily, the four of them made their way toward the wreck. Edna turned and called, "Sarah! You come and help too."

But Sarah was engrossed. "Now you *know* that stubbornness is your worst fault, 'n'at right, Sim? And if you hadn't insisted on taking that rear seat . . ."

"Keep your eyes open for fire," Roland said as they got closer. "Be ready to run."

Not a wisp of smoke could be seen. Did I dream up the whole extinguisher bit? Roland wondered.

Edna, Apple and Angus started to unload the luggage compartment, while Roland hoisted himself into the plane. Gloomy, like trespassing in a crypt. He threw off his fright and worked feverishly, heaving everything down to Angus, who pitched it to Apple, who tossed it to Edna, who flung it as far from the wreck as she could. Roland didn't consider value; if he could move it, it went. Time enough later to decide what they could use.

Ash trays. The folding table. Cards. Picnic basket and canteens. Blankets. Heavy tarpaulins. The tool kit. Their plastic raincoats. Magazines. A guidebook, *Where to Dine in Nairobi*. He stuffed a box of safety matches in his pocket.

After he'd stripped everything he could from the passenger cabin he moved to the cockpit. There was the fire extinguisher; flecks of foam were dissolving on the floor. He kicked out the windshield and tossed down maps, manuals, a letter from Keri's wife, Keri's sunglasses, a small first-aid kit.

The radio looked and smelled badly burned. But Edna had insisted, so Roland tackled it. He pulled, pushed, kicked; it wouldn't budge. The crash had buckled the plates.

As he worked he marveled at Edna. The way she'd

whipped everybody into shape! God, he was proud of her. He braced his feet against the instrument panel and yanked hard. One of his shoes came off . . . what was it Keri had said about his shoe?

After five more minutes of struggling, he still hadn't freed the radio. The smell of gasoline had gotten stronger. Roland's head began to swim. He snatched the rear-view mirror off the sun visor and stumbled out of the cockpit. At the hatchway he took one last look, then snapped his fingers. He dove under Farragut's seat and dragged out the camera case. Christ, it weighed a ton.

Roland leaped from the plane and gulped in the rain-fresh air. Junk lay strewn across the ground.

Edna came to meet him. "The radio?"

"Impossible," Roland said.

Her voice rose. "I told you to get it *first!* The radio is the single most important—"

Roland reacted as if she'd slapped him. "It's completely ruined," he shouted. "The transistors are smashed, the wires are all burned. Don't you think I know when something's wrecked?"

"No, I don't!" Edna nearly screamed. "Let me be the judge of that!" She thrust the tool kit at him. "If you had used your head in the plane, you would have used this to get the radio out."

She managed to control herself and tried another tack. "Don't you see? Once the radio is in our hands there's always the possibility that we can repair it. These tools will help you get it free. Roland, we're depending on you."

"Oh no!" Apple pointed to the right engine. "I think I saw—"

Edna lifted her binoculars. "I don't see anything."

"If the radio is ruined, what is the point in risking his

life?'' Apple said. "Roland, it is too dangerous now. Smell the gasoline? You must not go.''

Edna grabbed Roland's arm and half-shoved him toward the plane. "Roland, remember, our lives may well depend on that radio.''

Roland nodded blankly. "Yes, ma'am,'' he said and started back toward the *Solar Bark*. He knew he could never free the radio, even with the tools. But he could never convince Edna. The whole thing was hysterical. Here he was, about to be charbroiled, and he couldn't stop laughing.

"*Roland!* Why are you stopping?'' Edna called. "Don't be frightened. Go on.''

Roland remained rooted. Balanced on the balls of his feet, he stood eyeing the *Solar Bark*. How much time did he have? Thirty seconds? Ten seconds? Suddenly, unbeckoned, came the memory of walking the rails. And with it a recognition so overwhelming that Roland felt freed forever. It was Howie's choice! He *could* have jumped! He *should* have!

"Go on, go on,'' Edna urged him.

Before Roland could turn back, a burst of fire mushroomed up, wrapping the plane and him in a blinding shroud.

33

The explosion hurled Roland through the air. He felt as if his eyes were melting. Then somehow Apple was all over him, beating at his burning clothes. They crawled out of range and stared at the flames, orange and gold, snaking through the blown-out windows.

"*Dio mio*," Apple whispered, hugging him.

Roland fought off his shock. At last he sobbed, "I'm okay now. That's the second time you—" he snuffled and saw her smile.

Edna was shouting to them, her pharmacopoeia at the ready. Roland limped to the clearing, where she laved his burns with salve.

"You see? I *told* you," Roland complained. "I could be dead."

"But you aren't, thank God. That's the important thing. Some mean blisters, perhaps, part of an eyebrow singed off, but nothing too serious."

Edna bit her lip. "Oh, and Roland, after the fire dies down, see if you can't retrieve the tools you dropped? Apple, will you finish his bandages? We've discovered all our watches have different times. Magnetized, I suppose. But it must be late afternoon and we've an enormous amount of work to do before dark."

Despite her pleas, blandishments and threats, Edna was unable to galvanize the others into action. They were busy going through their luggage, pacing, and watching spectacular explosions reduce the *Solar Bark* to a charred skeleton.

Apple was the only one active. After tending Roland's burns she turned her attention to Keri. She leaned over him talking in a polyglot of English and Italian, urging him to open his eyes.

She motioned to Roland. "I will need your help," she said. "You have a steady hand?"

Roland held out shaky fingers.

"Never mind," Apple told him. "You *must* have a steady hand. Bring me Edna's little drugstore, please? It is much better than this silly first-aid kit. And my valise also?"

Edna, wisps of white hair sticking out of her plastic raincap, was tearing a sheet of paper into strips. She looked up at Roland. "And pencils. I'll need pencils."

"What for?" he asked, concerned at her wild look. But Apple was calling. Edna grudgingly relinquished her pharmacopoeia, telling Roland she held him personally responsible for it.

Apple sterilized her eyebrow tweezer in alcohol. Instructing Roland to hold Keri's head steady, she began picking the glass splinters out of his face.

"It is not so awful as it looks," she said as she worked. "All superficial. A few stitches, perhaps." Apple kept up her patter but worked so intently she might have been in an operating room.

"He might have glass in his eyes too," Roland said softly. "After the bird smashed the windshield he couldn't see at all."

She nodded and pulled back Keri's lids. The involuntary reflex made the membrane flutter like a wounded butterfly. As Apple irrigated the eyes specks of glass washed to the corners. Roland blotted them away. To be certain all the glass was out, she leaned down and flicked her tongue over the unseeing hazel eyes and the underside of the lids.

Roland's mouth fell open.

Apple blotted her tongue. "Primitive," she said, "but one must do the best with what is at hand."

She squeezed antibiotic ointment into Keri's eyes and taped a gauze bandage over them. "So he will move them as little as possible," she said. "Eyes are marvelous. Given the slimmest chance our little peepholes to the soul heal themselves."

Apple wished she felt as optimistic about Keri's other injuries. Growing up in a medical family had given her enough experience to know they were critical. Without doubt he had broken ribs, massive shock, perhaps internal bleeding. He needed transfusions, intravenous feeding, if he was to survive.

She tucked the blanket under his chin and stared at the lank blond hair that fell across his forehead, the hollow cheeks, the visor of white gauze. A wave of tenderness swept over her. How different this feeling was from what she had once believed to be the core of love. She could never tie this man to her, nor did she wish to. She only wished him life.

"Come," she said abruptly to Roland. "Now we must take care of Farragut."

As she stood up Apple was seized with a spasm. She

fell against Roland, brushing aside his anxious questions, and clung to him until the pain passed, leaving a heaviness around her pelvis. It would happen soon. An hour, perhaps, a day. She steadied herself against Roland and pressed on to Farragut.

"Now, Angus, I depend on you," Edna said, pushing a slip of paper into his hands. "It will be dark very soon."

Angus had been watching Apple fawn over Keri, and ugly suspicions were forming in his mind. His hand tightened on the bottle of scotch he'd slipped from his valise and put under his jacket.

"You're right," Angus said to Edna, "but excuse me a minute. Got an important phone call to make if you know what I mean." He strode off beyond a clump of boulders.

Exasperated, Edna hurried to Sarah, who was hovering over Simeon, buttoning his shirt, recombing his hair.

Edna thrust paper and pencil under Sarah's nose. "Now listen, Sarah. Simeon would have wanted you to carry on, to bring credit to his name."

Sarah looked up, her interest captured at last.

Apple snipped open Farragut's pant leg to the knee. Her fingers probed. Good, only a simple fracture.

But Roland's eyes told him more. Farragut's leg was misshapen with rickets. Suddenly all the carping Roland had done about him seemed stupid. And very young. Farragut's bones had been shaped by years of hunger. Who am I to pick out his faults? Roland thought.

"Will it hurt?" Farragut asked Apple.

She nodded. "But only for a moment. Here, bite on this wood. Roland, hold his thigh above the knee."

With one hand braced under Farragut's knee she pulled hard on his ankle. Farragut screamed as the broken bone scraped together and meshed. Apple applied splints, two branches Roland had found, then bound the leg with bandages Roland had ripped from her pink slip.

"Tight enough to keep the leg immobile, not tight enough to cut off circulation. *Finito*," she said with a flush of confidence. She thought of her parents and their dedication to healing. How closed off she must have been to have never understood them.

Roland admired the job. "Neat," he said. "Ever think of becoming a nurse?"

"Not until now," Apple said. "And you? You want to play 'Doctor and Nurse,' eh?"

Roland turned crimson.

"You must not move this leg," she warned Farragut. "When we get to Nairobi they will put plaster on it and we will all sign our names on the cast."

"None of us will ever get to Nairobi, or through this night alive," Edna called, "unless we get organized."

"Yes, you're absolutely right," Sarah was saying, fixed on the idea of what Simeon would have wanted. "I will dedicate my life to spreading his message. I don't want any glory for myself. That's not the kind of person I am."

"Sarah, this maudlin self-pity has got to stop," Edna said. "It's almost dusk. Pull yourself together, woman, and stop acting like a weak sister."

Despite his pain, Farragut laughed. "A weak sister," he repeated.

Sarah sprang to her feet and glared at him. "Well, Mr. Farragut, if you're finished laughing let's see how much work *you'll* contribute. Leg's probably not broken at all. The excuses some people will invent just to get out of a little honest work!"

"That will be quite enough," Edna said, stepping between them. "We've got more urgent things to do."

Sarah turned on her. " 'N' why are you pestering us with these silly strips of paper?"

Angus, just coming back from the bush said, "Yeah, what's that all about?"

"We must have a council of war," Edna began. "We've got to choose a leader. Somebody to assign duties, to organize a plan. Otherwise we'll do nothing but flounder about, the way we've been floundering for the past hour."

"You know, that's a good idea," Angus agreed. "Now I think the women ought—"

"Not quite so fast," Edna interrupted.

"Of course, Sim would have been our natural leader, smart as a trout and a *great* outdoorsman and—"

"I've prepared these ballots," Edna said. "First, though, we must all agree that whoever is elected—"

"What hogwash," Sarah retorted. "We're sure to be rescued before dark."

"Fine, Sarah. We'll just count you out," Edna said. "But when we've finished building a shelter for the night you'll stay outside. I warn you, Sarah, we've no room for grasshoppers in this group."

Sarah shrugged but reached for a slip. "Let me have Sim's too. We did pay two fares!"

Roland smacked his head. "Where have you been, Sarah? Haven't you heard? One man, one vote!"

The others agreed that Sarah rated only one ballot.

"This is in no sense a speech," Edna began. "Yet you must all decide who is best suited to lead us—at least until Keri regains consciousness. I know your natural instinct is to vote for yourself. But surely you realize that would lead us into hopeless anarchy? I urge you to *think*. Decide who is most intelligent, who can—"

"This is rough country," Angus interrupted. "Somebody with stamina, strong—"

Farragut cut in, "Roosevelt had polio, Kennedy a bad back. A physical handicap doesn't mean anything anymore."

"Edna?" Roland said, "you didn't give me one."

Edna looked puzzled. "But Roland, you're too young to vote."

"What? Are you kidding?" Roland choked. "I wasn't too young to drag everything out of the plane!"

"That's entirely beside the point," Edna said. "You failed at the one really important job you had—getting the radio. You can't be given the same responsibility as an adult."

"That is nonsense!" Apple exclaimed. "He risked his life. He must be allowed to have his say."

Edna shook her head. "I for one wouldn't think of jeopardizing our survival by allowing an immature—"

"Definitely immature," Sarah agreed. "Don't you remember how he jumped off the roof of the car? Scared us all to death on the Nile?"

"It's only for one night, Roland," Farragut said. "You wouldn't be elected anyway."

Angus grinned. "Tough, guy. Remember that old saying, 'You scratch my back, I'll scratch yours'?" He shrugged eloquently.

"But you are all missing the point," Apple insisted.

"We're wasting valuable time," Edna said. "The majority is against him participating, so there's no reason to argue. Write down your choice, fold the slips and—"

"Who's going to do the counting?" Sarah demanded.

They eyed each other suspiciously, and finally decided to tabulate the results together.

They're cutting my nuts off, Roland thought, and I don't know how to stop them.

Edna collected the ballots and held each slip up for group inspection as she read the results.

34

"Sarah," she read in a crisp voice. "Edna. Angus. Edna. Edna."

Edna leafed through the papers again and looked at the others. "Why, I'm overwhelmed," she murmured. "I shall do everything in my power to justify your faith." Her face glowed as she put the slips into her carry-all. She bowed her head for a moment. "I can only ask the Lord for His blessing and guidance."

"Amen," Sarah said, determined to be a good loser.

Edna assigned duties to each member of the group. Roland's tasks: (a) Gather thorn bush. (b) Drag it back to camp. While he was at it, (c) Reconnoiter.

He managed to drag back a small load of thorn bush but got badly scratched. Got to be another way, he thought. Then, clipping the ends of a tarpaulin together with a clothespin from Apple's skirt hanger, he made a kind of ground sled that could hold ten times as much as he could carry alone.

During his first couple of forays Roland was so angry

about the election that he dragged his heels. Then the rhythm of work took over. After all, what difference does it make? he thought. I'd have voted for Edna anyway.

Edna assigned the task of building an enclosure to Angus. Various sites were discussed. Roland pointed out that they'd save time, and his back, if they built a semicircle with the open end to the cliff, since nothing could get at them from there.

You really had to hand it to the old girl, Angus thought, as he intertwined the scrub Roland brought in. She was really pulling them together. Why not go along with the gag?

After a few more loads of bush the corral began to take shape, a low crescent enclosing a thirty-foot area. In the center, Farragut scratched at the rocky earth with a screwdriver, digging a firepit.

The three women were pitching a lean-to with the heavy tarpaulin. Their twine snapped under the weight and a wail went up.

Roland yelled to them, "Braid three strands of twine. When you've got three separate braids, then braid those together."

" 'N' will that hold?" Sarah asked.

"If it doesn't, the George Washington Bridge is in a lot of trouble."

Roland went off on another search. From the east came occasional flashes of lightning. The rain would soon be over. He passed the glowing wreckage and got the shakes again.

Down a scoured slope, bare save for the hardiest vegetation, and onto a plateau strewn with giant boulders. He climbed the largest one to get a better view but rain and mists cut visibility to a few hundred feet.

"Well, I've reconnoitered," he said, climbing down the rock. The farther away from camp he went, the more scared he got. Come on now, he told himself, Angus is waiting for more bush. He pushed farther into the unknown territory. A few yards away he almost stepped in spoor droppings. What kind of animal had made it? Antelope? Cat? If only Keri was there to read the signs!

Pushing across the plateau, Roland felt his skin crawl with the uncanny silence. Everything's been frightened away by the explosion, that's all, he told himself. How different this was. Without a plane, without a car, without a guide.

A sticky mass clutched at Roland's face, and he fought it off, terrified. He felt like an idiot when he saw the ruins of a rain-diamonded spider web. Lord, he thought, feeling the tears again, what's going to happen to us?

"Here's what'll happen," he told himself. "Keri'll be okay. We'll spend a peaceful night under the stars in enchanted Kenya. In the morning a plane will rescue us and everybody will make a big fuss."

And if the plane doesn't show?

Then Keri'll tell us the best direction to strike out for help. Got to be *somebody* living around here.

Like the Shifta?

He buried that thought as deep as he could and began the trek to camp.

When he got back Roland was amazed how well Edna had organized everything. Keri and Farragut were lying beneath the lean-to. So was Simeon. How freaky, Roland thought, staring at the body. Just when he'd begun to show signs of life, what with the mud balls and all. Was there a lesson there somewhere? Throw your mud ball when you wanted? Because the next minute—zap!

"Has Keri come to yet?" Roland asked.

Apple shook her head. "He groans and sometimes tries to turn. But when I speak to him he doesn't answer."

Farragut's forehead was beaded with sweat. His leg had begun to ache so badly he'd had to leave off digging. After her firewood-gathering chore, Sarah had taken over his job.

She chattered as she dug, "He can't even dig a little ditch."

"What did you say?" Farragut challenged her.

"I wasn't talking to you," she sang back.

Edna's most ingenious bit of planning was a water-collection device. She'd zipped up a plastic raincoat and suspended it upside down from a bush, the circle of hem up to the falling rain. The drops funneled down the neck and into a wide-mouthed thermos. Apple's job was to oversee that operation.

Edna knew that water was the most vital consideration. Without it, once the rain stopped, they couldn't last more than a day or so.

"Hey, Ms. President?" Angus yelled, "I'll be out of thorn scrub pretty soon." He jerked his thumb to a large gap in the enclosure.

Edna looked at Roland.

"I've carted in everything that's around," he said.

"You'll have to go further down the escarpment," Edna said.

Apple looked at the sky. "It will be dark soon. Perhaps if we all helped?"

"Not necessary," Edna said. "We all have our jobs. Yours is water collection and storage. Roland, the quicker you go—" she took him aside. "You and I have to set an example," she whispered. "These people will fall apart if we don't."

Roland started out again, boiling. "The quicker you go," he mimicked, just out of range. Next she'll be asking me to make bricks without straw.

Apple's voice threaded after him. "Be careful. Remember, it gets dark very fast."

Roland worked his way down the cliff, talking to himself to keep up his courage. "It's getting darker. Spot some signposts. There's a rock. And there's a rock. Great. All the rocks look like rocks."

He was about to tear up a bush when an orange streak swooped down around his head. He fought off a red-crested, yellow-breasted bird that hung in the air on fluttering wings.

"Saw your picture in Edna's book," Roland said. Then he spotted the nest, in the thorn bush, about to fall; loosened by the storm, probably. "Sorry," he said, "but it's you or me. How long will it take you to build a new one? Couple of hours?"

The bird dove, pecking at Roland's face. He was about to swat it when he saw the speckled eggs in the tipping nest. Food! He reached eagerly for them, but his hand hesitated. Something Keri had once said came back to him. Scramble those eggs and you'll fuck up the universe, or something like that.

"Okay, lady. No reason you and the kids should suffer just because we were dumb enough to crash." Cheered by this sign of life, Roland reached through the brambles, wedged the nest into place, and got away before the bird attacked again.

Farther downhill, he stumbled across an enormous thicket that had been uprooted by the storm. See that? he told himself. St. Audubon put that in your path for leaving his eggs alone.

·203·

He jumped clear of the bushes when he saw the ants' nests, the size of walnuts, built around the thousands of spines. A certain species of army ant, Keri had once told him, built their colonies around the thorns so anteaters couldn't get at them.

Sometimes, Roland thought, it is essential to inspect God's gifts.

Five more minutes of scrounging and he had another load of brush. Before beginning the steep trek back he stopped to take a leak. His stomach gurgled a loud complaint, and he patted it. "Sorry, but we are not going back for those eggs."

Hauling the loaded tarp behind him, he started the climb. Faster, getting too dark. He tried a shortcut through a stand of razor-sharp grass and came out—nowhere! Nothing but sheer drops on three sides. He stood on the ledge, frozen with fear, while the twilight drifted over the mountain.

35

Roland forced himself to take a step, and an avalanche of pebbles rolled down the cliff. He backtracked and came on another dead end. A hairpin turn around the cliff wall, just wide enough for the tarpaulin. Don't look down!

"Apple! Edna!" he yelled hoarsely. Then Apple's voice was calling from behind him. Carefully, he backed away from the ledge. Another turn in the path, a short climb, and he sagged with relief. There was the campsite ahead.

He gave Apple a hug. "If it had been any darker I'd have tumbled off that ledge."

Everyone pitched in to complete the enclosure. Four feet tall, patchy in spots, but at least it gave them a feeling of protection.

Sarah had outlined the firepit with a cunning design of rocks. She whispered to Edna, who nodded and called to Farragut, "Will you start breaking up branches for kindling? It will keep your mind off the pain."

Before they put the final section of thorn bush into place Edna insisted they all go to the bathroom.

"Don't have to," Roland told her. "Fact is—"

Edna insisted, they must at least try. "There are no predators now, but who knows what night will bring? We cannot leave ourselves vulnerable by constantly opening the *boma* gate around the *shamba*."

Incredible, Roland thought, one visit to that Masai village and she'd sponged up those words and made them hers.

One by one they went through the gate, Farragut using a forked stick as a crutch.

A little while later Sarah announced, "I'm hungry. Roland, didn't you see any fruit or anything while you were supposed to be scouting around?"

"Not a thing," Roland lied.

Edna began dispensing pills—antimalaria, antiamoebic, and vitamins. "Not exactly *cordon bleu*, but they do meet the daily minimum requirements," she said, doling out half a cup of water to each of them.

Sarah refused. "Pills don't agree with me. I've got the most sensitive tummy. 'Sides, my doctor says vitamins are a waste of time, and they can make you sick."

"That may be," Edna replied, "and you can discuss it with him when you get back. But meanwhile you'll get a lot sicker if you come down with any of these exotic bugs."

Sarah stamped her foot. "No is what I said, and no is what I meant!"

The insurrection rocked Edna momentarily. Then she said, "Sarah, if you get sick I'll make sure nobody helps you. If we have to move on, we'll leave you behind. I give you my solemn word on that."

The women glared at each other.

"Sarah," Farragut broke in, "if you don't want to go along with the majority, why don't you secede?"

In the burst of laughter that followed Sarah swallowed the pills. Tears sprang to her eyes. "Silly old woman with silly old pills," she muttered. "*I* didn't vote for her. What difference does any of this make when Sim is dead?" Sobbing, she whirled on Farragut. " 'N' you wouldn't be so free with your mouth if my Sim were here. Just you wait, you'll see, the Lord will smite my enemies."

Before they could finish gathering wood, night came down, making the compound seem makeshift and pitiful.

"Angus," Edna said, "light the fire."

Angus fumbled with his cigarette lighter, but the fluid had leaked out. He threw it down in disgust. "I'll get a light from the wreck. There ought to be some embers left."

He opened the gate, got a few feet outside, then dashed back, wide-eyed. "There's something out there!" he cried, pointing in the direction of the plane. "I don't know what, I couldn't see, but it was there."

"It's your imagination," Edna scoffed.

"Oh, yeah?" Angus said. "Then *you* go get the light."

The others looked through their belongings for matches. Panic spread when they discovered nobody had any. Roland suddenly remembered the box he'd pocketed in the plane and produced it.

He ripped a blank page from his journal, rolled it into a torch, and lit it under the wet kindling. Everyone's prayers centered on the curling smoke. Tiny tongues of fire licked around the twigs and ignited the heavier wood. The group's faces relaxed.

Edna held out her hand. "I'll take the matches."

"That's okay," Roland said, "I'll just—"

Her fingers swooped down to snatch the box from his hand and in one fluid motion drop them into her carry-all.

·207·

Roland lunged for the bag, but Apple restrained him.

"What does it matter who holds them?" she whispered. "As long as they are safe? And if we voted on it she would surely win."

Apple was right, Roland knew, yet he couldn't help feeling resentful.

"Now I suggest we try and get some rest," Edna said.

"What about a sentry?" Roland snapped.

"Of course," Edna said hurriedly. "Farragut, you take the first two hours. Then I'll give you a morphine tablet and you can sleep the rest of the night. After that, Roland, and then—" Edna detailed the rest of the watch.

Except for the glow in the center of the compound, darkness was everywhere. The air grew colder. The marooned travelers huddled beneath their blankets, but sleep would not come. They watched fire play across the jagged thorn and wondered what peril stalked beyond the flames, ready to spring.

Trapped by their civilization, they lay shivering in their separate cloaks, too weaned from tribal wisdom to comfort each other with the simple reaching out of a hand.

Many miles distant, hostile eyes had seen the plane crash. With darkness, the band mounted their horses. Perhaps there would be food to salvage, guns or other booty. There might be survivors they could hold for ransom. By riding at night and avoiding government outposts, they could reach the escarpment in two days.

36

The dull pain in Farragut's leg had him mesmerized. Why couldn't Edna have given him the pain-killer *first*? A broken leg put him at such a disadvantage. Yet it was about par for his luck. Wincing, Farragut managed to turn his cold side to the fire. He thought of Sarah and her persecutions. Now he almost waited for her to attack so he could retaliate.

"Why don't you secede," he chuckled.

If there was anything good about their crash, it was that they'd been stripped of every social pretense. The only thing left *was* equality. "And if you think I'm not going to keep pushing *that* in your face, Sarah—" That's why he'd voted for Edna. Even though he mistrusted her wealth, she was the only one strong enough to keep that Southern bitch in her place.

Hugging his camera case, he stared into the flames, conjuring another Farragut, carefully groomed, lecturing in the auditorium of the Photography Institute while his slides of Africa filled the screen. There were rounds of applause from faculty and students, and each of them had the face of Sarah Shallott....

Pain shot up from his shin and left him gasping. No matter how much it hurt, Farragut knew the trip had been worth it. Whatever bond he'd hoped to establish with this country hadn't materialized, and he now understood that he was more a son of the Mississippi than of the Nile. Yes, that's where the real confrontation would have to take place— on home ground, with the red-necked, Bible-quoting, hypocritical . . .

So intent was Farragut on the battle that he never heard the pad of paw, nor saw the beast's effortless leap over the thorn fence. Only the sight of Simeon chivvying his way along the ground made Farragut bolt upright and scream.

For an instant eyes like coals burned into his. Then they were gone. Everybody was up and shouting.

"I saw it! Right there!" Farragut yelled.

"Saw what?" Edna demanded.

Sarah snickered, "Dozing off on the job again? You know how *they* are."

"Can't you smell it?" Farragut said.

Angus sniffed. "I do smell something queer."

"Shouldn't be at all surprised," Sarah said. "It's a known fact that certain types—not even deodorants—"

"You shut up," Farragut yelled in a rage. "I saw it, after Simeon's body. It tried to drag him off."

"You're a no-good liar," Sarah spat. "You saw nothing."

Roland knelt by the body. "Look, it has been moved. And this leg's got teeth marks all around the ankle."

A high-pitched "Whahaha, whaha-ha" sounded just beyond the barrier, echoed down the escarpment, and was answered by another distant wail.

They looked at each other, terrified.

Roland swallowed hard. "Hyenas, I think." He grabbed a firebrand and cautiously searched the enclosure.

"Don't you think Farragut's making sense?" Angus said. "You all saw what happened with the zebra. It wasn't down more than a couple of minutes before the hyenas got there."

"What's a zebra got to do with Sim?" Sarah demanded.

"They're after Simeon's body," Farragut insisted. "We've got to do something, right now."

Sarah bared her teeth. "I'll see you in hell before you lay a finger on my Sim."

"Bury him," Farragut cried. "You're such a good Christian? Well, then, give him a decent burial!"

"I'll never leave my Sim on foreign soil," Sarah said. "We'll be rescued tomorrow for sure. I've paid for this trip, two fares. 'N' Sim's going to rest in peace in our family plot. Sim and me planned our eternity together. Why, our crypts are even marked."

"That's the stupidest thing I've ever heard!" Farragut shouted. "Come on, Sarah! You'll wear your widow's weeds maybe a month before you hook somebody else."

Sarah faced Farragut, fists clenched. *"Mrs.* Shallott, to you, boy. 'N' you better learn this too. You can't meddle in everybody's affairs and always get your way, just because *you* want it."

"But that corpse will draw every predator within miles!" Farragut said, looking around at the circle of faces.

"I'm not burying Sim here, and that's final!"

Edna stilled them with her hand. "There's no question in my mind that we'll be found come morning, so we probably won't have to do anything. But if it *should* take a few hours longer, Sarah, are you willing to put him someplace safe?"

"What do you mean?" Sarah asked suspiciously.

"What about putting him in the plane?" Angus said. "We could barricade the windows and the door."

Edna nodded at him. "Excellent idea, Angus. Sarah, we won't do it unless it's absolutely necessary. And you have my word that we will take his body back."

Sarah kept shaking her head. Farragut argued for immediate burial. But Edna rammed through a vote and Angus's plan carried.

Sarah went back to the lean-to and huddled in her blanket on the cold ground. They were all against her. Well, the game wasn't over yet. I'll get you, Farragut, she swore.

Edna said, "The only sensible thing is to double the guard. Whose watch is it?"

Roland's hand shot up.

"Then mine," Apple said. "So we will watch together?"

Angus slipped his arm around Roland's shoulder. "Hey, guy, why don't we switch watches? You can grab some more sleep."

About to agree, Roland caught the desperate look on Apple's face and changed his mind. "Thanks, Angus, but I couldn't get back to sleep now."

Angus wasn't about to be put off. "Then I'll stand your watch *and* mine."

Edna insinuated herself between Apple and Angus. She linked her arm through his and drew him aside. "It's better not to confuse schedules, don't you think, Angus? Besides, our watches coincide." Her eyes went to Keri and then to Apple. "And Angus, there's a great deal I need to discuss with you."

Roland and Apple took up their sentry posts, while the others fell into an uneasy sleep. Under his blanket, Angus took another pull from his bottle. Damned kid! He wondered what the old dame wanted; when he could get Apple alone ... Angus killed off his first quart before he was able to sleep.

After everybody else had settled down, Edna positioned the water jug in her field of vision. Perhaps they would be rescued tomorrow, as she had assured the group earlier. But Edna was too much of a realist not to recognize other possibilities. It might take two days, even longer. It was easy enough to go a few days without food.

But the water.

She had measured the demand against the supply, and always came back to simple arithmetic. In the infernal heat that day would bring, seven people might live for a day or two on their meager supply. Four people, however, might last two or three days. And so on.

Edna wondered about the Masai. Did their daily intake of blood fulfill their need for liquids? Or did the salt content in the blood make them more thirsty? Pity she hadn't had the foresight to have questioned Keri on this.

She closed her eyes. Best to get some sleep, even though she did not feel tired. No, *she* would not crack when the going got rough.

Her left shoulder and arm began to throb. Thinking, planning, she arranged the alternatives in their proper order.

Well, she would wait and see. Whatever tomorrow brought, she would be ready.

37

Roland and Apple were a half hour into their watch when a moan from Keri brought them to his side. "Livvie! . . . Altitude!" His lips frothed with blood.

Apple ran her fingers over his chest. If only she could help! Keri quieted and lay still.

"He's not going to die, is he?" Roland asked, his breath ghostly in the cold air.

"We all must die," Apple murmured.

"You treating me like a two-year-old also?" Roland said. "I mean *now*."

Apple turned to him. "How can I know such a thing?"

"You know more about it than the rest of us," he answered.

She thought a moment. "He will die unless we get him to a hospital. We *must* be found tomorrow."

Apple put another log on the fire, hoping it would help keep Keri warm. "Will the wood last the night?" she asked.

"It'd better. I'd hate like hell to go out scrounging for more." Roland got up and walked around the enclosure.

In her mind Apple stepped beyond the circle of thorns. A sound from the bush froze her. A whimper of mortality ... then silence. She hugged her knees and wondered at the sequence of events that had brought her to this time and this place.

Her pain had eased somewhat, but the heaviness remained as a reminder of what must come. She hoped that moment would find her alone, for it would be terrible and sad. Would losing the baby mean that she'd failed as a woman? she wondered. Or might it also contain a germ of hope? That she would be scourged of the past and could begin again?

Roland's return interrupted her thoughts. "Don't look so sad," he said, leaning back on his elbows and stretching his legs toward the fire. "The planes are bound to find us. Once they get Keri to the hospital he'll be okay. Then you and he—" he paused, embarrassed.

"It is not as you might think," Apple said. "Sometimes you must taste the ice cream to know the flavor is not for you, no?"

Roland nodded. Outside of one or two times with Keri, he'd never felt closer to anybody in his life. And this wasn't even sexual.

After a silence he said, "Apple, am I being paranoid or has Edna got it in for me?"

Apple shrugged. "A little of both, I think."

"Why?" he said. "I'm doing my share. Did you see her snatch those matches away from me?"

Apple patted his hand. "What good does it do to pick at that scab? Think of it this way. If the powers were reversed would you not have done the same?"

"Not me," Roland protested. "I'd be the one benevolent dictator!"

"No, I *would*," Apple insisted. "And I will fight you to the death to prove it!"

They laughed then, smothering their giggles.

Roland stared at the sky, darkly patched with clouds whose luminescent edges heralded the emergent moon. Then all at once the escarpment lit up.

"Moon's almost full," Roland said. "No wonder everybody's so nutty."

Once more the moon retreated behind the clouds and the mercurial light flowed over the cliff. In another quadrant of the sky, stars shone in their animal patterns. The Bear. The Scorpion. The Dog.

Roland said, "It's like they're saying, 'We're here all the time, storm or no, night or day. Only the sun hides us, and the blindness in men's eyes.' "

Again the air bristled with the rising and falling laugh. The sound seemed to circle the base of their mountain.

Roland's neck hairs stood up. "Nothing except that mangy fence between us, and even I can hurdle that. Tomorrow I've got to build it up, do something about weapons."

"Like what?" Apple asked.

"Maybe salvage a strut from the fuselage, hammer out a spear? I don't know, I'm just talking to keep from passing out. But I'd feel a hell of a lot better with something in my hands."

"Is it worth the trouble?" Apple said. "Surely tomorrow the planes will—"

"Everybody keeps saying that! But what if they don't? What are we supposed to tell the animals, don't bite, because the planes *should* have been here by now?"

Apple looked at Roland intently and cleared her throat. "Roland, there is something I must tell you. You will not hate me?"

Roland shook his head.

"I can tell you now because it is no longer true," Apple went on. "But when I first met you? Forgive me, it was as if you were a *foruncolo*—a great big boil. Angry, festering, ugly in your mistrust. And now you are almost your own man."

Roland felt the blood rush to his face. Impulsively, he leaned forward and kissed her.

The fire crackled and popped. Roland threw another log on.

"If not Keri," he began, "will you and—?"

Apple shook her head slowly. "No, I will go back home, I suppose. Try to start again, something worthwhile. Then someday, perhaps, somebody worthwhile."

"Ever hear of Eleanor of Aquitaine?" Roland began, but before he could go on a desperate rattle came from Keri.

Apple leaned over him, her ear on his chest. "He is scarcely breathing. He is like ice."

"Can't we get him closer to the fire?"

"That is not enough," Apple said vehemently. "He will die unless—do as I do. Quickly!"

38

Apple slipped under the blankets and wrapped her arms around Keri. "Roland, he is going into terminal shock," she said. "The cold will kill him. If you love him, then quickly, go to his other side."

Roland hesitated a second, then crawled under the blanket and pressed his body against Keri's. He *was* cold. Was he dead already? But then Roland felt the beat of Keri's pulse and his own heart pounded back. Don't die, I do love you.

Apple reached across to clutch Roland, pressing Keri tightly between them. The shock of blond hair was an inch from Roland's eyes. ... Apple's arm was around him ... it was almost too much to stand. He closed his eyes and drifted into a reverie. Don't die ... need you around ... ask you things ...

Roland was swallowed into deeper sleep. Dimly, he realized that something was stalking him. He looked to Keri for help but Keri couldn't speak. The unknown presence crept closer and closer.

A shadow fell across Roland's face. He opened his eyes. Somehow, Edna was looming over them. Caught, condemned, executed, Roland saw it all in her expression.

Edna listened to Apple's explanation with contempt. She touched Keri's forehead. "His temperature seems fine to me."

"Now, yes," Apple said. "But he would have died."

"I suggest that you leave him in peace," Edna said. "Now get to your own blankets, your watch is over."

Apple's temper flared, "He must be kept warm. I will sleep near him and you can go to hell!"

"Do as you like, miss. But Roland, out! This instant!"

Roland looked to Apple, who was checking Keri's pulse and temperature.

Apple nodded at him. "It is all right, Roland. For the moment he is out of danger."

Roland crawled under his own blanket feeling guilty as hell. But as he dropped off to sleep, a feeling of happiness washed over him. They'd managed to give Keri more time.

Edna and Angus put more wood on the campfire and settled down to their watch. Edna waited until she was sure everybody was asleep, then turned to Angus.

"I consider you my good right arm, Angus," she began. "The others?" she waved her hand in dismissal. "Without you this group would fall to pieces."

Angus nodded, his eyes still bleary with booze and sleep. He wished she'd stop lecturing long enough for him to get away and have a little hair of the dog. Not that he was afraid of drinking in front of her. Hell, no! But that would mean sharing it with everybody. And he had just one bottle left.

"There are a number of things you should know," Edna went on.

Angus stood up jerkily. "You can depend on me. But right now, I'd better patrol."

"Angus!"

"Be right back," he said, his fingers to his lips.

Angus followed the curve of the thorn fence to the cliff's edge. He looked back at Edna's firelit profile. She was doing something strange. Emptying her bag on the ground? Now was she putting the stuff back into it? Hell, he couldn't figure it. While Edna was occupied Angus had three or four deep swallows and once more surfaced to a buoyant spot. He stared at Edna for a moment, wondering what the old girl would have been like in the kip. Stainless steel. And Sarah? God, no. She'd only talk it down.

All he needed was a couple of minutes with Apple. He was so primed—hell, it'd been almost a week, no, more! "No wonder I'm going nuts," he said. How do I get her alone come morning? Go looking for wood? Water? Whatever. But early, before the planes come.

Angus started back toward the fire. The morning seemed so far away. Where was she anyway? Then he saw her— lying there with Keri! A jolt of pain shot from the base of his spine. He stumbled toward them, his mouth working. Edna reached out and clutched his leg. "You don't want to do that. Not just now."

Angus tried to pull free, but she was stronger than he guessed.

Edna stood up. "Didn't you know? I assumed that you just didn't care. It's been going on for quite a long time."

This *couldn't* be happening! Not to him! But the alcohol and Edna's voice kept mixing in his head.

Once more Angus lunged toward Apple, but Edna blocked his way, pointing to the dawn that was about to break. Their eyes met. Though they exchanged no further words, he took her pat on his arm as approval for what he knew he must do.

39

With the first light of day, the group made their meager ablutions, inquired after each other's health, and exchanged nightmares. The site, a concave shelf, hung suspended between the sun's haze and the morning ground mists.

Roland yawned mightily and went to Apple. "How's Keri doing?"

"A little better, I think," she said.

"Know something?" Roland asked. "Seeing a day like this I could almost believe in God."

"That is not too hard," Apple said. "But can He believe in us?"

Roland scratched his head. "Is that one of those cryptic remarks that really don't mean anything?"

Apple laughed. "If we believe in ourselves, then we believe in Him."

"Even if you are right," Roland said, "there must be a little something extra. You know, like a little body English to get the whole thing going."

Edna came by rationing water and pills. She was humming.

> Father Time is a crafty man,
> And he's set in his ways . . . .

"What I wouldn't give for a batch of my buttermilk flapjacks," Sarah grumbled. " 'N' you needn't be so stingy with the water, Edna. I got less than a quarter of a cup."

"That's all anybody got," Edna said.

"Shouldn't we lay in some wood for a signal fire?" Roland said to them. "For the rescue planes?"

"How come they aren't here yet?" Sarah asked.

Farragut said, "Any fool would know it takes a couple of hours to fly here from Nairobi."

Angus ran his hands through his hair. "Hey, Apple, how about you and me going for the wood?"

Keri stirred and everybody clustered around him. His hand moved feebly to the eye bandage, and Apple stripped the gauze away. Edna's spirits of ammonia pried Keri to full consciousness.

Keri blinked his lids, raised his head a fraction and whispered, "I can see."

Roland squeezed Apple's arm.

Keri sank back to the ground. "Where are we?"

"You're the one's supposed to know!" Sarah gasped. "Because of your carelessness my Sim is—"

"For the love of God, shut up!" Farragut bellowed.

Roland told Keri the situation so far. "Some water, no food," he ended.

"We were just getting ready to build a fire to guide the rescue planes," Edna added.

"No," Keri moaned. "No fire."

"Why? We had one last night," Sarah reported. "Been eaten alive if we hadn't."

Sweat broke out on Keri's forehead. "Shifta . . .torture . . . Roland?"

Edna looked to Roland. "What is Keri talking about?"

Roland explained about the Shifta bandits and the torture of the joints. The group reacted with stunned silence.

Keri nodded feebly and again warned them not to light a fire. Commit suicide rather than be captured. No fire . . . down into a red whirlpool he spun, shouting from the funnel's end about a cactus whose pulp could be chewed for water, an edible ground melon, and then the spinning waters choked him off.

Apple pressed her fingers against his temples. "He is still alive, thank God. But for the past minute has anybody understood one word?"

"One thing is clear," Edna said, "we can't have a beacon fire."

"Then how will the planes know where we're at?" Sarah looked like she was ready to cry.

Edna ran her hand across her brow. Then her face lit. "We'll spell out a large S.O.S. that can only be seen from the air."

"Great idea," Roland said, and everybody agreed. "But wait a second, that'll work only if the plane flies directly overhead." He waved his arm around. "We're smack in the middle of a thousand square miles of nowhere."

" 'N'at's right."

Edna shook her head. "Roland, if you used your intellect then you'd have realized that they certainly have our location."

Should he tell them? Roland bit his lip. Yes, the information was too important to withhold. "Lightning knocked out the radio before Keri could give it to them," he said.

"What a venomous thing to say!" Edna exclaimed. "Just because you failed to salvage the radio is no reason to frighten us like that!" She turned to the others. "Of *course* Keri gave them our position. It's the first thing any responsible pilot would do. Now you all heard Keri, no fire."

"Think of your magnetized watches," Roland said. "Look, I'm not knocking Keri, but he *is* delirious. And I don't think he's thought the whole mess through."

Edna laughed. "Are you equating your rather dubious logic with Keri's considered judgment?"

"If it's so considered, how come we all wound up here?" Roland asked.

" 'N'at's right!' "

Apple cut in. "Roland, what do you think we should do?"

"You said Keri couldn't last another day without a hospital, right? We can't wait until a plane accidentally flies overhead. We've got to make *sure* we're found."

"Look, guy," Angus said, "it's too dangerous keeping a fire going with those bandits around."

"Right," Roland agreed. "So what we do is post lookouts. Light the fire only when we've spotted the aircraft. And for extra measure—" he rummaged through the salvage and held up the visor mirror.

"Really, Roland," Edna said, shaking her head, "you think of the most frivolous things."

Waggling the mirror, Roland caught the sun, reflected it across the campsite and stabbed the rays high onto the mountainside.

"And draw every bandit within miles?" Edna cried.

"It's a calculated risk," Roland agreed. "But if there are bandits around they're less likely to figure this out. We'll flash the mirror at the plane the minute we see it."

"Bravo!" Apple said. "Roland, you are another Leonardo."

Roland swallowed his smile.

"Now just one minute," Edna interrupted. "This whole thing is ridiculous. Just because you're intent on getting killed is no reason for us to be exposed to unnecessary danger. I can't believe that Keri didn't radio our position. The mirror and the fire are out. Now for the SOS rock detail—"

"Now damn it, wait a second," Roland said. "Why don't we vote on it?"

"Must I remind you that you've no voice in these matters?" Edna said.

"*I* have a voice," Apple said. "I call for a vote."

Edna couldn't hide her shock when she read the results of the vote. Three to two in favor of Roland's plan. Her arm trembling, she got very busy working out a lookout schedule and sign detail.

An insurrection was brewing, she knew. She would have to stop it. Quickly. For the safety of them all.

40

They exhausted themselves lugging the volcanic rock and shaping it into the twenty-foot S.O.S. Their sign was finished by midmorning.

By that time the obscuring mists had burned away and Edna surveyed the terrain. Their escarpment, slashed with gorges, dropped abruptly. Above the crash site rose wind-carved cliffs, and the thin belt of bamboo. To the north a mantle of lava glistened like scar tissue and dormant cones pockmarked the desert. A land as barren as an Old Testament curse, Edna thought.

All evidence of yesterday's freak storm had been sucked back into the dry, dusty air. Insects buzzed. The bowl-like campsite held the heat, and a definite odor began to drift from Simeon's corpse.

Edna overruled Sarah's tears and insisted they carry out Angus's plan. Muttering, Sarah wrapped Simeon in a tarpaulin. Angus and Roland hoisted the body on their shoulders and carried it to the plane. Sarah led the procession, her fingers laced through Simeon's petrified hand.

They laid him out in the aisle. Around him were the smashed seats and fire-scarred instruments.

"I will keep a prayer vigil," Sarah informed them, a scented handkerchief clutched to her nose.

"You're out of your skull," Angus told her. "You'll roast to death."

"Come on out, Sarah," Roland pleaded. "You'll only make yourself sick."

Sarah tossed her head and knelt beside Sim.

Outside, Roland knocked a six-foot spar loose from the wing and began to sharpen it on a boulder. He thought how much simpler it would have been if they'd treated Sim like a Viking, sent him on his way to heaven or hell in the purifying flames.

Keri had told him the Kikuyu left their dead for the animals and thus renewed nature's cycle. Come to think of it, what good did it do anybody to be sealed away in a glass-lined casket? A parts bank—could that be the answer?

Roland caught himself short. Strange, that he could think about death now without going ape. Even a few weeks ago they'd have had to tie him in a straitjacket. Well, he was still scared of dying, though not in the old insane way—not fascinated with it.

Roland balanced the crude spear in his hand. "Nuts," he said as it flopped over. But when he hurled the javelin in a practice throw, it flew within a foot of its mark. "Not bad for a do-it-yourself," he said.

Edna watched his activity with apprehension.

Roland threw it again and Apple called, "And one day will you beat that into a plowshare and lie down with the lambs?"

·227·

"Not after what happened to that lamb at the Tented Camp," Roland called back.

Sarah staggered from the plane, blotting her brow. "Those damned pills, I told you I had a sensitive tummy." She straightened. "I have prayed, and sung Sim's favorite hymns. 'N' now I feel it's my duty to help out here. Has the plane come yet?"

The lookouts scanned the horizon, straining to hear the hum of an engine. Nothing. Only the molten sun that turned the site into a rock oven.

"Well, where are they?" Sarah demanded every ten minutes. "Why don't they come for us?"

Farragut stamped his crutch. "Knock, knock. Who's there? Rhino. Rhi*no* they come for us?"

Sarah gave him a murderous glance. "Silly chimp," she muttered. "Playing games at a time like this."

Too hot to wear a hat, too brain-roasting without one. Sarah demanded another cup of water. So did Farragut. When Edna tried to explain that they must conserve, Sarah insisted on a vote. Why make them suffer when the planes would soon arrive?

Edna lost. Under protest, she rationed out a half cup to each of them, leaving the thermos half-empty. Her fears were being realized faster than she'd anticipated.

Angus and Sarah took their turns at the lookout posts while the others sought shelter beneath the sweltering lean-to. The sun beat so damnably they fell into a stupor. Apple moistened Keri's lips with wet cotton. His body had begun to dehydrate; skin was flaking off.

Angus hunched in the shade of a slab of rock, binoculars at the ready, sweat crawling down his crotch. For the first few minutes he scanned the sectors religiously. Often his spyglass focused on Apple, her swelling breasts brought into touchable closeness. He remembered what Edna had told him, and his lust turned mean. She would pay, he promised himself. Nobody did that to him and got away with it.

He put the binoculars on the ground and gulped from his flask. Once more he searched the sky. But by the time Angus had finished the liquor he didn't even care that the shadow of the rock had shifted, exposing his head to the sun.

Roland decided that if he sat under the lean-to a minute onger his blood would boil. Maybe he could scrounge up something to eat, before they all started hallucinating. No wonder those old mystics had visions—just try fasting.

Roland left the lean-to and headed across the clearing. Nobody paid any attention to him.

Don't go back to that bird nest, he thought. He didn't trust himself with those eggs now.

Skirting the wreckage, Roland climbed up the incline toward the bamboo belt. Small avalanches slid from his toes. He hauled himself over a jutting ledge and looked down at the camp. The people seemed fixed in the heat.

He kept on climbing. Into the yellow-green cover of the bamboo stand that rustled with his every move, then through haunts of denuded baobabs and finally into a denser cover of green.

Queer, Roland thought, that on such a barren mountain this tiny Eden could exist. Probably because it's on the windward side, he told himself. Why didn't they come here to get out of the heat? No—the climb was too steep for any of them to make it. Besides, how would the planes ever spot them among the trees?

He picked his way over fallen branches molding with foxfire, past a strangler vine snaking its way down an acacia. It's like walking underwater, he thought, but steamy hot. An occasional beam of sunlight lanced through the canopy of leaves to touch the humus carpet. Hanging over everything was a smell of growth and decay.

He stumbled across a sausage tree with one lone breadfruit within jumping reach, just waiting to be picked. Roland smacked his head with disgust. Why hadn't he brought his spear along?

Roland stepped back, took a running leap, and missed. Once more, and this time he caught a branch and chinned himself up—only to confront a monkey that bared its teeth and screamed at him.

With a bellow of terror Roland thudded to the ground. The fall set up a buzzing in his head.

A hidden squad of monkeys took up the alarm. Unseen birds chided, and then from far off came the whining laugh that had surrounded the camp last night.

Roland jumped to his feet and started running, crashing through the bush. He shook his head to stop the buzzing. If anything, it was getting louder.

It wasn't his imagination, there it was again.

As if in confirmation the forest noises ceased, and only the droning sound of engines continued.

Wild with hope, Roland fought his way through the underbrush, tripping over roots as he raced back down toward the clearing.

41

Roland sent up a column of dust as he bumped down the steep incline. He imagined Angus at that moment flashing the mirror, Edna lighting the fire. The plane would spot them and it would be all over. Keri would have a chance.

But when he reached the edge of the clearing—he couldn't believe it! Nobody was moving. Here in the cup of the mountain the sound was muffled. He could barely make it out himself. But it *was* there. He stumbled toward camp, yelling frantically, "Get up! There's a plane! Can't you hear it, you idiots?"

He raced to the woodpile. Damn! Edna had the matches. He saw her, standing near the cliff's edge, staring in the direction of the sound. But she wasn't making a move.

Hearing Roland's shouts, Sarah and Apple ran into the center of the campsite. Farragut limped after and joined them, shouting and waving at the sky. Angus grabbed the mirror, discovered he had the coated side to the sun, and fumbling to turn it, dropped it.

For a second Roland saw the sun glint off the tiny metal

cross in the sky. He snatched up the biggest fragment of mirror just as the plane disappeared into the sun.

Roland grabbed Angus's shirt. "Why didn't you signal? Asleep, weren't you?" The reek of alcohol hit him. "How in the hell did you get drunk?"

Angus stared dumbly at him.

Roland slapped him as hard as he could. Angus blinked, then his fist shot out and sent Roland sprawling. Roland got up shakily, charged again, but Apple was pulling them apart.

Edna hurried from the cliff toward them. "Stop this instant! Roland, have you gone completely mad? You won't bring the plane back by fighting."

" 'N'at's right."

"Say, wait a minute," Farragut said. "Sarah, it was your watch too. Where were you hiding?"

Apple said quickly, "Roland, you are right to be angry. But truly, we could not hear. The mountain—"

"What about your eyes? That's what you've got binoculars for!" he shouted. Their faces blurred in his swimming vision as he bent down for the pieces of the broken mirror.

He looked up at Edna. "You saw it. Why didn't you yell?"

Angus doubled his fist. "Cut it now, guy, or I'll really paste you. The plane was too far away. No pilot could have possibly seen us."

"That's why the mirror," Roland choked. "And the beacon fire."

Angus lunged at him. "I said shut up!"

Roland dodged away and kicked stones all the way to the tool chest. "What's the use? I might just as well be stranded with a bunch of lemmings. Where the hell's the glue?"

Edna brushed wisps of hair from her face. "Now come on, everybody. There's no reason to be discouraged. At least we know they're definitely looking for us. It's simply a matter of time, certainly no more than a few more hours, before they find us."

Her optimism revived everybody. Sarah hurried to her valises, fluffed a new coat of powder on her face, and refurbished her lipstick. "No reason not to be presentable when they pick us up."

Though it was now Farragut's and Apple's watch, everybody kept scanning the sky. Minutes gave way to hours.

Roland, his anger subsided, ripped the cover off his journal and glued the shards of mirror onto it. Almost as good as new. He wasn't as confident as the rest of them about being found that fast. Thousands of square miles of irregular mountain and desert surrounded them. It might be another day, maybe two before the planes searched this sector again. That meant another night here. And *that* meant they'd better have one high thorn fence.

While the others watched listlessly, he began to build it up. His pace slowed as the midday heat clobbered him. He twirled a handkerchief into a sweatband and knotted it around his forehead. The sun climbed toward its zenith, leaving everybody weak and gasping for breath. In the next hour there were three false alarms and countless complaints of hunger, thirst and heat. Apple recognized symptoms of hysteria in all of them.

Orange and red lichen seemed aflame; the hum of insects ceased. Creatures of the desert holed into shadowed places, even those with cold blood avoiding the direct sun that penetrated the porous terrain. But Wing Safari #7, terrified of missing another rescue plane, stood under the relentless sun, searching, hoping.

Sarah pointed an accusing finger at Edna and said, "You promised us an hour or two and here it is, afternoon." Her makeup, melting in pink streaks, made her look like an oversized paraffin doll. "You can be sure I'm going to protest to the consulate. The very idea! Why don't they come for us?"

Farragut choked with laughter. "Sarah?" he called. "If you don't like it why don't you secede?" He looked from face to face for the laughs that did not come.

Sarah struck like a cottonmouth. "I'm Mrs. Shallott to you. No amount of fancy cameras is going to change the color of your hide."

Farragut scrabbled around for something to throw at her.

Heading for the plane, Sarah suddenly turned. "Nigger!" she cried, then ran the rest of the way.

Angus shook his head. Muttering, he ambled off into the bush, climbing down slope until he came to a clearing dotted with giant boulders. In the shade of one he refilled his flask from the last quart of scotch and finished off what was left in the bottle. Tough missing the plane. But in a way it had its compensations. If they weren't found before nightfall—well, this time he was going to get Apple alone no matter what anybody said.

Farther down slope Roland continued collecting thorn scrub. He looked to the sun that had grown huge feeding on the day and now stood balanced on the western ridge.

"Dear sweet Jesus," he breathed, "make it go down fast, or we're all going to go fruity."

He passed the spot where he'd found the bird's nest, and this time he couldn't resist. "I'm sorry," he said, "but we've just got to have them."

He stood on tiptoe and peeked into the nest, only to be

met by a quartet of fledglings demanding to be fed. "Well, what do you know!" Roland laughed aloud.

Sarah hoisted herself into the wreckage of the plane, smiling with the satisfaction of having bested that nigger. "Cleansed, that's the only way to describe it, Sim," she said. "Oh, you would have been proud."

She picked her way along the aisle. The fuselage had stored the day's heat and felt like the inside of a broiler. Sarah paused and listened. She thought she heard a faint chirring sound, but she couldn't make it out. The odor almost drove her back, but intent on a moment of meditation with Sim, she pressed on.

"It's going to be a big service," she said. "I'll have the large chapel awash with flowers. Don't you worry, Sim, I'll do you proud."

When she lifted the tarpaulin she tried to scream, but the sound rattled in her throat. Simeon's head seethed with safari ants, tunneling in and out of his nose and eye sockets. The last of his face was being stripped away, and the bony ridge of his teeth grinned at her.

Alas, poor oryx, was all Sarah could think of as she stood, her mouth wide with horror. She was so overcome that she never saw the column of safari ants advancing toward her Hush Puppies. Hundreds of them swarmed up her pants leg and needled her flesh with minute doses of formic acid. An advance guard crawled out her shirt collar, intent on her eyes.

Wailing and beating her hands against her face and body, Sarah hurled herself from the plane and thrashed on the ground.

Farragut saw her first. Though he couldn't figure out what she was doing, she did look hilarious. He grabbed a camera and hobbled toward her. Edna and Apple also heard the cries and came running.

Farragut advanced, snapping shots as Sarah tore at her eyes. "Sim! Eaten alive! Because all of you—murderers! Oh, help me, please!"

The shutter click caught her attention. Eyes widened, she flung herself at Farragut, who hopped away from her windmilling arms.

"Stop, you perverted nigger! You stop that!" Sarah cried, shielding her face. "Won't somebody please make him stop?"

Edna and Apple ripped at Sarah's clothes while Farragut circled them, his hands and brain working in a perfect marriage. Time exposures, light, everything was right. All the missed opportunities on the trip vanished as he took frame after perfect frame. He laughed. He even had the caption for this series of photos, "Only Two Species in the History of Evolution Practice Slavery. Ants, and —"

Sarah flung off her blouse. Her pink bra stood out against her white skin, her eyes bulged from their sockets. "It was *you* who wanted him in the plane, nigger! You knew the ants were there!"

Suddenly Edna let go of Sarah and turned toward the lean-to. "Don't worry, Farragut," she cried, "your camera bags are not in danger."

Sarah stiffened with recognition. Breaking away from Apple, she raced to the lean-to, snatched up a leather bag, and held it high in the air.

Farragut limped after her. "What are you doing? All my film! Somebody stop her!"

"Apple, run and get the insect repellant," Edna ordered. "Quickly, or we'll all be infested. I'll take care of these two."

Apple winced as an ant bit her hand, then went to her luggage for a can of repellant.

Sarah held the pouch toward Farragut. "Want it?" she asked, waving it before him. She danced toward the edge of the cliff, making Farragut limp after her. "Come get it!" Sarah whirled the bag over her head, faster, and with all her might hurled it. The case sailed over the edge, bounced down the chasm, and flew open. Colored canisters of film sprayed out like fireworks.

Stunned, Farragut crawled to the edge and peered down the cliff. "I can get them back," he shouted. "When they come to get us I'll pay the pilot. He'll get down somehow. A helicopter, maybe."

He turned to see Sarah doubling back toward the lean-to. She grabbed the other camera bag and raced back toward the edge. As she tried to dodge past Farragut he caught hold of the leather strap. They pulled and tore at the bag.

Farragut swung his crutch and hit Sarah on the side of the head. She and the bag thudded to the ground. Without the stick Farragut lost his balance and fell also. He dragged his way across the ground to get the case.

Apple, carrying the insect repellant, ran toward Sarah and Farragut, who were in a tangle on the ground. Before she could get to them Edna's fingers closed around her wrist. " Let them get it out of their systems," Edna said. "Or we'll never have any peace."

Apple stared at her. "Are you insane?" she cried, fighting to break free.

Dazed from the blow on her head Sarah saw two Farraguts crawl past her. She kicked at a pink-bandaged leg and saw Farragut scream and roll over in anguish.

Scooping up the case, Sarah stumbled toward the brink, which moved back and forth in her shifting sight. She gouged at her eyes to kill a stinging ant. Behind her, the sun loomed like an enormous blood clot.

"The first bag went over for me," she cried, throwing her head back and laughing victoriously. "And this one's for Sim." She drew back her arm.

When he'd first heard the screams Roland had dropped his load of thorn bush and had gone tearing up the hill to the clearing. Just as Farragut lunged for Sarah's legs, he saw the rain-weakened ledge crumble under their weight. They dropped, fingers clawing each other as they fell, their screams still echoing even after their bodies were broken against the outcroppings of rock.

Roland rushed to Apple and grabbed her shoulders.

"Why didn't you stop them? Couldn't you—?"

Apple stared at the camera bag lying on the ground, then turned toward Edna. She tried to speak but sank to her knees, moaning.

Roland crawled to the edge. Craning his neck he could see the two bodies. Canisters of film, red and orange and yellow, lay scattered about them like bits of confetti.

Sick at heart, Roland dragged his way to Edna. All his questions went unanswered. She just stood there, staring into the flaming ball of the sun.

42

A wreath of vultures materialized in the darkening sky and spiraled down into the chasm.

Apple began to pray, an endless stream of words degenerating into a babble, until she was pulling at her hair and raving against Angus, Edna, God.

When Roland and Angus tried to quiet her she kicked and punched at them, moving toward the cliff's edge in her distress. At last, exhausted, she lay still, making the small, gulping noises a child makes after crying, but Apple had no tears.

"Are you okay now?" Roland relaxed his grip but stayed ready to hold her again.

She nodded and stood up. Across the clearing Edna was taking inventory of Simeon's, Sarah's and Farragut's belongings.

"Look at her," Apple hiccoughed. "Our ragpicker of souls."

Edna swung her gaze to Apple and said, "I'm simply collecting their personal items to send to the next of kin."

"Hah!" Apple cried. "And whose personal items will it be next?"

Edna unzipped her pharmacopoeia and took out two white pills. They lay in her palm, perfect in their roundness, branded with the letter M.

"I know you're upset, my dear," Edna said. "And believe me, I'm heartbroken. I was only trying to warn Farragut—" she shrugged and shook her head. "We're running very low on water but we'll make an exception and let you have an extra ration. If you take these."

Apple shrank back. "I will swallow *nothing* you give me!" She made the sign of the cross.

Edna's fingers closed into a fist. Her hand opened and the crumbled pills fell to the ground.

Angus said, "Come on, Apple, it's horrible, we know. But nobody could have saved them. It was an accident."

"And where were you?" Apple demanded. "Drunk again?" She glared at Edna. "An accident? No. To think it in your heart, that is evil enough."

"That will do," Edna warned. "We have more important things to do than indulge your childish behavior. If you say one more word, I'll have you gagged."

Apple bit her knuckles and backed away.

Dusk rapidly gave way to darkness. With search planes no longer likely, Edna canceled the lookout watches and directed Roland to close the gate.

Despite the danger, they decided to have a small fire; it didn't seem possible to get through the night without one. To cut down the chances of its being seen from afar, they built a rock wall around it. Edna reorganized the sentry details to two half-night spans. And though Angus argued against it strenuously, the first watch fell to Apple and Roland.

For a long time Roland left Apple alone. He busied himself pricking the blisters on his hands. When it got colder he took the spare blanket and tucked it around Keri. His breathing was now very shallow.

"How do you think he is?" Roland asked Apple.

Apple went to Keri and pulled back his eyelid; the reflexes were there, but weaker. "Maybe a little worse," she said.

Then she reached out and touched Roland's arm. "Forgive me for fighting you. When I saw them fall, I lost my mind."

"I think we all cracked up a little this afternoon," Roland said with a shiver. "No food, brains baking, missing the plane." He rubbed his forehead. "You know what keeps popping into my head? All the things I should have said to them. Like, Gee, Farragut, sure wish I could handle a camera like you. Or, My, Sarah, you're looking especially pretty today. And, Simeon? If you'd have been around this afternoon you would have spotted the plane for sure."

Roland stoked the fire. "I tell you, Apple, if we get off this mountain alive I'm going to say an awful lot of nice things to an awful lot of surprised people."

"They will believe that you are *pazzo*—nuts!"

"So what? They think I'm nuts anyway."

Apple rested her head on her knees, her profile framed by her hair. "If only I could cry," she whispered.

Roland placed another branch on the fire. A spider scurried along the bark, whirled in a fire-dance, and before Roland could pull the log free, crisped into the flames.

"Sad," Roland said. "I didn't have anything against him. Hmm. I wonder if Somebody is thinking the same thing about us?"

Apple's smile was melancholy. "You are right, death *is*

sad. But to hang onto life out of fear? That is the greatest sadness of all."

"You're talking about Edna, aren't you?" Roland said.

Apple shrugged. "I mean everybody—Edna, Angus, me."

Roland looked to where Edna lay sleeping, her carry-all beneath her head. "I just decided I'd only nice things about people, right? And she is a sweet, helpless old lady, right? But then how come she's always got to be on top of everything?"

Apple nodded. "It is very difficult to understand the old. But believe me, you have much to admire in your Edna. Planes will crash, worlds will crumble, but she? A born survivor."

Roland jumped to his feet and began pacing. "I feel so helpless! You know what I could go for right now? A joint. Just light up and forget we're stuck in this here and now."

Apple felt a stab of fear for him. "Roland, if you took all the drugs in all the world, they would not be enough to make you forget. Believe me, I know. Happiness must come from within you. If not," she gave a little shrug, "then you might as well be a drunk like Angus. Collect people the way Edna does. Or invent excuses for yourself the rest of your days."

The fire crackled and popped. She sounded a little like Keri just then, Roland thought. Did that happen to everybody when they got old? When he'd first met them he'd have sworn they all had it made. But now—Christ, they were all so miserable about their lives.

"Besides," Apple murmured, "everything you are looking for is waiting for you." Her hand moved in an arc across the sky. "You will inherit all of this, and it's your body English that makes it go."

They sat quietly for a bit. Apple yawned and curled toward the fire. The full moon was high before Roland spoke again. "Apple, in line with all the nice things I wish I'd said? Well, I just want you to know I'd never have let Edna gag you."

The only answer he got was Apple's heavy breathing. Roland leaned over her. Fast asleep. Edna would have kittens if she found out, but Roland decided to let Apple go on sleeping.

He took a strand of Apple's hair between his fingers. I love you, he thought. I may never be able to say it to your face. If only I could cancel out that night at Treetops. We could begin like nothing had happened. You wouldn't have to love me at first . . . .

He looked into the fire for a long time, thinking over what she'd said. In all this dark vastness, on the edge of the unknown, for a solitary moment he felt a part of it all.

He hugged his knees and looked up at the Milky Way. If you let Keri live, I'll give up grass for a year. Five years. All right, forever. Don't worry, I can do it. You'll see. Just let him live.

Shortly before their watch was up Roland shook Apple awake. Her eyes looked hurt, and she felt hot to his touch.

"Are you sick?" he said anxiously.

"It is nothing," she said. "Some female trouble. It will be over soon."

The sentries changed.

Apple crawled under the lean-to and fell asleep almost instantly. Roland burrowed under his blanket, his fingers curled around the shaft of his home-made spear. As he dropped off he could see Edna and Angus hunched over the fire, their shadows flickering across the ground.

The moon cast its glow on the compound and silvered the sands that stretched away at the base of the escarpment. Angus and Edna stared at each other.

Is she trying to stare me down? Angus thought, trapped in a fog of whiskey. "Screw off," he muttered. "I'm not afraid of you."

If Edna heard him she made no sign.

Angus blinked. The way she was staring made him feel like he was still sitting out in the sun. He ran his tongue around his swollen lips. Where was Apple? There. Curled up in a question mark. Waiting.

God damn! The old bitch was still looking at him! In defiance Angus took out his flask and drank. After each swallow he deliberately locked eyes with Edna.

Edna's gaze never faltered. She looked beyond Angus's sensual face to his brutish core... raw, tied to the earth. Everything she had fought against all her life. His eyes, so dulled with excesses that not a flicker of intelligence remained. Yet he was a necessary part of nature's plan.

Edna reached for the flask and took it from Angus's yielding fingers. Never taking her eyes off him, she brought it to her lips and drank. Her intent gaze shifted to Apple.

Angus followed her eyes and felt his body come alive. Through the blur of alcohol the moon pulsed, do it, do it. And Edna's hollow eyes glowed with the same message. Do it now. I know what you want. Do it.

Edna handed the flask back to him and he finished it off. Now. He'd found the perfect spot this afternoon. Downslope, not too far from camp, but private enough.

The weeks of fear and failure disappeared as Angus got to his feet. He opened the gate enough so he'd be able to slip through, then circled back toward Apple.

Roland lay a few feet away, stirring restlessly.

Angus crouched down. Just as Apple opened her eyes he clamped his hand over her face. She thrashed and struck at him but he pressed her head into the ground. In ten seconds she was unconscious. Slinging Apple over his shoulder, Angus stumbled past the fire and out the gate.

Roland turned in his nightmare and cried out, "Sadly!"

43

Outside the protection of the enclosure, Angus felt scared.
He peered uncertainly at the shadowy slope. Better go back,
he thought. But then feeling the warmth of Apple's body, desire and confidence returned.

I'll just go down a little ways, he told himself. Then
even if the kid wakes up, he'll never find us.

The thorn scrub scraped across the ground as Edna
struggled to close the gate. Apple and Angus, gone. Keri?
A miracle if he lasted the night. She crept to where Roland
lay sleeping and cautiously inched the spear from his hand.
The honed point reflected the moonlight.

The barest moan made her whirl. Keri lay looking at her,
too weak to speak. Edna realized that he'd witnessed everything that had happened. She calculated plans and alternatives
for some minutes. Then she walked near the cliff's edge and
buried the spear beneath a thin layer of earth, came back and
took up her vigil by the fire.

Apple hung from the chinning bar at the convent school,
head down, feeling the weight of her hair. No, she was

bouncing along on her father's back in some childhood game. The ground had a life of its own, rocks and trees and strange suspended shadows. She caught sight of a red glow, retreating, yet so familiar.

The campfire! Remembering the eyes that had knifed through hers just before she'd lost her senses, Apple remained perfectly limp. Her mind raced like a doe before the dogs.

Angus struggled down until they reached the flat stretch of ground strewn with giant boulders he'd discovered that afternoon. Plenty far enough, he thought, and dumped her. He clutched at his reeling head and finally got his bearings back.

He squatted beside Apple and threw aside her wraparound skirt. Angus fumbled with his pants, got one leg out, hopped about like a stork trying to free the other leg.

Now! Apple thought. She rolled aside and scrambled off.

Angus made a grab and tripped, sitting down heavily. "Goddamn! You're not getting away this time!" He hitched up his pants and took off after her.

Apple dodged around the boulders. If only the moon weren't so bright! She came to another slope and leaped, bumping and sliding all the way down. A rock hyrax scurried out of her path. Angus couldn't have carried her very far from camp but Apple knew she couldn't call for help. Angus was insane, and if Roland came he would get hurt.

Angus leaped a divide, dropped six feet and caught her near the base of the escarpment. Panting for breath, they circled each other. He grabbed for her, his lips curled in their crooked grin, and she raked his cheek. He twisted her arm, forcing her to her knees. She caught his thumb between her teeth and bit. Angus crashed his fist into the back of her neck, and Apple toppled forward into blackness.

When her senses returned, she found herself pinned to

·247·

the ground by his heavy rhythm. Again and again his body gored into hers. She butted her head up against his and he jammed his forearm on her neck, forcing her back to the ground.

"Why fight?" he snarled. "You like getting it this way. So you can make believe you're still pure, make believe we haven't—how many times—like this?"

She writhed to break free, but her struggle only made him more brutal. With his free hand he tore open her blouse, an exultant mood fired him and in the moonlight of his mind he stood aside, watching himself perform. All night, he thought, I could go on all night!

"Think you can put—horns on me? Well, *mia figlia*, I'm going to—ram you till morning. And when I can't—get it up—I'll shove it to you with anything you can take. I'll show you." Yes, deeper into the fountain of youth he would go. His bones ground into hers, his teeth drew blood. Apple felt herself slipping, losing control. With a final wrench she felt her insides rip away. She could not stifle the wail that tore up from her loins and rose to the moon.

Roland bolted upright. "What?"

"Hush," Edna said, at his side immediately. "You've had a nightmare, dear, that's all. Now go back to sleep."

He slumped with relief. "I was dreaming, of Sadly. Then I heard—"

"Only an animal, darling. Back to bed now. You want to be fresh for your next watch, don't you?"

Then Roland spotted the empty blankets. "Where is everybody? Apple?" he called. When he got no response he sprang to his feet. "Angus?" He looked at Edna. "Where are they?"

·248·

"They've . . .gone for a walk, I suppose."

Roland dashed to the campfire. In his haste he didn't see Keri, who was trying to speak. Roland picked up a burning branch and held it aloft.

Edna snatched the firebrand from his hand. "You want to draw every bandit within miles?" She threw the stick back on the fire.

Roland raced to the gate. "Apple? Angus?" he yelled into the darkness. He glared at Edna. "How come the gate's shut?"

"I closed it after they left," Edna said. "No reason we should all be endangered just because they wanted to—" she grimaced.

"For God's sake! What happened?" Roland cried.

Edna dropped her head and gave a little shrug. "Well, maybe it's best that you know. Believe me, dear, I'd have done anything to keep it from you. The simple truth is . . .she went off into the bushes with him."

"That's a lie!" Roland spat.

"Is it?" Edna asked gently. "Don't you realize we all knew what was going on?" She shook her head slowly. "Remember how I tried to warn you, way back at Treetops? Well, when she couldn't get what she wanted from Keri she simply went back to Angus."

Her voice softened. "Roland, I know how bitter this must be for you. But please, don't torture yourself. They're not worth it. Don't you see? She needed a man who was like her. And you—you're still a child."

Roland bit his lip, trying desperately not to believe her. He *couldn't* have been wrong about Apple! But, she *had* been doing it with Angus. And he'd *caught* her doing it with Keri. Why *not* try Angus again?

Then from the base of the escarpment came another echoing scream. Roland whirled on Edna. "That's not anybody having any fun!"

She reached out for him. "Listen to me, child. It's their affair, let *them* settle it. It has nothing to do with you or me."

"You're really out of your head," he blurted. "It has everything to do with everybody!"

"Roland, I warn you. Don't go. He's stronger than you."

She was right there, Roland thought. He ran back to the lean-to.

"My spear," he called. "What did you do with it?"

"What? Oh, I saw Angus hide something." She pointed. "Over near the cliff."

No time to hunt. Roland tore through the pile of salvage for something he could use. He grabbed Farragut's camera bag, dumped some of the contents to make it lighter, then swung it through the air like a slingshot. It was next to useless, he knew, but it was *something*.

When he ran back toward the gate Edna grabbed his hand. "Roland, you *must* listen. Stay here, *please*."

She hurried on, kneading his fingers. "We'll forget everything that's happened between us. We'll start fresh. If I can forgive then surely you—? Roland, *please*! I know you're capable of love. Why, when I saw you with that antelope—Roland, we've only got each other left! It will be a good life, I promise you. And when I'm gone—"

Her eyes held him hypnotized with their loneliness. He wanted to please her, he'd spent a lifetime trying ... impossible. Roland pulled free and in a frenzy yanked at the bramble gate.

Gate! He bit the back of his hand to keep from whimpering. Gate. Sadly's pen . . . the boat on the Nile.

"Roland! For the last time. I'm warning you. If you go out there—"

Another scream. Roland ran out into the darkness.

Edna listened to him crash through the thickets as she closed the thorn barrier. Setting her shoulders, she took the canteen and poured a tiny bit of water into her hands. Then slowly she rubbed them together and shook them clean. She had given him his choice. He had chosen his way. Her conscience was clear.

When she came back to the fire she was startled to see Keri trying to drag his body forward, his fingers digging into the earth.

"What have we here?" She lifted his fingers from the ground and stroked them. "Now you know you mustn't go anywhere. You've got to rest. After all, we want you well when you and I are picked up."

Edna nodded and went on talking as if to a little boy. "That's right, just you and I."

As if in confirmation a distant baying laugh rose toward the moon.

She sat by his side. "You don't want to get cold. *She* says it's very bad for you. And you chose *her* way, didn't you. Shall we help you get warm? Now how did she do it last night?"

Edna lifted the blanket and moved next to him. "Close your eyes and I'll sing you a song. Don't be frightened. You'll be warm in a moment, I promise. Let's see . . ."

Edna paused to reach into her carry-all and take out her lipstick. Very carefully she outlined the thin slash of her mouth with brilliant red.

In her thin, true soprano she sang:

> And we know that we never can
> Ever bring back past days ...

Keri's breath rattled in his throat.

"There," she said, "isn't this the way she did it? And isn't it nice? So tired, aren't you. Wouldn't it be pleasant just to close your eyes? Not to worry anymore? No more pain? Come on, we'll put out the light."

Keri's eyes widened to the beckoning constellations. Edna reached out and brushed his lids shut.

44

Roland plunged down the slope. From far off came the sound of deep whimpers. He sprinted faster.

Suddenly the crying stopped. He listened to a silence even more terrifying. The strap of the camera bag bit into his shoulder. He shifted its weight and ran on to the clearing with the boulders.

A rustle in the bush and a crazy laugh—that had come from even farther down the mountain. Roland raced on, zig-zagging through the scrub, unmindful of the thorns tearing at him. He'd almost reached the base of the cliff when he came on them.

Apple lay on the ground, her face profiled by the light of the moon. Angus, fumbling with his pants, looked up at Roland. "How the hell did you ever find us?" he asked good-naturedly.

Roland gagged at the sight of the purple blotches staining Angus's clothes. Angus, still trying to zip up, didn't see the slingshot arc of the camera bag. It caught him on the shoulder and knocked him to the ground.

He hiccoughed, slapped his thigh and laughed, "Okay, you owed me that one. But right now, nothing can bug me. I've just had me one of the best—"

Roland swung the bag again, shouting, "You killed her!"

Angus barely had time to duck. He charged to his feet and caught the boy in the gut with a left. Roland doubled over, his stomach heaving.

"That's for openers," Angus breathed heavily. "Shape up, now. I don't want to have to cream you. She's not dead. She's had some girl trouble, nothing serious, and not even trouble if you look at it from my angle."

Roland gulped for air, searching Apple's face for some sign of life. He fell to his knees and shook her shoulder. "Apple, *please*." He couldn't find her pulse. Tears sprang to his eyes.

Angus lowered his fists. "I told you, she just passed out." Then his crooked smile brought out his dimples. "Hey, guy, you've been wanting to try it on again, right? Just to show you there's no hard feelings, why don't you hop on?"

But Roland was still searching for a pulse.

"Need a couple more lessons?" Angus asked, and started to unzip.

When Angus made his move toward Apple, Roland sprang. He got his fingers around an ear, his teeth an inch away from Angus's throat. Angus chopped down with a punch to the kidneys that dropped Roland to his knees. Paralyzing pain radiated from his spine but Roland leaped again.

Angus wrapped his arms around Roland's scrawny chest and squeezed. "Do I have to bust your ribs before you let up?" He increased the pressure. "Come on, guy," he coaxed. "You've been the good little hero. Time for some fun now—"

Roland crashed his head into Angus's jaw, and Angus reeled away. Roland swarmed over him, crying, punching. His leg shot out to kick Angus's groin.

Angus hunched over to protect himself. "You trying to kill me?"

He brought his fist up from the ground. Blood fountained from Roland's nose as he pitched forward.

Angus stood, heaving with exertion. When he got his wind back, he glanced at Apple, who was still unconscious. Beautiful, available and no back talk.

Angus rubbed his groin. Damn. If she wasn't out cold she'd have known what to do. A couple of more tries and he gave up. "Screwy kid's cost me a lay."

No use standing here, Angus thought, starting back toward camp. He got about twenty feet when he stopped. Now why in hell am I going back there? For more of Apple's bitching when she comes to? That queer old dame staring at me? And that demented kid'll try to throttle me in my sleep.

He studied the moon. In less than an hour it would get light. That gave him at least six hours before the noon heat. Dimly, he remembered something about never leaving the ship. But this ship was sinking. No food, almost no water. Waiting for a plane that might never come. No, he thought, his chances were better if he struck out on his own.

The euphoria of alcohol persuaded him that he'd find somebody before the heat set in. A native tribe. A patrol out searching.

"I've never been one to wait for anything," Angus said. With the breeze at his back he set out across the sands.

Apple shook Roland to his senses. He groaned, turned over, blinked at her. Then they fell into each other's arms. He hugged her, touching her face, her hair, laughing at her through his swimming eyes.

She pulled away. "You mustn't. I am all covered with— but look at your face!" She ran her fingers over his swollen eye and blood-caked nose.

Roland tottered to his knees. "Where's Angus?"

"I don't know. When I came to I saw something walking in that direction," she pointed toward the desert. "Would he be that crazy?"

Roland poked at his chest. "I think he broke my ribs. No, just my nose. Hey, what's the matter?" he asked. She was shivering and he drew her close again.

"It's okay," he said. "He's not here. I tried to get to you in time, honest. Before he ... I didn't think you were alive."

A tremor shook her. "I thought I had died. Part of me has. Oh, Roland," she whispered, and buried her head in his shirt.

She began to cry then, slowly at first, softly, then wailing like a child. She cried for her husband, for Angus, for Keri, all the stored weeping of all the countless desolate months. She cried until she thought she had not a drop of fluid left and still the tears came.

Roland whispered reassurances as she cried herself out in his rocking embrace.

After a bit Roland nudged her. "We'd better get back." He helped her to her feet and looped the camera bag over his shoulder.

"Leave it," she said. "Farragut will not need it anymore."

He shook his head. "Maybe he's taken some good shots that are still in the camera. If we ever get back I can have them developed. At least get him some credit."

She started to cry again.

"Come on, Apple," he coaxed. "Lean on me. We'll take it slow."

They stumbled along for a few yards trying to find the easiest path up the incline.

In response to Roland's questions, Apple told him what had happened. When she had finished he said bitterly, "Why didn't Edna stop him? Why did she lie to me? I could just *kill* her!"

Apple sank down on a rock. "Don't even say that," she pleaded. "There has been enough."

"You mean just let her get away with it? Like she's gotten away with everything all her life? Oh, no."

Apple started to argue with him but her voice cracked. "I am so weary," she whispered. "I could lie down here and sleep forever."

Roland tried lifting her under the arms but her ankles buckled. "I cannot," she said. "I must sit."

"You can rest all you want when we get back to camp," he said. "We mustn't stay here. I've got this awful feeling."

Apple looked around uneasily. "There *is* something," she agreed. "I feel it too."

"I know," he said under his breath. "For the past couple of minutes something's been following us."

"There are many of them," Apple said

Roland broke into a sweat. "Now don't lose your head," he croaked. "If an animal smells that you're scared—"

"Smell," she repeated, wrinkling her nose in disgust. "We know that smell."

A melancholy cry from their left stopped them in their tracks. They veered away but an answering call came from the right also. And the lunatic giggle wove through the bush.

"Can't you go any faster?" Roland urged Apple. "We can't let them cut us off. I don't know if they attack people but let's not find out."

He fought his way up the slope, dragging Apple behind

him. She gasped with pain as they crawled, inch by foot, into the clearing of the giant boulders. The laughter pursued them, sounding closer and closer.

"I cannot go any faster," Apple moaned.

Roland panted, "It's not much more. I remember this spot."

Suddenly Apple stiffened and pulled back. "There!" she cried, her arm sweeping out in a wide circle. "And there! And there!"

45

A half-moon of hyenas skulked toward them, uncertain of this strange prey. For this puny animal had no horns, no hooves, no claws, no fangs, nothing for defense, and ran awkwardly on its hind legs.

The leader of the pack, the matriarch, appeared on a rise. The blunt snout on the powerful neck turned toward them, ruby eyes burning.

Roland dug his fingers into Apple's arm and pulled her along. "At least eight of them. Come on!"

She stumbled and fell, sobbing, "I can't!"

Roland dragged her up. The insinuating laugh eddied on the night air, "Whan, waa, wa, whan," growing in intensity like the howl of police sirens.

"It's the blood," Apple whispered. "It's all over me. They are drawn by it. You go on. They will let you pass."

One hyena broke from the shadows and charged. Roland scooped up a rock and hurled it. The animal slunk away, but the rest of the clan circled closer, tightening the noose.

Roland rubbed away his tears. "We can't let it end this way! We just can't!"

He searched desperately for a tree, anything they could climb, but this barren stretch supported nothing but scrub.

"If only Edna let me keep the matches!" he said. He knew Apple was right, it was the blood. But she had saved his life. On the Nile. When the plane exploded. He *couldn't* abandon her.

Less than twenty yards away a huge boulder loomed in the moonlight, maybe eight, nine feet. He'd climbed it yesterday when he was reconnoitering. If they could get to it— but even now three of the pack blocked the way.

These hyenas looked scrawnier than the ones that had gotten Sadly. That might mean they were weaker. It could also mean that they were hungrier. Roland snatched up a branch and threw it. The hyenas scattered.

Roland weighed the camera case. It would last a couple of seconds against those jaws. Furiously, he groped through the bag. Maybe Farragut had stashed a knife in there. *Anything*. His fingers touched cameras, flashcubes, binoculars, then instinctively went back to the flashcubes.

"Because when Keri switched the headlights on and off," he told Apple excitedly. But she was too terrified to listen.

There were four flashcubes, each with four shots. His hands shook with panic but he managed to jam a cube into the camera socket.

"Let's go," he said through gritted teeth. "We've got to keep moving or they'll ring us."

Apple clung to his shirt. Step by step they advanced toward the slinking beasts who blocked their access to the boulder.

"Shield your eyes," Roland warned her and aimed at the nearest hyena. The brilliant flash lit the clearing. For an instant phosphorescent holes burned where the animal's eyes had been. Startled, the creature scampered away, tail looped between its legs.

Helpless with fright, Apple cried, "Did you see the eyes? *Diabolo!*"

"Shut up and save your breath!" Roland ordered and yanked her closer to the rock.

The pack reformed, wary now. Strings of saliva swayed from their jaws. One hyena spun off from the ring behind them and galloped in. Apple saw it from the corner of her eye and screamed. Roland whirled and fired directly into the animal's face. The hyena hung suspended in the flash-white, then, dazed, stumbled off.

"You did good." Roland squeezed Apple's arm to encourage her and to stop his own shaking. "Stick close to me, only a few more yards." Roland fired twice in rapid succession and the hyenas scattered from the rock.

"Now!" he yelled, and half-dragging, half-carrying Apple, made a dash for it.

Apple flattened herself against its face, fighting for a grip on the cold, abrasive surface. "I cannot climb there," she said, tears coursing down her cheeks.

"Shut your mouth," Roland gasped as he fumbled to replace the used flashcube. "You haven't even tried, you chicken-hearted—go on! I'll boost you. Jump!"

She gave an ineffectual hop and then sank to the dirt. The pack closed in, their eyes a ring of fire. The bedlam laugh went up again.

A trio drove in at once. Roland triggered the flash, three, four times, pressing long after the cube had been burned out. Once more it stopped them, but just. The effect was wearing off, and the smell of blood overrode any fear.

Roland jerked out the hot melted cube and reloaded. Two cubes left, only eight more flashes.

He dug his fingers into Apple's shoulder. "Now listen to me, goddamn it! I'm going to get down on my knees. When I do, you climb up. Put your feet here and here," he said, slapping his shoulders. "Then I'll stand up very slow. Don't panic now, you'll be leaning against the rock so you won't fall."

Apple shook her head. "Just leave me."

He slapped her face and shook her. "Your grandmother probably dropped triplets and an hour later went back to work in the fields! Where's *your* body English or whatever bullshit you handed me a while back? *Now come on!*"

He stuck the camera in his belt, got on one knee, and held his hands in a stirrup so she could climb onto his shoulders. Her legs shook as she grabbed at the vines and roots growing from crevices in the rock.

One thing to say it, another to do it, Roland thought, as he struggled to stand. His thighs ached under the load. He was sure his back would accordion, but slowly, groaning with the effort, he began to raise himself.

Apple tottered, Roland braced her knees with his left hand. With his right he pulled the camera from his belt and held it ready.

"The ledge," Roland panted. "Stand up straight and get your knee over the top."

A thick vine had sunk its roots into the rock's crevices untold decades before. Apple clutched it, managed to throw an elbow over the ledge, then her knee, and as Roland heaved she fell over the top.

"Good girl!" Roland shouted. "Catch this." He tossed the camera up to her.

He backed off a few feet and made a running jump. One hand closed around the gnarled vine, the other groped for the ledge, and slowly he chinned himself up.

Apple pulled at his sleeve. She stifled a scream when she saw the hyenas racing in again.

Sensing the prey's imminent escape, the pack roiled under Roland, leaping at his thrashing feet.

"The camera!" he shouted.

Flat on her stomach, Apple leaned over the ledge and fired the cube. A curse streamed from her mouth. The hyenas stopped, noses twitching at the acrid odor, eyes momentarily blinded.

Roland's arms were straining their sockets as he kicked against the boulder for a foothold. Apple stretched down and managed to hook her hand under his belt. They seesawed in a static balance, fighting for every inch.

A hyena sprang for his flailing legs. Apple snatched up a heavy rock and flung it down, hitting the animal in the chest. The beast toppled backwards, stunned. Its huge, vulnerable genitals were exposed, and in a second the clan closed in, tearing the sex organ off, then ripping into the underbelly, while the grunting animal gobbled the intestines that spilled from its own stomach.

Roland hung there, hypnotized by the sight. But the momentary diversion gave him the breather he needed.

His right knee scraped over the ledge as the pack sprang, jaws gnashing the air where he'd hung. Then he was over, his heart threatening to burst as he lay against the rock.

The pack hurled themselves at the two who huddled in a tight ball on top of the boulder. They kept up the attack as the moon waned to a ghostly disc. The sky gradually lightened. Then the wind shifted, fresh and strong with the promise of the new day. One by one the hyenas stopped leaping, craning their necks, nostrils twitching to the new message on the wind.

One hyena laughed, and then the others took up the howl

in a chorus. The clan loped away, on the trail of an easier prey.

After an endless time Roland got up enough courage to peer over the edge. He couldn't see them anywhere, but he was still afraid to make a move. He also knew that if he and Apple stayed on the rock the sun would soon broil them.

Shakily, he got up on his knees, and after a couple of tries was able to stand all the way. Apple tried to get up also but collapsed against him. Roland reached down and touched her head.

She looked up. They stared at each other's grimed, streaked faces.

"I don't believe it," he said weakly.

"We are alive," she whispered.

Farragut's camera bag lay at the foot of the boulder. The binoculars were in it. Ready to scramble back at the slightest sound, Roland began to climb down.

He found the binoculars and scanned the area, sweeping across the stretch of desert and the black mantle of volcanic rock. "I don't see anything."

The sun's blood-red crescent appeared on the horizon and then Roland did see the hyenas, strung out like a moving frieze.

"There they are. Must be more than a mile off. I think they've got wind of something else. But it's too far to make out what."

He waved at her urgently. "Come on. This is our chance."

46

It took them more than an hour to make their way back to camp. Roland had no strength left but he drove himself on, pushing Apple before him. When at last they stumbled to the edge of the clearing, Apple gave out completely. Roland took her under the arms and dragged her the last hundred feet.

The breeze was gentle, the sun warming the land. Edna was nowhere in sight.

Heaving with exhaustion, Roland leaned against the thorn fence. Then he saw her crouched under the lean-to. The contents of three suitcases—Apple's, Angus's and his own—were neatly stacked on the ground. Her brow was knitted in concentration as she read from a notebook lying in her lap. Roland recognized the torn cover.

Edna whirled as he ripped open the gate. She stood up slowly, not quite believing the haggard figures.

Of all the things Roland had planned to say, what finally came out was, "That's mine. You've got no right."

Edna opened her fingers. The pages spilled to the ground.

"Thank God you're alive," she said. "You don't know how worried I've been. Then, tentatively, "Angus?"

"Took off," Roland choked. "Across the desert, I think."

Edna shook her head. "Oh, the fool. So he did it after all? He told me he was planning to go bring back help. I tried to warn him, but he wouldn't listen."

Before Roland could throw the lie back in her teeth Edna pointed to where Keri lay. "During the night," she said softly. "Without ever regaining consciousness."

Roland and Apple staggered to the lean-to. Roland peeled back the blanket covering Keri's face and looked at him for a long time. The lids were closed, the worry lines all smoothed in a look of peace.

Apple put her forehead on h¹s chest and rocked back and forth. But Roland was beyond tears. He stared at Edna, his vision blurred with exhaustion, his heart urging him on with each beat.

As he moved toward Edna, Apple grabbed his leg. "You must not," she begged. "Whatever has happened, Roland, forgive, forget. A new beginning."

"She did it all," he muttered. "You know yourself she did."

Apple's fingers tightened around his ankle. "Roland, must it always be an eye for an eye?"

"Let me go," he said, never taking his eyes off Edna.

"If you harm her," Apple gasped, "I swear, I will tell."

Roland jerked his leg free.

Then Apple raised her eyes to a faint buzzing. Her hand shook as she pointed to the tiny speck glinting in the sky. The three of them looked up, watching the plane grow larger.

Roland clenched his fists. "Give me the matches," he said to Edna. "Right now."

She handed them over without protest. He struck one to

the tinder, and black smoke began to billow up. Roland found the mirror and flashed it at the approaching craft.

The plane circled the escarpment in a tight arc, its sound reverberating across the clearing and down the chasms.

Without strength or joy they watched the pilot give them the thumbs-up gesture, then fly off to direct the rescue party.

Apple crumpled to the ground, barely distinguishable words coming from her caked lips. "Comfort us . . . in the hour of . . ." Her head sank.

Roland grabbed her hair and pulled her face out of the dust. He emptied the thermos and forced some of the water between her lips.

"It may take hours for them to reach us," Edna said. "Why waste it? It's perfectly obvious that she isn't going to—"

Roland's shout came out a croak. "She *is* going to live! You think she went through all this just to die?"

Edna's eyebrows arched. "How touching. And how very naive. Now, Roland, we've things to do. They've seen the two of us and—"

"Three, damn you!" he yelled.

She shrugged his remark off and lifted her carry-all onto her lap. "I suggest you clean up as best as you can. Use some of the fresh clothes I've laid out for you. There's no reason to look like a barbarian."

She searched her bag for her cosmetics case, couldn't find it, and carefully emptied the contents on the ground. Locating it, she began to repair her face, first washing it with a foil-sealed cleansing pad, then dusting a thin layer of powder over the hollows.

Roland was so exhausted he could barely keep his eyes open. He was also too scared to close them. He felt himself slipping in and out of hallucinations.

"I told you to get ready," Edna called to him.

Things slowly refocused in his swimming vision. His eyes picked out something familiar resting against Edna's carry-all. Only when he touched it, saw the familiar worn spots, could he admit to himself that it was the mate of the sneaker he thought he'd lost.

He crumpled the soft canvas in his hand and saw a lamb bleating while its liver was cut out, a gate swinging open through which Sadly flew into the open jaws of the Nile.

Roland locked eyes with Edna. For an instant she knew panic, and then she recovered.

His throat worked in spasms. "Why?" he managed at last. "Why?"

Edna's veined fingers tightened around her empty carry-all and then dropped away.

Why indeed, she thought, suddenly disgusted with his blatant, faked display of innocence. As if he hadn't tried to push her through the gate on the Nile. As if he hadn't left the roof hatch open when the lion had bounced onto the Land Rover. As if he had not deliberately left the plane's radio behind and kept them from being rescued immediately. As if he hadn't plotted to expose them all to the Shifta. As if all his life he hadn't thwarted her, tormented her—

Roland laughed crazily, "You know what? I'm going to have you put away."

Edna's voice came out crisp and sure. "We shall see who puts whom away."

He came at her then, the shoe in his outstretched hand like an indictment. His repeated "Why?" hounded her retreating steps. His voice found strength with each sentence. "I don't know how. I don't care how long it takes. But I'm going to see that you get what you deserve."

The lilting laugh that came from Edna belied her years. She backed toward the cliff's edge, her eyes searching the dusty ground. "Why, Roland, *you* are what I deserve. You are my justice and I am yours."

Suddenly her hand darted down and unearthed the hidden spear. She clutched the shaft and held the honed point toward him in a move somewhere between defense and attack.

Only then did Roland realize the magnitude of her plan. She would be the only survivor! Then a feeling he did not understand, very close to pity, swept over him.

She stopped retreating, still pointing the spear at his stomach. Their eyes locked.

"You're mad!" both cried simultaneously.

I've got to do it, Roland decided. Force her off the cliff. Before she gets me. She said the plane only saw two of us. Apple and me. I've got to. Otherwise she'll twist everything that's happened. I've seen her do it before. And in the end she'll come out right. Like she always does. I can't let that go on. I've got to stop her, I've *got* to!

She thrust at him. He dodged and hurled the shoe as she jabbed again. The sneaker hit her wrist and knocked the spear from her hand. Before she could retrieve it he kicked it over the edge.

Her hands flew up in front of her face to ward off his blow. When he didn't strike her fingers slowly parted, then dropped. Her face was livid.

"Roland! You don't know what you're doing! You're crazed with heat and thirst and fatigue. I love you! How can you stand there—in my flesh and blood—and even think of doing such a thing? What will you accomplish?"

"Justice," he whispered. "Your justice." Confusion raged in him. She *was* a part of him. But she was guilty of so much.

Her words lashed him again.*"Roland*! I love you. Your mother had these lapses. Roland, they're only temporary. I'll see that you get the best doctors, the best—*Roland*! What good will it do? Don't you hear me? I love you!"

Instinct had driven him to a point where he could not stop, and he felt his lips thin to a snarl.

"There's no other way, Edna!" he shouted.

And when the chasm called back her name, Roland began to tremble. For it was her voice, *her* voice coming from his mouth.

He looked to the wheel of the sun and struggled with the awful question. Have I become the very thing I hate?

Sweat and tears ran down his cheeks.

And if heaven is shaken by a crushed flower, then what of murder?

His fists unclenched. He reached his hand out to her. "Come away from the edge," he murmured.

She did not move.

"Trust me," Roland whispered. "You *are* all I have."

But Edna's eyes said she would never trust him. Inching toward the campsite, she began to think, to plan.